THE
HENCHMAN

MARK LEE LUTHER

1st WORLD
LIBRARY
Literary Society

The Henchman

Mark Lee Luther

© 1st World Library, 2007
PO Box 2211
Fairfield, IA 52556
www.1stworldlibrary.com
First Edition

LCCN: 2006936265

Softcover ISBN: 978-1-4218-2728-5
Hardcover ISBN: 978-1-4218-2628-8
eBook ISBN: 978-1-4218-2828-2

Purchase *"The Henchman"*
as a traditional bound book at:
www.1stWorldLibrary.com/purchase.asp?ISBN= 978-1-4218-2728-5

1st World Library is a literary, educational organization
dedicated to:

- Creating a free internet library of downloadable ebooks

- Hosting writing competitions and offering book
publishing scholarships.

Interested in more 1st World Library books?
contact: literacy@1stworldlibrary.com
Check us out at: www.1stworldlibrary.com

1st World Library Literary Society

Giving Back to the World

"If you want to work on the core problem, it's early school literacy."
- James Barksdale, former CEO of Netscape

"No skill is more crucial to the future of a child, or to a democratic and prosperous society, than literacy."

- Los Angeles Times

"Literacy... means far more than learning how to read and write... The aim is to transmit... knowledge and promote social participation."

- UNESCO

"Literacy is not a luxury, it is a right and a responsibility. If our world is to meet the challenges of the twenty-first century we must harness the energy and creativity of all our citizens."

- President Bill Clinton

"Parents should be encouraged to read to their children, and teachers should be equipped with all available techniques for teaching literacy, so the varying needs and capacities of individual kids can be taken into account."

- Hugh Mackay

TO

GEORGE RICE CARPENTER

OF COLUMBIA UNIVERSITY

Those familiar with the early history of Western New York will know the "Tuscarora Stories" of this volume for twice-told tales which the author has ventured to adapt from the suggestive "Pioneer History of Orleans County," by Judge Arad Thomas.

BOOK I

CHAPTER I

It was the custom of the geographers of a period not remote to grapple somewhat jejune facts to the infant mind by means of fanciful comparison: thus, Italy was likened to a boot, France to a coffee-pot, and the European domain of the Sultan to a ruffling turkey. In this pleasant scheme the state of New York was made to figure as a couchant lion, his massy head thrust high in the North Country, his forepaws dabbled in the confluence of the Hudson and the Sound, his middle and hinder parts stretched lazily westward to Lake Erie and the Niagara. Roughly speaking, in this noble animal's rounding haunch, which Ontario cools, lies the Demijohn Congressional District whose majority party was now in convention assembled. In election returns and official utterances generally the Demijohn District bore a number like every district in the land, but the singular shape lent it by the last gerrymander had settled its popular title till another political overturn should distort its outline afresh.

The spokesman of the defeated faction had been recognized by the chair, and was moving that the convention's choice of the gentleman from Tuscarora County be declared unanimous. His manner was even more perfunctory than his words.

"The name of Calvin Ross Shelby," he ended colorlessly, "spells success."

"Screws it out as if it hurt him," whispered the Hon. Seneca Bowers to the nominee. "I tell you, Ross, there's no argument like delegates."

Bowers was a thick-set man of the later sixties, with a certain surface resemblance to General Grant of which he was vain. So far as he could he underlined the likeness, affecting a close-trimmed beard, a campaign hat, and the inevitable cigar; when the occasion promised publicity sufficient to outweigh the physical discomfort he even rode on horse-back; and he was a notable figure on Decoration Day and at all public ceremonies of the Grand Army of the Republic. Shelby was his protege.

The present member of Congress from the Demijohn District, whose seat Shelby coveted, may be most charitably described as a man of tactless integrity. His course in Washington had been a thorn in the side of the organization by whose sufferance he rose, with the upshot that the Tartar neared the end of his stewardship backed by a faction rather than a party. The faction clamored for his renomination and pushed their spirited, if poorly generalled, fight to the floor of the convention. In debate they were eloquent, in logic unanswerable; nor did any one attempt to answer them. With the best of possible causes they lacked but the best of possible worlds to insure success. The whole story of their failure was packed into the Hon. Seneca Bowers's succinct phrase, "There's no argument like delegates."

The vanquished clustered in a little group apart marked by a suggestion of tense nerves, but the gathering was noticeably of a kind. Country lawyers, bankers, merchants, stockmen, farmers, in its units, it was sealed as a whole with the seal of New England which had sent forth these men's grandfathers and great-grandfathers in their ox-carts to people and leaven the West. The transplanted New Englandism had sloughed certain traits of the pioneers who laid the axe to the forests of the Genesee Country and the Holland Purchase. Only the older people of the Demijohn District now computed their dealings in shillings; mentioning one's conscience on week-days was an eccentricity; the doctrine of Original Sin had lapsed from among burning topics of conversation; family records were less and less scrupulously kept; and the *Mayflower's* claim to consideration as the Noah's Ark of the only ancestors worth reckoning had assumed a mask of comedy. Yet, all said, the Yankee blood cropped out in face and limb and speech—particularly in speech; the folk of the Demijohn District did not employ the dialect of Hosea Biglow, nor a variant of it, but the insistent drawling R to be heard on every second lip was of no doubtful lineage.

The victor, who sat with folded arms as the perfunctory motion was seconded and carried, was bone of their bone and flesh of their flesh. Not a few there could recall his sturdy grandfather, a pioneer of Massachusetts birth, and everybody remembered his spendthrift father who had squandered the substance of three generations in drink. The man's own story was an open page which needed no thumbing of the Tuscarora County history to find. Born under the administration of Buchanan, the lad's palm was callous with work by the surrender of Lee, and it knew no softening till his seventeenth year; yet somehow he got the marrow from the common schools, and in good time won a competitive scholarship in a narrow little sectarian college which boastfully called itself a university. Here he acquired two wholesome things: a perception that the college is but the beginning of education, and a lasting disgust with bigotry of every stripe. There followed some years of school-mastering by day and law-book drudgery by night, whose end was his admission to the bar and a partnership with the man sitting by his side. Then politics drew him, and, step by step, through rough and ready service at the polls, in town caucus, county convention, what not, he secured his footing and finally a seat in the lower house of the State Legislature. In politics a hobby is often a useful piece of property, and Shelby, who had a hobby, rode it to success; it made him a marked man in the first month of his term, it gave him a popular title, it compelled his renomination and reflection. Nowadays chairmen always introduced him as the "Champion of Canals," and even at this moment the catchword with cries of "speech" greeted him from every quarter of the dingy convention hall. He unfleshed his strong teeth in a wide-mouthed smile, rose, squared his shoulders, and walked alertly down an aisle to the platform. Brought thus into the open, under the yellow glare of a gas-light chandelier, he showed for a simply clad, businesslike person, with a well-set head and a shaven jaw, whose firmness a cushion of superfluous flesh could not disguise.

"Thank you, boys," he said.

The offhand fashion of address provoked a fresh demonstration which the nominee acknowledged with a good-humored nod. His eye sauntered over the delegates, and with a shrewd twinkle halted on the dejected group which had fought his nomination.

"This happy occasion reminds me of a Tuscarora County story," he began, with a little drawl; "the story of Tired Tinkham's election as overseer of highways at Noah's Basin—a pioneer classic which some of you have doubtless heard. It happened in the early days of Noah's Basin, when that interesting village contained perhaps a score less people than walk its changeless streets to-day. Tired Tinkham was the local Rip Van Winkle—the children's friend and labor's foe. No one could whittle green willow whistles in the springtime like Tired Tinkham, or fashion bows and arrows with such fascinating skill. Like Rip also he drank whenever a drink was forthcoming, but unlike Rip he did not hunt. Minks, coons, and squirrels were plentiful, with here and there a deer or bear, but Tired Tinkham was too weary to hunt. He fished; fished day in and day out in the canal basin, which gives the place its name; fished till the packet captains came to know him and point him out as a fixture in the scenery. But, lazy as he was, Tired Tinkham didn't monopolize all the laziness in Noah's Basin. In one particular laziness was epidemic, even among the otherwise industrious, and it took the form of shirking the road tax. No roads were wretcheder than theirs; nobody cared less than they. In his personal view of life Tired Tinkham was a fit exponent of the local theory of public duty, and some village humorist accordingly hit upon the idea of nominating him for overseer of highways. Tired Tinkham looked more than commonly fatigued at the suggestion, but did not put the crown away. His election was unanimous. Then Noah's Basin woke up. The jubilee bonfires were scarcely ashes before Tired Tinkham delivered at the corner grocery what he called his inaugural address. 'I cal'late I know why I wuz 'lected; he said. 'T' loaf 'n' let ye loaf. I cal'late ye've mistook suthin'. Ye'll work.' And work Noah's Basin did as it had never worked before."

Shelby noted that the anecdote won even a thin-lipped grin from the hostile camp.

"The Tired Tinkhams aren't so rare in politics," he went on. "We sometimes put them in the White House. Americans have a way of growing up to their responsibilities, and perhaps even I shall prove another sort of man than I've been ticketed." His tone quickened suddenly, and his glance fastened on the defeated anew. "I should count this honor less had it fallen as a ripe fruit falls, the prize of the first comer. We've had our battle; we wear our scars; no battle worth the name is without its scars; but I assume to speak for every man present when I say that the blows we give and take do not rankle to the prejudice of the common cause. Our quarrels are wholly in the family, where speech is free, for it is a fundamental article of our party creed that the will of the majority should prevail. The will of the majority made plain, it is our healthy custom to strip off our coats, and go to work: The party, not the individual, is of moment;—the historic party of our fathers, the party of the living present, the party of the future whose bounds no man may set."

As he dropped into his seat, Shelby added a foot-note.

"If that didn't jam their duty down those soreheads' throats," he told Bowers, "I'll take another guess."

CHAPTER II

Meanwhile the nominee's fortunes and traits of character underwent dissection in his own town at the first autumn assembly of the Culture Club which, as always, met with Mrs. Hilliard. There were two profound reasons for this constancy to Mrs. Hilliard,—her house boasted the largest double parlors in New Babylon, and her husband had a billiard table. The intimate association of billiards with the pursuit of sweetness and light may at first seem grotesque, but Mrs. Hilliard proved it to be not without warrant in sound philosophy; by her simple formula billiards stood to culture as the Salvation Army to the decorous body of the Church Militant, both alliances resting on the basic truth that some souls will prick ears only to the beating of tom-toms.

Theory aside, the fact was not to be blinked that she knew how to clash cymbals to the unregenerate and drum up in the name of culture such a varied company as no other woman could muster short of a silver wedding. In the winning of the cultivated, Mrs. Hilliard took no pride. They lent their countenance to any educational project, and she owned to herself that given a like cause any capable woman with double parlors could have them for the asking. It was rather in the hooking of men of the stamp of the Hon. Seneca Bowers and her own husband that she gloried, for in their candid souls they styled great Shakespeare rot and voted Ibsen and Tolstoi sheer bedlamites at large. While mind met mind below stairs these honest gentlemen contentedly knocked the balls about the green, smoked hospitable Joe Hilliard's cigars, and sampled the choicest liquors of his sideboard. By such diplomacy every important walk in the town's life came to have its representative in what in her heart of hearts Mrs. Hilliard called her salon.

The first autumn meeting should have gladdened the hostess. Her house had never lighted to better advantage; everybody admired the new decorations; she herself felt no impulse to quarrel either with nature or her dressmaker; the programme had run with consummate smoothness,— Volney Sprague, the editor of the *Tuscarora County Whig*, reading a scholarly paper on Shakespeare's anachronisms, and his fast friend Bernard Graves leading the discussion in his usual clever way; furthermore, the ices which had been ordered for this very special occasion had proved everything that ices should be. Yet Mrs. Hilliard was dissatisfied.

"The club positively loses a vital something of its individuality when Mr. Bowers and Mr. Shelby are absent," said she.

Mrs. Bowers, a large placid personage of indefinite waist-line, remarked that nothing except politics could have dragged her husband away.

"What a pity that the Hon. Seneca had to miss your anachronisms, Volney," murmured Bernard Graves, who was a personable young gentleman of thirty.

"And Shelby," queried the editor, "hasn't that choice spirit your pity too?"

Mrs. Hilliard caught nothing of their sarcasm save Shelby's name.

"I miss his criticism," she declared. "It's so practical."

The editor fell to polishing his eye-glasses for lack of a reply.

"And so helpful," pursued the lady. "He has the faculty of ending a tangled discussion with a word."

"The dear man usually changes the subject," muttered the editor savagely under cover of an amiable platitude put forth by Mrs. Bowers.

"Or fogs it round with one of his Tuscarora yarns," dropped Graves.

The topic apparently knew no bottom for Mrs. Hilliard.

"How he will shine in Congress!" she went on. "Of course he'll get the nomination?" She referred the query to Sprague.

"Probably." His reply was lukewarm.

"And isn't there news of the convention? You ought to know, who get straight from the wires what ordinary mortals must wait to read. Has he won?"

"There was nothing definite when I left the office. They hadn't begun to ballot."

Mrs. Hilliard sensed an increasing dryness in the editor's manner.

"We're not talking literature, are we?" she laughed.

Bernard Graves considered the moment ripe for a paradox.

"The by-laws of the ideal literary club would forbid all

literary talk," he declared. "Then there would be nothing else."

"Cynic," rebuked the lady, threatening punishment with her fan. "We shall talk politics if we choose."

Disseminating culture and an odor of patchouli she drifted down the drawing-room to join another group, and the two men caught a fragment of feminine comment from a divan hard by.

"Cora Hilliard is handsome," asserted a voice. "Look at those shoulders."

"She manoeuvres to show them. Besides, she's too stout."

"What can you expect, my dear, after thirty-three years of idleness?"

"She's thirty-six," came the scrupulous correction.

"You don't mean it? And a blonde!"

"Oh, I know it's so. We were classmates in the seminary. Besides, her Milicent is a year and two months older than my Georgie, who will be thirteen in October, and when Milicent was born her mother was twenty-two."

"She says she feels twenty-two now."

"Well, she looks—" the gossip languished to an indistinct murmur.

"More literary discussion," said Sprague.

"It's as literary as politics."

"You're capable of saying it's as interesting."

"Why not? It's very human."

"So is politics."

"We are drifting on the rocks of an argument. You and I can't agree about politics, and we'd better stop trying. What absorbs you bores me—this tiresome Shelby above all."

"Oh, surely you're not serious," protested Sprague, eagerly. "It isn't possible that you care nothing whether Shelby or the honest man he's scheming to supplant represents you in Washington."

"He attracts me neither as a man nor as a problem in ethics. But don't be harsh with me. The fault is congenital, I'm sure. Every masculine American is supposed to be interested in politics,—I wonder if the Irish invented the notion,—but I can't conform; I don't know why."

"Gad," fumed the editor. "Your indifference is criminal."

"I like to hear you say 'gad,'" Graves observed. "You remind me of Major Pendennis."

Sprague shrugged his thin shoulders impatiently.

"I tell you it's a crime for you to sit by as unconcerned as a mud idol while other men struggle for civic decency."

"Picturesque as usual," applauded the delinquent, unruffled; but he added, more seriously: "It's natural that you should feel strongly after your newspaper war on Shelby. Is he so sure of the nomination?"

"If he's not sure, there's no virtue in packed caucuses."

"There, that interests me," cried Graves, brightening. "I'd like to see a caucus packed. The slang attracts me somehow. Is it very shocking?"

Sprague laughed in spite of himself.

"In things political your artlessness is prehistoric," he said. "You belong in the Stone Age. All in all, you and Ross Shelby aren't far removed: he's politically immoral; you are politically unmoral."

"We'll go and talk to Ruth Temple," decided the younger man, his eye lighting on the central figure of a group, chiefly masculine. "Who can look at her and maintain that the higher education of women is a mere factory for frumps?"

"Ruth has a quaint rareness all her own," Sprague answered, watching the play of the girl's mobile face. "She had it as a mere tot. Is it her mouth, her simple dress, her hair?—One can't say precisely what."

"Don't try. You're squinting at her like an entomologist over a favorite beetle. Take her for what she seems, and chuck analysis. She is decorative. She satisfies the optic nerve."

"Which is intimately allied with other nerves, my bachelor." He counted the men around the sofa where the girl sat beside little Milicent Hilliard, and announced, "Seven; it's Queen Ruth always."

"And, like a true monarch, bored to extinction by her courtiers. Behold Dr. Crandall browbeating the Rev. Mr. Hewett like a hanging judge. I'll warrant they're talking politics too. The atmosphere is drenched with it."

Sprague bent his head to listen.

"Wrong," he chuckled slyly. "It's literature this time, or what passes as such. They're threshing out the immortal ode on the 'Victory of Samothrace.'"

Bernard Graves laughed, also, at some jest well understood, and moved to watch this eddy in the astonishingly widespread discussion of an anonymous poem, of a certain rhetorical vigor, which had been Interpreted by some critics as a plea for woman suffrage. At this juncture Mrs. Hilliard suddenly bore down upon them, flourishing a yellow paper.

"Such news, such news!" she called. "Here's a telegram—a telegram from our candidate. He is nominated! Mr. Shelby is nominated. Think of it! One of our members! And he has wired the good news to us first of all!" She searched vainly for her glasses—her big blue eyes were astigmatic—and finally, with an impatient "You read it to them all," thrust the message into Volney Sprague's reluctant fingers.

He unfolded and read the paper, in lively quandary whether her choice were as haphazard as it seemed:—

"Nominated on first ballot. Home ten-thirty. Coming directly to club. It stands first.

"C. R. SHELBY."

"Isn't that simply dear of him?" demanded Mrs. Hilliard. "*We* come first. He remembers us in his hour of triumph. It shows the true nature of the man."

"It does indeed," grumbled Sprague, shifting within pinching distance of Bernard Graves, whom he had seen grinning in the background during the reading. "It's a barefaced bid for votes."

Mrs. Hilliard's enthusiasm demanded a vent.

"He'll be here in five minutes," she exclaimed, peering at the hall clock. "The message was delayed somehow, and his train is due now. We must devise a reception. We owe it to him. He thought of us. We must think of him. What shall we do? Think, think, you clever people!"

"That preposterous woman means to turn this into a ratification meeting," groaned the editor under his breath. "I must get out."

His hostess was of another mind, however, and barred retreat when he attempted to make his excuses.

"You shan't desert us," she declared roguishly. "You can't," she immediately added, at the sound of carriage wheels on the gravel of the drive. "He's here! The hall, the hall! Into the hall!" And into the hall Mrs. Hilliard masterfully bundled the Culture Club of New Babylon, grouping it theatrically around the newel-post and up the winding stair.

"Gad," muttered Sprague, struggling to efface himself, "knock me in the head."

Bernard Graves gleefully struck an attitude behind a friendly palm, and Mrs. Hilliard threw wide the door.

"Welcome to your own people," she cried, and Shelby, closely followed by Bowers, crossed the threshold into the light. Then big Joe Hilliard, whom the unwonted commotion had attracted from the billiard room, led a boisterous cheer, which the candidate received with modestly bowed head. He flushed, and wrestled with his diffidence like a schoolboy, as the house grew still and they waited for him to speak.

"I—I don't claim the credit, friends," he stammered. "It's your victory."

CHAPTER III

Midway in the following forenoon Shelby sat in his law office revising for the seventh time the last will and testament of the Widow Weatherwax. It was the seventh revision of her third last will and testament, to speak by the card, for the widow had a bent for will-making, which the lawyer had noticed was of periodic intensity. Once, in a moment of drollery, he entered a jocose memorandum in the "tickler," under the first week-day of several successive months: "Revise Mrs. Weatherwax's will;" and such was his foresight that twice only during that term did she frustrate his prophecy.

This day, as always, she attained the topmost step outside his office door breathless, and, as always, Shelby gravely lent a hand to deposit her plump little person in the softest of his old-fashioned office chairs. The ceremony ended regularly with the panting announcement, "The Lord has spared me for another month."

It was the man's custom at such times to allot equal praise to Providence and the widow's marvellous vitality for this happy issue, and to hazard a guess that she had thought of important changes for her will. The widow would nod assent over a heaving bosom, and slowly fan herself back to normal respiration. The relict of a leather-lunged Free Methodist preacher, she affected a garb of ostentatious simplicity. No godless pleats or tucks or gores or ruffles or sinful abominations of braid defaced the chaste sobriety of her black gown; buttons were tolerated merely as buttons, without vain thought of ornament; and the strange little bonnet, which she perched above hair whose natural coquetry of curl was austerely sleeked away, was of a composition so harshly ugly that more worldly-minded women shuddered at the sight. The worldly-minded, indeed, were prone to the criticism that the material of Mrs. Weatherwax's garments was beyond cavil, but this surely was her own concern. It were sheer impertinence to finger the texture of a zealot's sackcloth.

Shelby busied himself with his papers, pending her recovery.

"Them stairs alluz give me sech a turn," she sighed, at length. She enunciated her R's with the merciless fidelity of her section at its worst, saying stair-urs and tur-urn.

"Too bad the town's boom stopped short of elevators," sympathized Shelby.

"Shouldn't use 'em, anyway," returned the widow, firmly. "They give me a wuss turn than the stairs."

"They're trying moving stairways in some places,—a French invention, I believe."

"Shouldn't use them contrapshuns neither. The French are a godless people, full of vanity and all uncleanness."

Shelby's imagination balked at suggesting another alternative, and he held his peace. The visitor's jetty eyes forsook his face and pounced upon the clerk, who, with tongue in cheek, was filling out narrow slips of paper at a battered table clothed in a baize of a dye traditionally held to have been green.

"How's your ma's lumbago, Willie Irons?" she demanded.

The youth stammered a husky reply, and blushed far into his brick-colored hair. He was of an age when a babyish diminutive becomes a thorn unspeakable. Mrs. Weatherwax glanced tranquilly past his writhings to the ancient table.

"Ross," she asked, "wa'n't that your grandfather's?"

"Yes. He used it in his place of business."

"I call to mind seein' it in the old distillery when I was a girl," pursued the widow, who never called a spade an agricultural implement. "Distillin's a wicked business."

"People thought differently about many things in my grandfather's day."

The widow sniffed. "Wrong's wrong. Is that Seneca Bowers's roll-top desk?"

"It was Mr. Bowers's. I bought it when we dissolved partnership."

"Law books, too?"

"Yes."

"Threw in the pictur's, I s'pose?" indicating some dingy lithographs of political worthies past and present.

"Yes," admitted Shelby with superhuman good nature; "they came to boot."

The widow sniffed again. "'Pears to me," said she, "you've got nothin' new."

The man wheeled in his chair to a neighboring safe and took a tape-bound document from a pigeon-hole.

"Shall we begin?" he asked.

"Yes—if you're so rushed," she returned, and composed her features to fitting solemnity. As the lawyer slowly read the instrument, which he could have rattled off from memory, Mrs. Weatherwax punctuated the pious phrases of its exordium with approving wags. "'Frail and transitory,'" she interpolated; "that's jest what life is. I might be took any minute." At the reference to the payment of her lawful debts she recovered her spirits sufficiently to put in that she did not owe a "red cent," as everybody knew. Finally she called a halt. "Needn't go any farther," she directed. "The first part's what I like to hear best. Exceptin' one thing, all the rest about my green rep sofy a-goin' to Cousin Phoebe, the pickle-caster to Brother Henry, the old dishes what can't be sold to my beloved nephew, Jason Weatherwax, and my best tablecloths and sheets and pillow-slips to his little Ann Eliza when she gets a husband what's a good provider, is fixed jest as it hed ought to be. What I want now is a postscript."

"Another codicil? Very well."

He made note of her wishes concerning a cherished feather bed which it had struck her was too good for that "shiftless coot," Cousin Phoebe's husband, to lie upon, and, bidding her bring her witnesses on the morrow, bustled the will into his safe and fell upon his papers after the manner of all lawyer kind since Chaucer's sergeant of the law who "semed besier than he was."

The widow eyed his movements placidly.

"In a stew to hev me go?" she asked.

"Of course not," Shelby protested. "What put that in your head?"

"Your squirmin' round. Seein' I'm entirely welcome, I'll set a piece."

Shelby restrained the delight he said he felt and returned to his papers under her relentless scrutiny.

"Telegraphs of congratulashun, I s'pose," the visitor presently observed.

"Yes; my friends are rejoicing with me."

"Everybody tickled?"

"All but the common enemy, I trust."

"I ain't hed a chance to go about much and ask," said the widow, with a preliminary sniff; "but I've met some as wa'n't tickled or enemies neither."

"No? Well, after all, this isn't paradise, but New York politics."

"At Tompkins's—I alluz go to him for my Oolong—I heard that Doc Crandall won't vote for you after your dead set at the place. He's one of your party, isn't he?"

"Yes. The doctor is one of us. Good fellow, too."

"And at Brady's, where I get my corn meal, I heard somebody say you've got the Irish down on you."

"Oh, I hope not," returned the candidate, cheerfully. "They're a most respectable and industrious factor in our town's life. I like the Irish."

"I s'pose."

He searched her face and concluded that her irony was unconscious; she undeceived him.

"Butter wouldn't melt in your mouth now you're runnin' for office," she said, laboring to her feet. "I'm s'prised you hevn't wings."

Shelby affected to relish the hoary jest, and escorted her gayly to the door. "I'll look for you to-morrow," he assured her.

"Don't strain your eyes," said the widow.

The Hon. Seneca Bowers passed her on the stairs. Greeting the lawyer, he seated himself behind the clerk's back, with a meaning slant of his Grant-like head.

Shelby understood. "Leave those notices of trial for the present, William," he ordered, "and get this stipulation signed. If the man isn't in his office, try the county clerk's."

Bowers pulled with clock-work precision at his cigar, while the boy uncoiled his long legs from his chair, and with furtive little pats at his necktie and fiery shock, made ready to go out. Shelby stumbled upon the waste-paper basket as the door slammed at his clerk's heels, and with vicious satisfaction he kicked it to the room's far end.

The caller's eyes twinkled.

"The Widow Weatherwax been administering spiritual balm?" he asked.

"I could wring her neck," Shelby averred.

"Her will again?"

"Of course."

"You'll have it as long as you practise law. I did. It goes with the office. Remunerative as ever?"

"Talk about 'benefit of clergy,'" exploded the younger man; "that mediaeval bonanza isn't to be mentioned in the same week with the ministerial half-rates, donations, and hold-ups we moderns put up with. This pulpit pounder's shrew pays me no more than she pays the doctor, the grocer, the butcher, and the rest. What a ukase I could issue if I were Czar of these United States."

"Cousin Phoebe's 'sofy,' beloved Nephew Jason's unsalable dishes, and Brother Henry's pickle-caster still extant?"

"Yes, yes," groaned Shelby.

"And little Ann Eliza's sheets and pillow-slips, I dare say. It's astonishing how they endure."

"It's astonishing how I endure."

"You must—at any rate, till the Tuesday after the first Monday in November. Did the pious gossip tell you any pleasant personal news?"

"She has heard talk that the Micks are sore and that Doc Crandall has had an attack of virtue."

"You needn't lose sleep over the handful of Irish in our camp; they know who butters their parsnips. And I'll take care of the doctor. He's an innocuous mugwump. She didn't mention Volney Sprague?"

"Sprague," said Shelby, wearily; "what is that man up to now?"

Bowers rose, paced the room, and returned, big with news.

"The *Whig* has bolted," he announced.

CHAPTER IV

Shelby's amaze spent its force in an oath. In a moment he asked, calmly:—

"What does he say?"

"Not much; mainly that the manner of your nomination debars his printing your name at the head of his editorial page."

"Endorses the rest of our party ticket, doesn't he?"

"Yes; it's a personal bolt."

Shelby ruminated earnestly.

"It's only a one-horse country daily," he declared finally. "The *Whig*! You'd think Henry Clay still above ground."

"Strikes you that way, does it?" Bowers emitted with a cloud of smoke.

"Why, yes. You don't consider such a paper dangerous?"

"All newspapers are dangerous in politics; there's none too mean to have its following. The *Whig* has influence."

"It's a one-horse paper," reiterated Shelby.

"M-yes; it is a slow coach," Bowers admitted; "but it suits a lot of people. They respect it because it keeps the old name and jogs along in the old gait it had under Volney's father before him. It's been a stanch party paper, too, and that without soliciting a dollar's worth of public advertising or political pap of any description. The *Whig* doesn't often kick over the traces. The Greeley campaign was its last bolt."

"Well, the milk's spilt," said Shelby, with strenuous cheerfulness; "we've one reason the more to make next week's ratification meeting a rousing success. What did you think of our little welcome at the club last night?"

Bowers grinned.

"Mrs. Hilliard managed it first-class," he said; "but I felt cheap when we came in."

"So did I. The scheme seemed a good one when she suggested it, but when it came right down to pulling it off I would have sold out for thirty cents on the dollar. It takes lovely woman to do those things. She has her uses in politics, eh?"

"M-yes," Bowers answered in half assent; "but she's an uncertain quantity. Like grandsire's musket, she's as likely to kill behind as before."

The vine-screened window in which they now talked overlooked the neighboring Temple house, a dignified sentry at the point where the leisured street forsook the chaffer of the town to climb amidst arching elms and maples, above whose gaudy autumn masses rose the dome of the courthouse and the spires of many churches. It was an old-fashioned Georgian structure with white columns clear-cut against its weathered brick; at either side of the low steps a great hydrangea, its glory waning with the summer, lifted its showy clusters from an urn; while walk and carriage drive alike sauntered to the street through hedgerows of box. The mouth of the driveway at this moment gleamed white from the kerchiefs of a knot of Polish children estray from the quarry district, who, at a laughing nod from Ruth, swooped, a chattering barbaric horde, on the fallen apples dotting a bit of sward with yellow and red. Shelby smilingly watched the scramble to its speedy end, and turned to the giver of the feast, who sat in a sheltered corner of her veranda with a caller. The latter proved to be Bernard Graves, sunning himself with a cat's content.

"Industrious young man," Shelby observed with the irony of whole-souled dislike. "Inherits a comfortable property, goes to an expensive college, dawdles through Europe, and then comes home to play carpet knight and read poetry to girls. Why doesn't he go to work?"

Bowers made no reply to the gibe. He was watching Ruth. Presently in his slow way he checked off her qualifications:—

"Handsome girl, good education, kind disposition, rich, no airs, and no incumbrances, barring her companion, the old maid cousin, who could be pensioned. Ross, she'd do you more good than a brace of married women."

Shelby threw off the laugh of a contented man.

"I'm not in the marrying class."

"Then you'd better enter." His hand on the door, Bowers asked, "Your contribution for the county campaign fund ready?"

"Draw you a check any time," the candidate returned jauntily.

Nevertheless, when the county leader had gone Shelby gave a diligent quarter-hour to his bankbook. By and by he took an opera glass from a drawer and focussed it on the pair below. So his clerk came upon him, compelling a ruse of adjusting the instrument.

"One lens has dust in it," he declared. Perceiving Bernard Graves pass down the box-bordered path, he left his office for the day.

That evening Shelby took certain steps to prosper his coming rally at the court-house, one of which was duly noted by Mrs. Seneca Bowers. It was this lady's habit in summer evenings to discuss the doings of her immediate neighbors from her piazza, but now that the nights were cool she had shifted to the bay window of a room styled by courtesy the library from a small bookcase filled with Patent Office Reports and similar offerings of a beneficent government. This station embraced a wide prospect of shady street flanked by pleasantly sloping lawns and dwellings of various architectural pretence. Most proximate and most interesting to Mrs. Bowers was the Hilliard house, and while she rocked placidly over her darning, she contrived to hold this gingerbread edifice in a scrutiny which permitted the escape of no slightest movement of chick or child. She saw the newsboy leave the evening city papers; Milicent Hilliard dance down the leaf-strewn walk to a last half-hour's play; a white-capped maid sheet the geranium beds against possible frost; and, finally, the householder himself emerge and light a cigar whose ruddy tip winked for a second in the thickening dusk. Listing from side to side, big Joe Hilliard tramped heavily down and away to his nightly haunt in the billiard room of the Tuscarora House. As the quarry owner's great bulk vanished Shelby entered the scene, briskly crosscut the Hilliard lawn, and bounded up the steps just quitted by the substantial Joe.

"There; he's done it again!" exclaimed Mrs. Bowers.

"Who has done what?" grunted her husband, from the lounge. He was coatless and shoeless, and had spread a newspaper over his bald spot to the annoyance of a few superannuated yet active flies.

"Ross Shelby. He's gone to Cora Hilliard's again!"

"Well, let him," said Bowers, from beneath the news of the day. "It's a free country."

Mrs. Bowers smoothed a mended sock and rolled it into a neat ball with its fellow by aid of an arc light which sizzled into sudden brilliance among the maples.

"'Tisn't his going that's such a scandal," she discriminated. "All the men run there. It's the way he goes. This is the ninth time I've known him to wait till Joe Hilliard had left the house."

"Looks as if he didn't dote on Joe's society," chuckled Bowers. "I can't say that I do myself."

"It's a scandal," repeated Mrs. Bowers, firmly. Her husband remaining indifferent, she assumed her wifely prerogative to pass rigorous judgment upon his conscience. "And it's your plain duty, Seneca Bowers, to speak to him."

The old man flung off his newspaper with a snort.

"What call have I to set up as a censor of public morals?" he demanded testily. "I'm not Shelby's guardian. He's of age. He's cut his eye teeth. Talk sense, Eliza."

Mrs. Bowers essayed a flank attack.

"You're the Tuscarora boss, aren't you?"

"Yes, I'm county leader."

"What you say goes?"

"I suppose so."

She pushed her Socratic pitfall a step farther.

"When you say run so-and-so, he runs, doesn't he?"

Bowers permitted himself a dry smile in the dark.

"Most generally."

"Then you're responsible," she argued triumphantly. "You got Ross Shelby into politics; you've run him for this and that; he's your charge."

The Hon. Seneca Bowers turned his disgusted face to the wall.

"So you've the Sunday-school idea of politics," he threw over his shoulder with heavy sarcasm. "I'm to teach a Bible class and pass out dinkey little reward-of-merit cards to the prize pupils! Bah!"

His wife presently fetched her outdoor wraps and adjusted them before a mirror in the dimly lit hall.

"I'm going to take a tumbler of jelly to poor lonely Mrs. Weatherwax," she announced from the door.

Bowers roused suddenly.

"I hope, Eliza, you don't intend raking them over the coals with her," he protested, rummaging for his slippers; but his consort was beyond hail.

A literal transcript of the talk in progress over the way would have confounded the evil thinking; to illustrate the blameless text with an equally faithful record of Shelby's actions might salt the narrative. He had a lawyer's perception of the values of words as words, and through extended practice with Mrs. Hilliard excelled in that deft juggling of pregnant trifles without which Platonic friendships must die of inanition. He now thanked the lady for her successful coup at the club without specifically naming it—to hint at prearrangement were too fatuous; and Mrs. Hilliard admired his tact. Parenthetically she reflected that Joe had no tact. Without specifically naming it, Shelby contrived to suggest that she could do him yet greater service by shepherding society at his ratification meeting.

"To be significant, that sort of thing should be broadly representative," said he.

His words were impersonal, but there was no misreading his look.

Mrs. Hilliard offered her aid with equal thrift of speech and prodigality of glance. She rejoiced in transparent subtleties. Joe was never subtle.

"But I've no right to ask it of you—I don't ask it," Shelby deprecated with his lips.

"You have every right, dear friend," she reassured. "Friend! We are more than friends, you and I. We are spiritually akin. We fairly speak without words."

"Exactly." His business despatched, Shelby prepared to go.

"My time isn't my own now," he explained. "It belongs to the party."

"Selfish party," she pouted. "I hate it."

CHAPTER V

By the night of the meeting it was clear that that bugaboo of politicians, a general apathy, had blanketed the candidate's own community. Shelby should have stirred local pride. Not for years, in fact not since Bowers himself sat in Congress, had the nomination come to Tuscarora County out of the several counties which the Demijohn District comprised. Nor had the interval since the convention been a time for folding of hands. Mrs. Hilliard rounded her social circle, rallying the members of the Culture Club to stand by their own, and appealing to such outside its membership as seemed desirable on the ground of local pride. Shelby became all things to all men. To the club people he was the Club Candidate; to the unclubbed townsfolk he was New Babylon's Candidate; while among the quarry workers and other socially impossible flotsam and jetsam of the voting public other agencies than Mrs. Hilliard's heralded him as the People's Candidate. Yet the fog of apathy refused to lift.

There can naturally be little of the herdlike crushing at the doors of a political gathering in the country which marks the urban rally. The rural citizen has elbow-room to take his politics sedately and order his going with temperate pulse and judicial mind. Of such mettle normally were the New Babylonians who took their leisured way beneath the fluted columns of the court-house into Shelby's rally; but this audience felt itself more than normally temperate and judicial. Despite Mrs. Hilliard, despite the Hon. Seneca Bowers, despite Shelby's own striving, it had come less to encourage than to try and weigh.

The high places were immutably fixed. The bench of the courtroom, surmounted by a pitcher of ice-water and adorned by crayon portraits of New Babylonians learned in the law, of course stood consecrate to the speakers. The arm-chairs within the railed precinct set apart for members of the bar were by unwritten canon the peculiar haunt of citizens of light and leading, while the jury-box and its neighboring benches by custom immemorial bloomed with the pick of feminine good society. It was a privilege of the socially elect to enter such meetings at the court-house by way of the court's own staircase behind the bench, and so came Bernard Graves. Spying a vacant seat beside Ruth Temple, the young man slipped into it as unobtrusively as Mrs. Hilliard's acute sense of her responsibility as society's chief whip would permit.

"The club has responded nobly," she confided in a stage whisper across the intervening millinery. "That eccentric Volney Sprague is positively the only recreant. And isn't the audience representative?"

She beamed impartially round upon the just and the unjust through her jewelled lorgnon. Mrs. Hilliard rejoiced in her lorgnon. It compensated fully for her defect of vision, and lent her a distinction which she felt to be wholly cosmopolitan. She aspired to be cosmopolitan.

The New Babylon Brass Band fell lustily upon a popular two-step at this moment, and an usher thrust a bundle of campaign leaflets into Graves's hands. One of these pamphlets contained a half-tone portrait of Shelby, with an account of his career and a few phrases from the more noteworthy of his public addresses. Graves gave these latter a caustic scrutiny, and read aloud one of the italicized quotations.

"'It has been said, that Egypt is the gift of the Nile; Tuscarora County is no less the gift of the Erie Canal!' Now what can you say of a man who couples those two ideas with a sober face? He is aesthetically dead."

"At least, he's enthusiastic," smiled Ruth, "which is refreshing nowadays. The canal is his master hobby, the poetry of his prosaic existence. Mr. Shelby is nothing if not practical."

"Offensively practical."

"Practicality achieves."

Graves thought he detected an implication levelled at himself, and laughingly accused her.

Ruth made no denial.

"The world weighs achievement," she returned, "not barren cleverness."

Outwardly serene, the young man was inwardly ruffled. It was no new thing for her to reproach him with napkined talents, and he was wont to count it as an earnest of her liking. The novelty of this situation lay in her presenting Shelby as a pattern of fruitfulness, and it irked him. The agile leap of the brass band from the half-finished two-step to "Hail to the Chief," suddenly put this out of mind, and he watched the speakers of the evening file up the judge's staircase to the rostrum. With the subsidence of the musicians the Hon. Seneca Bowers aligned himself with the water-pitcher.

"How much he looks like Grant!" exclaimed Mrs. Hilliard, with originality.

With soldierly calm Bowers waited for the applause to cease, and submitted a slated list of officers for the meeting. It was straightway manifest that he had made good his promise to take care of Dr. Crandall. Speech-making was the breath of the worthy, if pompous, physician's nostrils, and Bowers had shrewdly judged that to offer him the chairmanship would clinch his wavering allegiance. The crowd which always relished his grandiloquence, voted him into office with a shout, and cheered his soaring periods to their peroration. A quartet of young voters now proceeded in catchy doggerel to laud the virtues of the party and the commanding genius of its candidates, thereby giving the blown doctor a much-needed respite. He came up in good form presently, winged another flight with Shelby's name as its climax, and while Mrs. Hilliard split a new pair of gloves in ineffectual applause, the candidate rose and faced his well-wishers and his foes.

"Mr. Chairman," he began, "men and women."

Bernard Graves was surprised into approval of his unexpected good taste, never dreaming that a chance remark of Ruth's had moved Shelby to discard the more hackneyed form of address. Before ever he presented himself as a candidate for public office, Shelby had been rated in the note-book of the Secretary of the State Committee as an effective speaker on "canals, local issues, and currency," with the further information that he was "strong in rural neighborhoods." This entry foreshadowed the development of an art which he had since rounded to high facility. He was considered a spellbinder of uncommon power.

"There are some among you who think harsh things of the way by which the honor of a congressional nomination has come to the community we love," he went on boldly. "I ask all such—my honest critics, I make no doubt—and I ask my avowed supporters to listen to a story. It's an old story, nearly as old as New Babylon itself, and many of you must have heard it from the honored lips of the Tuscarora pioneers whose deeds it chronicles. It is a story of our town in that rough-hewn past before railroads were dreamed of, before 'Clinton's Ditch' had touched our wilderness with its mighty wand and made it blossom like the rose. We owe a vast debt to De Witt Clinton," he digressed to add. "He was our Moses, and I can never think upon his great achievement without a thrill of gratitude. I confess to a mania for the Erie Canal."

A man in the body of the audience whom Graves recognized as a canal bank watch whose appointment Shelby had brought about, called for three-times-three, but Shelby interfered, saying, "I'd rather you'd listen than cheer."

"I speak," he continued, "of New Babylon before the coming of the canal put an end to the log cabins, the spinning-wheels, the ox-sleds, the corduroy roads, the miasmatic swamps, the wolves, the bears, the fever, the ague, the blue pill, and all the rude makeshifts and back-woods' evils which to your forefathers and mine were stern reality. These were the days when men wore their coat collars high in the back and small clothes were lengthening into trousers; when veterans of the Revolution still walked the land hale and strong, and the second war with the mother country was an uncicatrized memory. In short, I mean New Babylon of the critical hour when the Legislature wisely saw fit to erect Tuscarora County, and appointed a commission to choose a county-seat. 'Then was the tug-of-war.' New Babylon coveted the award, pined for it, panted for it as the hart for the water brooks. But so did Etruria, our strapping rival."

A ripple of appreciation of his version of the familiar legend ran from jury-box to door, and Shelby, a psychologist, like every real orator, perceived it with stirring pulse. The instrument he knew best lay attuned to his hand.

"How little could we boast," he said, adroitly identifying his listeners with the past. "The surveyors assured us that the canal was pointed our way, though no one was sanguine of its speedy coming. We did occupy the geographical centre of the new county, and with that ends the tale of our pretensions."

"We had Penelope Chubb!"

The suggestion came from an old man in one of the arm-chairs immediately below.

Interruptions never disconcerted Shelby.

"I forgot Penelope Chubb," he admitted smilingly. "Yes, we had her, the best dress-maker in Tuscarora, whom even Etruria was keen to employ. But you wouldn't have had us offer Penelope Chubb to the commissioners as an induce-ment," he added, and won a laugh for his readiness. "It was far different with Etruria. It lay on the great Ridge Road, and the stages from the East tooled and trumpeted straight through its long main street. It had stores and shops and factories, it had a grist-mill, a distillery, a tavern—"

"Two taverns," corrected the hoary critic below.

"Two taverns, a bona fide doctor, a licensed preacher, the only academy, the only meeting-house, the only printing-press, and the only newspaper within the county limits. The Etrurians were so cock-sure of victory that they raised the price of village lots. Yet we presumed to hope. Great emergencies focus on individuals; so with ours. New

Mark Lee Luther

Babylon found its saviour in Israel Booth."

Booth's name was the signal for an outburst. The older generation held him in equal reverence with the fathers of the republic.

"It was Israel Booth who saw that our one hope lay in a natural resource, and set himself to conjure one from Red Jacket Creek. Genius has seldom worked with less promising material. Red Jacket Creek isn't an imposing stream to-day as it skirts our town,—I am told few of the historic streams are imposing,—and there was hardly more of it then. It yielded adequate power to run the sawmills only during the spring freshets when the swamps over-flowed, and it was our ill luck that the legislative commission decided to visit Tuscarora in dog-days while Etruria's stage line was doing a land-office business and our poor little resource was wasted to a long-drawn-out puddle choked with cat-tails and lily-pads. But what dismayed other men seemed to spur Israel Booth, and one night, a bare fortnight before the commissioners' coming, his great conception saw its birth. Before he slept he took counsel with the leading settlers."

Shelby broke off to address one of his audience.

"Your father was in the secret, Mr. Hewett," he said; "and yours, Dr. Crandall—and my grandfather, and many another upright citizen."

The gentlemen singled out for reflected fame stirred consciously in the effort to appear unconscious.

"Now Red Jacket Creek woke from its summer sleep. The spiders in the mill yards were dispossessed; lumber that had been hauled away was replaced and piled conspicuously; the dams and flumes were repaired, and the water-gates were shut; the backwater began to flood the ponds and agitate the colony of frogs; prominent men were heard to pray for rain, and Israel Booth was seen carrying water by night from his well to the raceway; New Babylon was big with mystery. You all know the sequel. You know how the commissioners came to us hungry from Etruria; how Booth and his helpers met them in Sunday butternut and shirt frills without spot; how we flattered our visitors' distinguished yet entirely human stomachs with the toothsome dishes of our grand-mothers; how we cracked dusty bottles of Madeira brought years before from New England; and how we brewed a waggish punch from the output of our rival's own distillery. You know how they were driven presently about our cleanly streets, every dooryard raked spick and span against their coming, and were brought at last to the mills. You know how the Red Jacket, pent to bursting from a providential thunder-storm of the night, blustered down through the race with the pride of a Danube; how the saws sang, the logs rolled, the teamsters shouted, and the commissioners admired. You know, too, that the guests left before the waters abated or the punch-bowl knew drought; and that by the same token we won our fight. Does any of you in his inmost heart censure the pioneers for their stratagem? I think not. They worked with what tools lay to their hands, and the profit is their children's and their children's children's."

He wisely left it to his listeners to point the parallel, and turned to discuss the larger issues of the campaign. His canvass chanced among one of the several battles waged over the national currency, a thorny topic at best, but Shelby threw a life into the juiceless principles of his theme which roused the dullest. At the last, referring to the hardships a depreciated currency might entail on the nation's pensio-ners, he turned to the Hon. Seneca Bowers as if his Grant-like figure typified the great war's heroism, and delivered an impassioned eulogy upon the soldier dead. It was naturally, convincingly done, and the audience was loath to find it his peroration.

There was no doubt of his sweeping triumph. With its formal close the meeting transformed itself spontaneously into a reception, and, under the spell of his eloquence still, men prophesied that his brilliant career would halt not short of the governorship. Mrs. Hilliard would be satisfied with nothing less than the presidency.

"The world his oyster," said Bernard Graves. He had pocketed a sheaf of stenographic notes, with which he had busied himself during the latter part of Shelby's speech, and mounted a bench with Ruth, the better to watch the crowd surge round the foot of the platform. "Shall we go now?" he asked at length.

Ruth turned from the scene with shining eyes.

"I promised I would tell him what I thought," she answered.

"You promised Shelby!"

"He called the other day—after you had gone. He talks well of politics. I was interested."

Bernard Graves swallowed something unpalatable.

"And the speech?" he said. "What do you think?"

"That it was remarkable—even brilliant, as they're saying."

"Great is buncombe."

"Don't," she begged. "Why spoil it for me? If nothing more, it proves him a born orator, who can do what he will with men. I believe in him."

Shelby approached them presently, with the melting of the throng, and Graves had to listen to an antiphony of praise, sung by Ruth and Mrs. Hilliard. In a lull he asked Shelby if he admired the oratorical methods of General Garfield.

"Eh!" said Shelby, abruptly.

"Your manner suggests his at times."

"Yes—oh, yes. I see. Powerful speaker, Garfield. No bad model, you know."

"Yes, I know," Graves answered.

Shelby turned again to the circle of women, and Graves left the building. A few minutes later he entered the *Whig* office and made his way to Sprague's cluttered sanctum.

"Volney," he announced, as the editor peered genially from underneath the green drop-light, "I want to browse in your file of the Congressional Record. And you've Garfield's Works down here, too, haven't you?"

CHAPTER VI

Shelby stretched himself awake and contentedly surveyed his bachelor bedroom in the Tuscarora House. He had boarded at this establishment upward of five years, and his chamber had been decorated and, to a degree, furnished in accord with his notions of elegant comfort. The wall paper was a pattern which William Morris and his disciples would have writhed to behold,—a hideous terra-cotta ground overrun with meaningless scrolls and stiff garlands of roses of an unearthly pink. There were stuffy maroon lambrequins above the window casements, and two large blue vases, containing many-dyed plumes of pampas grass, flanked like rigid sentinels a pseudo-marble clock upon the truly marble mantelpiece which somehow suggested a mausoleum falling to decay; while the blue motive was further emphasized by a plush photograph album, with a little mirror let into its cover, standing in a metallic holder on the bureau, whose sombre walnut matched the bed and chairs. The pictures included a chromo, depicting an impossible castle set in an equally impossible landscape, a print or two of race horses, a lithograph of a poker game in supposably high life, and a photogravure of a painting familiar to the habitues of a great metropolitan hotel, popularly fancied in the country to be daring in the extreme. At first sight of the original, over the rim of a cocktail, Shelby had been fired with the resolve to own some sort of copy, and even now, after several years of possession, he esteemed it one of the world's masterpieces of pictorial art.

He dressed himself in the same content which had flushed his waking revery. The plaudits of last night's mass-meeting still rang harmoniously in his ears, and the praise of Ruth Temple and Mrs. Hilliard was sweeter in retrospect than it had been in reality. This happy serenity bore him company through the bare echoing corridors of the hotel to the office, to be heightened by the gratulations of the landlord and the help, who seemed to feel that a vicarious honor had been done the house, a most insinuating form of hero-worship which attained its climax in the homage of the true-penny who set forth his morning bitters on the bar.

Extended notices of the meeting had been telegraphed to the neighboring cities by local correspondents, and Shelby ran through the newspaper accounts in the cheerless dining room, which he thought to-day by no means comfortless. There was a flattering deference in the manner of the waitresses, and the lessening of their pert familiarity told him, more plainly perhaps than anything else, that he had become a personage. He failed to remind them that the oatmeal was burned, the rolls soggy, and the coffee reminiscent of chicory. He ate all that was set before him, and was still content. The hotel barber-shop seemed a blithe spot indeed, as he sat for his daily shave, and the admiring barber a prince of good fellows. Sweet also were the greetings of the market-place, as, cigar in mouth, he sauntered through Main Street to his law office. All his paths were pleasantness and peace.

The first discordant note was struck, oddly enough, by his faithful satellite, William Irons, who, at his employer's entrance, abruptly left off an attempt to coax his red shock into lovelocks, slid his pocket mirror under a heap of papers, and fell to hammering the typewriter with unnatural energy. Shelby accepted the subterfuge, and wished him a hearty good morning.

"Did you attend the rally, William?" he inquired, as he slit the envelopes of his morning's mail.

"Yep," said William Irons.

"Everybody seemed pleased?"

"Nope."

"No?" Shelby repeated, lifting his eyes. "And who was disgruntled?"

"The Widow Weatherwax."

"Ah! That's unfortunate," returned Shelby, blandly. "What is the widow's grievance?"

"She's put out because you told a story makin' light of drinkin' punch. She belongs to all the temp'rance societies doin' business, you know."

"No; I didn't know."

"And she says none of her church'll vote for you after your countenancin' such a cryin' sin."

"Her list of cardinal sins is extensive."

"Yep," agreed William. "Won't even let me play my fiddle in the house. Says it's a vanity."

"I'd forgotten that you had gone to live with her."

"Do chores for my keep," explained the clerk. "Have codfish three times a day, Monday morning to Saturday night, and no warm victuals Sundays. Makes me keep my fiddle in the barn and play it behind the woodpile."

Shelby laughed, and sought to woo back his mood of charity toward all, but it was futile. The widow's mite of hostile criticism had leavened the whole lump with bitterness. Nevertheless, he bridled his tongue.

Work came hard for the moment, and his eyes strayed past his papers through an open window and spied Ruth Temple's slender shape in the lawn below. The dewy freshness of the morning seemed to touch her youth as it did the asters and belated hollyhocks of the quaint garden into which she passed as he watched. Then Bernard Graves suddenly cut into the picture, and drew a newspaper from his pocket, directing her attention to something which amused him. But Ruth did not laugh. Shelby clearly saw her color change.

A heavy step outside his door heralded the coming of the Hon. Seneca Bowers. The county leader was in no mood for idle words, and looked as Grant may have looked when about to pass judgment on a disgraced soldier.

"Seen the *Whig*?" he asked curtly, when William Irons had been despatched to the post-office.

"The *Whig*! No, I don't take it."

"I'd advise you to subscribe."

Shelby's face sobered with a premonition of misfortune.

"What's to pay now?" he asked.

Bowers struck open a copy of Volney Sprague's newspaper, and with stubby rigid thumb guided the candidate's glance to an editorial.

"Read that, sir."

His tone was a new thing in their intercourse, but without remark Shelby read:—

"AN ELOQUENT THIEF"

"Before a crowded mass-meeting last evening, Calvin Ross Shelby, congressional candidate for the suffrages of an intelligent people, stultified alike his hearers and himself. We shall not dignify his specious appeal to local pride with the easy exposure of its fallacy; the victory were too cheap; but since he glibly sought to establish a parallel between his own questionable political methods and the legendary deeds of the founders of our community, we too will frame from his eloquence a parallel which we commend to the orator and to his electors. In the newspaper business we call it the deadly parallel.

"Do you realize what this about the dollar means, if true? It means that all you need do to increase the acreage of your farm is to change the figures in your title deeds; it means that your creameries will yield a better product if you water the milk; it means that when the housewife shops she will buy more linen, or gingham, or calico, if the merchant moves the brass tacks of his counter yard measure nearer together."

"When you can enlarge your farm by changing the figures in your deeds; when your dairymaid can make more butter and cheese by watering the milk; when you can have more cloth by decreasing your yardstick one-half; when you can sell more tons of merchandise by shortening your pound one-half,—then, and not until then, can you increase the value of your property or labor by decreasing your standard of values."

CALVIN ROSS SHELBY.

JAMES ABRAM
GARFIELD,
Faneuil Hall, Boston,
September 10, 1878.

"These fanatics say that if foreign nations don't want the sort of money we choose to coin they can go without, and that we should be glad that they don't. We've some other things that foreigners don't want. We've peaches with the yellows, and weeviled wheat, and rancid butter, and ancient eggs, but I've yet to meet a farmer who wants to corner the market. They remind me of a town that was moved to build a gallows because all its neighbors had them. I don't need to add that it was not an American town. And one of the wise city fathers was so carried away by his patriotism that he tried to make the council pass a resolution that the gallows be reserved for that town's inhabitants exclusively."

"But this is the first time I ever heard a financial philosopher express his gratitude that we have a currency of such bad repute that other nations will not receive it; he is thankful that it is not exportable. We have a great many commodities in such a condition that they are not exportable. Mouldy flour, rusty wheat, rancid butter, damaged cotton, addled eggs, and spoiled goods generally are not exportable. But it never occurred to me to be thankful for this putrescence. It is related in a quaint German book of humor that the inhabitants of Schildeberg, finding that other towns, with more public spirit than their own, had erected gibbets within their precincts, resolved that the town of Schildeberg should also have a gallows; and one patriotic member of the town council offered a resolution that the benefits of this gallows should be reserved

Mark Lee Luther

exclusively for the inhabitants of Schildeberg."

JAMES ABRAM GARFIELD,
House of Representatives,
June 15, 1870.

"If each grave had a voice to tell us what its silent tenant last saw and heard on earth, we might stand, with uncovered heads, and hear the whole story of the war. We should hear that one perished when the first great drops of the crimson shower began to fall, when the darkness of that first disaster at Manassas fell like an eclipse on the nation; that another died of disease while wearily waiting for winter to end; that this one fell on the field, in sight of the spires of Richmond, little dreaming that the flag must be carried through three more years of blood before it should be planted in that citadel of treason; and that one fell when the tide of war had swept us back till the roar of rebel guns shook the dome of *the* capitol, and re-echoed in the chambers of the Executive mansion. We should hear mingled voices from the from the Rappahannock, the Rapidan, the Chickahominy, and the James, solemn voices from the Wilderness, and triumphant shouts from the Shenandoah, from Petersburg, and the Five Forks, mingled with the wild acclaim of victory and the sweet chorus of returning peace."

CALVIN ROSS SHELBY.

Rappahannock, the Rapidan, the Chickahominy, and the James, solemn voices from the Wilderness, and triumphant shouts from the Shenandoah, from Petersburg, and the Five Forks, mingled with the wild acclaim of victory and the sweet chorus of returning peace."

JAMES ABRAM GARFIELD, Arlington, Va., May 30,1868.

"Of these three passages, rightly thought by Calvin Ross Shelby's audience the most telling of his speech, the first and second are unmistakably plagiarisms of ideas, while the third, differing from its original in but one telltale, damning word, is shameless, flat-footed theft. Either of the first two offences committed singly might be unconscious; conjoined they betray deliberation; united with the third they 'smell to heaven.' It is high time for the voters of this congressional district to ask themselves the question. Shall we vote for a thief?"

"Well, sir, well?" exploded Bowers at last.

Shelby tossed the paper aside with a laugh.

"It's well done."

"Well done!" Bowers dropped one of his infrequent oaths. "Have you nothing else to say?"

"Yes; it's true, more or less."

"You admit it?"

"Keep cool. It was this way: I was pressed for time when I prepared my speech,—you know that,—and it occurred to me to adapt one or two of Garfield's illustrations. I've studied him some, and he said many things that fit in nowadays as well as they ever did. Plenty of speakers quarry there I guess. I honestly meant to give him the credit of that soldier business in my peroration, but somehow the quotation marks were lost in the shuffle. There was but one chance in a thousand that anybody would notice."

"Somebody did," growled Bowers, and spat our his mangled cigar.

"Yes; I ran against a man with a memory."

"It wasn't on the square, Ross. It'll hurt you."

Shelby eyed him shrewdly.

"You read speeches in Washington that I wrote," he reminded.

"That's different. Lots of congressmen do that,—even senators. They're not posted on everything."

"No," Shelby agreed, with an irony too subtle for Bowers; "they certainly are not. However, there's no need to borrow trouble over this thing. People will laugh a little, say it was a good speech, wherever I got it, and vote the straight party ticket despite Bernard Graves."

"Graves," said Bowers. "What has he to do with it?"

"Everything; he's the little joker with the memory."

Bowers whistled.

"What is he after?"

Shelby jerked his head toward the Temple doorstep where Bernard still lingered.

"After her."

CHAPTER VII

"Humor a silk stocking according to his crotchet, that's my maxim," submitted Bowers as they threshed the matter out in its latest aspect.

"I can't see its application to Graves. He's outside politics; hates the very name, they say."

"Practical politics is applied human nature. If a rule is sound in politics, it will work anywhere this side of the pearly gates. Graves may not care a tinker's dam for politics, but evidently he does get queasy when another man's ideas are misappropriated. Perhaps that's his crotchet. Writes himself, doesn't he?"

"Some rubbish or other," returned Shelby, contemptuously.

"That's where he is susceptible, to my thinking. I don't cotton to your woman theory. I say leave women out of politics. So conciliate him; humor his crotchet."

"I can't see why I should kotow to him, or what further harm he can do," said the candidate, but he deferred to Bowers's judgment. "I'll look him up this afternoon," he agreed; "though I've no stomach for the job. I never liked the cuss."

He abundantly appreciated this long-standing antipathy as he cast about for some common ground of interest in the little reception-room of the house shared by Bernard Graves and his mother. It seemed to the waiting caller a drab and lifeless home, uninteresting in its appointments, and out of keeping with the wealth known to have been inherited by the widow and her son. The young man's study was visible down the vista of a series of low-ceiled apartments, and Shelby saw that it was crammed with books. None of the many pictures could cope in dash and color with his own collection and, what seemed to him singular in a Protestant home, they were chiefly of the Madonna; all in all, a tame assortment beside his copy of the secular masterpiece in the great metropolitan hotel. Over one of the crowded bookcases was the cast of a winged woman. It was armless and headless, and Shelby wondered by what accident it had become so damaged, and why it was not banished to the attic.

The maid came presently to tell him that Mr. Bernard had gone for a walk to the golf links.

Shelby was relieved. He felt ill at ease in this queer drab dwelling, and doubtful of the course he ought to pursue with its tenant. It would be another matter altogether in the open air. Returning to his law office, he bade William Irons to telephone the Tuscarora House livery-stable to send around his horse and buggy.

At the farm-house on the outskirts which served the golf devotees for a headquarters Shelby was told that Graves had gone yet farther, taking the direction of the Hilliard quarries—geologizing bent, the speaker thought. Unassociated with practical results, this had always presented itself to Shelby as a trivial pursuit akin to botany, embroidery, and other employments distinctly feminine. He forebore comment, however, and presently struck down a road which wound into a little suburb peopled by Polish quarry-workers. It was essentially an alien community in whose straggling streets and lanes one heard English but seldom. Tow-headed children, shy elves peeping from odd hiding-places, swarmed a half-dozen and upward to a house. Work was the key-note of Little Poland, as it was called. While the men toiled in the sandstone quarries the women did a man's stint in the fields of the outlying farms, and bore more children. Childbirth was a mere detail in these thick-waisted women's lives; some hours, a day perhaps, and they were stooping in the fields again. And the children early put shoulder to the wheel; those too small for the fields begged food in the streets of the town. Little Poland was virtually a fief of Joe Hilliard's. Men, women, and elves looked up to him as to a benevolent feudal lord, and the naturalized males voted Joe Hilliard's party ticket with mechanical precision.

The politician approached the quarries with an interested eye. Among his many irons in the fire he had acquired part ownership in another quarry to the westward, like this bordering the towpath of the canal. Bowers held the controlling interest, though neither his name nor Shelby's figured prominently in its management. They called it the Eureka Sandstone Company.

Shelby tied his horse near the office, and, putting his head among the morning-glories curtaining an open window, stated his errand to Hilliard, whose vast bulk was humped ludicrously upon a high stool. The big fellow stopped thumbing his ledger, greeted him with a jovial shout, and directed him toward a stratum of rock which the workmen had recently unearthed.

"Look it over," he called after him. "It promises to pan out scrumptious. We struck A-1 rock seven feet below the surface."

"That discounts the Eureka," said Shelby. "We've never done better than twelve."

He picked his way through the yards, the hammers of the stone dressers clinking out a not unmusical chorus from every shed, and skirting the docks where the ponderous cranes swung the great slabs to the canal boats, scrambled down a rough roadway into the quarry proper amidst all the hurly-burly of the teamsters and the hoarse steam drills. The walls of sandstone rose sheer around him, sliced down by the blasts like sugar with a scoop. Some of the formation was not unlike sugar little refined; some, lighter, with streaks of grayish pink, like sides of bacon; and some, a rich deep brown which architects specified the country over, was said to have no equal the world around save only in Japan. In the newly uncovered tract Shelby spied Bernard Graves pecking about with a little hammer.

"Prospecting for gold?" he asked jocularly.

"No; fucoids."

"Eh?"

"Fossils, you know; a sort of seaweed. The only kind we can discover in this formation."

"My little freshwater college wasn't strong on the sciences," said Shelby, speculating whether this particular crotchet required humoring. As the young man's own interest in the topic seemed languid, he decided against this course and frankly told him that he wanted to talk with him. "Suppose we move away from the clatter of the drills," he suggested.

Graves assented, and they shifted from beneath the overhanging bank of sandy loam to the shade of an unused derrick.

"Smoke?" queried the politician, affably.

Graves declined a cigar, explaining, "I merely take a cigarette now and then, usually after dinner."

Shelby's contempt for cigarettes was boundless, but he dissembled his opinion, and lit the strongest cigar in his case.

"It's up to me, Bernard," he confessed with a laugh. "It's my move, and I'm right on the spot like a little man, though humble pie isn't my favorite tidbit by a large majority."

"Meaning what?" asked Graves, without animation.

Behind the candidate's urbane mask rioted a lust to mar and maim, but his political self explained blandly:—

"Meaning that your checkmate in this morning's *Whig* was well played."

"I didn't write that editorial."

"I know you didn't. It had the Volney Sprague earmarks. But you did what is more important,—you inspired it."

"Well?"

"Just this: in a general way I admit its justness, and come frankly to tell you so."

"Why should you trouble yourself?"

Shelby throttled his mounting ire.

"Because," he returned slowly, "I recognize your ability and want your support. If you mean to interest yourself in politics, I can be of service to you. I know, of course, you don't think politicians are necessarily scamps."

"I judge no class of men so summarily," Graves opened his mouth to protest. "That is too much like Burke's indictment against a whole people, you know."

The allusion was not familiar, but Shelby said, "Exactly," with labored calm. He fancied that he detected a note of condescension, and resented it passionately.

"The average politician isn't such a bad lot," he went on. "His methods don't always square with the Decalogue, but he means well, and in the long run does well. I don't say this to pat myself on the back. You know me. I'm a plain, practical man, and try to steer by common-sense. If I'm elected to Congress, I'll do my best to make the district proud of me, and I'll promise you personally, right here and now, that I will deliver no man's speeches but my own."

Graves wished that he would make an end of his excuses and go away. The whole episode bored him, and his mind wandered even while he listened. He was thinking that that muscular Pole directing the planting of a steam drill below the sand-bank a rather statuesque figure for these prosaic days. The man had jumped upon the tripod of the drill in ordering the work, and loomed large and competent. Graves thought him in feature not unlike his great compatriot John Sobieski, and tried to picture him in the Polish king's armor which he remembered to have seen in some European collection. Shelby's silence recalled him.

"Really, there's no necessity for you to explain or promise anything to me," he rejoined coldly. "I'm not in politics, and I don't care to be."

Shelby had reached his last ditch.

"You think you're too damned good for it," he broke out. "It's the lily-fingered people of your stripe who make reform a byword and a laughing-stock."

Graves's face flamed, and he shrank inwardly with a scholar's repugnance from the rencounter. Outwardly, however, he was truculent.

"Such bar-room personalities are characteristic of you," he retorted. "Your place—"

But it was fated that Shelby should not learn his place. A sharp warning cry from a workman heralded the crumbling fall of a great section of the bank overhanging the drill which Graves had idly watched, and, as idly, watched still. A dreamer of habit, his will failed immediately to rally to the naked fact and its demands. It was unreal, a picture, a play, a poet's conception of chaos—that was it! The thing was Dantesque or Miltonic. The gaping rent, the jumbled rocks, the thick spurt of steam issuing from the buried drill, it was all tumultuous, primeval; and that grimy workman, heaving aside the dirt and scrambling to the air, was suggestive of Milton's earth-born "tawny lion, pawing to get free."

"Good God, man, wake up!" Shelby shook him roughly by the arm and dragged him toward the scene of the catastrophe. "There are men under that heap."

A little knot of Polish laborers forthwith congregated, ox-eyed and inert. Shelby tore a shovel from a paralyzed hand and began to dig, ripping out crisp oaths at their stupidity.

"Find shovels for these cattle," he commanded.

By signs Graves roused the unnerved men to action, but he could find no sort of tool for himself, and stood empty-handed apart, conscious of unfitness. The politician, burrowing like a woodchuck, showered him with red earth.

"English? Anybody speak English?" he panted without stopping. "How many are under here?"

One of the workmen understood, chattered excitedly with his fellows, and held up one soiled finger.

"Ein," he said. "Kiska, he vork here."

Shelby's shovel grated on the cylinder of the buried drill. From underneath its tripod protruded the booted leg of a man.

"Go easy, boys," he cautioned.

With his own hands he skilfully uncovered the victim's head and trunk. Graves saw that it was the giant of his daydream. The man's rugged face was earth-stained and still; his great chest motionless. Shelby mastered the situation with a glance, thrust his hand into the coarse shirt, and felt for the heart.

"There's life in him," he announced. "Over with him into the shade." Between them all they bore him to a shelf of level rock. "Off with his shirt," said Shelby to his helper, and they two stripped the body to the waist. It was the torso of a gladiator. Shelby rolled the garment and thrust it underneath the bare back below the shoulders. "It's not high enough," he decided instantly. "Something else—a coat—anything."

Kiska's compatriots could not have complied had they understood, being coatless to a man. Bernard Graves took off a new golf coat which Shelby ruthlessly crumpled and stuffed into place. An instant later he was astride the Pole's hips, his hands grasping the powerful chest on either side.

Bracing his elbows, Shelby bore his whole weight forward, counted three, sat back upon his knees, counted two, and so continued, down "one-two-three," up "one-two," with the quiet assurance of a surgeon.

The younger man watched his every movement with wondering respect. The operator interrupted his meditations.

"Get hold of his tongue with your handkerchief," he ordered. "That's right—hold it by the tip. On one side—on one side. Now take both his wrists and pin them above his head—so."

All the while the steady pressure and relaxation went on, compelling the lungs to their function. Presently came the faintest quiver of a nostril, and Shelby smiled.

"Kiska will do his own breathing pretty soon," he said. Presently he suggested: "Better fetch Hilliard now. And have him 'phone Doc Crandall to come to Kiska's house in Little Poland. I'll take Kiska home in my rig when his bellows gets well under way."

Graves did his errand, outlining the disaster and rescue as he hurried with the quarry owner to the scene. Joe Hilliard was divided between sympathy for Kiska, whom he declared was the pick of his men, and admiration for Shelby's presence of mind.

"He's got gumption, that man," he exclaimed, "gumption, simon-pure."

Graves's own impressions were mixed, and the stress of the accident passed, he resumed his ruined coat with a vague sense of personal slight. Something of this sort prompted him to say rather patronizingly to Shelby as they parted:—

"You made skilful use of that method of resuscitation. Where in the world did you pick it up?"

"Every schoolboy knows it," returned the politician, shortly; "or every schoolboy should."

CHAPTER VIII

Shelby's forecast of the effect of the *Whig's* exposure was brilliantly fulfilled. People did laugh over it and say that it was a good speech, whatever its source. In popular conception literary theft is at worst a venial sin whose very iniquity is doubtful unless found out. The culprit's average fellow-townsman accepted the incident as fresh evidence of his acknowledged cleverness and promptly forgot it in the nine days' wonder over his exploit at the Hilliard quarries.

The town's attitude mirrored that of the congressional district and the state. Volney Sprague's editorial occasioned some little paragraphing here and there among up-state newspapers and by brief mention in *Associated Press* despatches roused a metropolitan daily of opposite political faith to one of the satirical thrusts for which it was famous; whereupon one of its more serious contemporaries found a text for a thunderous jeremiad on the decay of political morality. Yet where one person read of Shelby's plagiarism, a score devoured the sensational accounts of his rescue of Kiska, while of those who read both, an illogical but human majority considered his atonement complete.

Sprague himself was disposed to gauge Shelby's vogue with the groundlings as greater than before, and lamented it to Bernard Graves, who fell wholly into his mood for once and deplored the fatuity of popular judgment with unlooked-for warmth.

His friend listened with unqualified approval.

"Thank Heaven, you're beginning to take an interest in politics!" he exclaimed.

The young man flushed.

"There are some things in this man's canvass one can't ignore," he carefully explained, and tried to think he meant plagiarism.

He had not discussed recent happenings with Ruth Temple. When he took her the *Whig* article the morning after the mass-meeting she had displayed a disconcerting willingness to cloud the vital fact and excuse Shelby. Indeed, he finally left with the disgusted conviction that she had pilloried not the sinner but himself,—a not uncommon outcome in a clash of wits between a woman and a man. After that, he told himself, she might form what fantastic opinion of this freebooter she chose without let or hindrance from him, and at the same time he resolved that she should see less of him. The latter resolution proved as flimsy as a New Year's vow, but while it needed less than a smile to whistle him back, the whole distasteful subject of Shelby became tacitly taboo.

As Ruth was a very woman, often saying less what she really thought than what she knew would stir dissent, her inner-most opinions were less stable than he fancied. She had not had speech with Shelby since the mass-meeting, but he had found time that night to ask her to drive with him, and she anticipated the outing with a zest whose disproportion to its surface cause she did not analyze.

On the appointed afternoon she saw his horse and buggy brought from the Tuscarora House and hitched at the curb below his office, and as it lacked little of the hour set she thrust home the last hat-pin and stood jacketed and gloved by a window, waiting his coming. The hour struck and brought no Shelby, though punctuality was the first article of his creed. Out in the drowsy thoroughfare a sprinkling-cart jarred heavily past, spurting ineffectually at the yellow dust which rose perversely under its baptism and surged beneath the awnings of the shops. It was Saturday, universal shopping-day in the farmland, and a ramshackle line of rustic vehicles—buggies, democrats, sulkies, lumber wagons —with graceless plough horses slumbering in the thills, stretched in ragged alignment down the curb. Shelby's smart turnout seemed fairly urban by contrast, and Ruth saw that it met with the critical approval of the loungers.

A quarter of an hour slipped by; no Shelby. His cob fretted at the autumn flies and whinnied to be gone. A half-hour elapsed, unfruitful; an hour. Then did Queen Ruth, on whose imperious nod a little world had hung from baby-hood, perceive the recreant come calmly down from his law office in company with some creature of relatively common clay, shake hands, chat further, shake hands again, take up his reins amid an interchange of badinage with the bystanders, and so, gossiping still, jog deliberately on—to her!

She spun on her heel as he turned in at the drive and rang for her maid.

"If Mr. Shelby should call," she directed, wrenching at her gloves, "say I'm not at home."

Shelby's occupations in the meantime had been absorbing. In the course of an earnest conference at the Tuscarora House the evening of the quarry accident, the Hon. Samuel Bowers had removed his cigar to let fall a sententious observation.

"As long as an all-wise Providence saw fit to dump that sand-bank on one of the Polacks," said he, "I call it a piece of downright Ross Shelby luck that it fell on Kiska."

"I should have worked as hard over a dago," rejoined Shelby; "or a dog either, I guess."

"M-yes; I reckon. But you're not complaining that it wasn't some dago who doesn't know a ballot from a bunch of garlic? No, I reckon not." His eyes twinkled, and Shelby flickered a responsive grin. "Note a rule for candidates: When about to effect the spectacular rescue of one of the toiling masses which are the bone and sinew of this fair land of ours, pick a man who holds a block of the foreign vote right in the pocket of his jeans."

It was perhaps appreciation of this aphorism's significance, perhaps sheer abundance of the milk of human kindness, perhaps a harmonious blending of both, which inspired Shelby's warm welcome to Kiska as he was about to leave his office to join Ruth Temple.

"You shouldn't have come out so soon, Kiska," he protested, urging the big Pole to a chair, and bringing him a glass of water. "Did you walk all the way from Little Poland to see me?"

"I valked," answered Kiska, simply, his face working. "I vould like to haf roon, Meester Shelby."

"Oh, I wouldn't run much just yet," laughed Shelby, kindly, trying to head off the man's expression of gratitude. "Have another drink? Perhaps you'd prefer some whiskey?"

Kiska declined, and harked back to his message.

"I vould like to haf roon to tank you, Meester Shelby. I got vife to tank you. I got mooch cheeldren to tank you. I no taalk good. Dat Eengleesh hard,—so? Eef I no taalk, I tink. I tink all day: Tank you, Meester Shelby, tank you, Meester Shelby."

"You speak English very well," said Shelby, patting him on the shoulder. "But you mustn't say any more about the matter."

He led him presently to talk of the quarry-workers and their families, their wages, their hours, their recreation, their parish church, their priest, their school; for Little Poland was sufficient unto itself; and Kiska saw that he questioned with sympathy and understanding, and was pleased. On the dial of his office clock Shelby noted the hour of his appointment come and go, and from his window he caught a fleeting glimpse of Ruth at hers. She wore his favorite hat, with a gleam of red, which became her dark hair so well, and he divined that she had put it on because of him. He longed to be out and away with her between the autumn hedgerows, but there sat Kiska, garrulous of Poland over seas and Little Poland by the quarries, and to Kiska the politician inclined a patient ear.

The Pole rose at last, after a delighted hour, and Shelby saw his eye light on a package of campaign lithographs of himself, which had come that morning from the printers.

"Want one?" he asked.

Kiska exploded in incoherent gratitude.

"Take several," said Shelby, snapping an elastic band around a sheaf of the pictures. "Give 'em to your friends to hang in their front windows. That's what we do with 'em in town, you know. It's American. You're all good Americans in Little Poland, aren't you?" A thought struck him, and from a roll of banknotes, destined for campaign uses, he extracted a ten-dollar bill. "I dare say Joe Hilliard will pay your doctor, Kiska," he went on, "but there'll be other things you'll want. Winter's coming; buy the yellow-haired kids some shoes; get the wife a warm dress. You can pay me when Poland gets its independence."

Kiska took the money. "I vould like to vork for you," he exclaimed.

"Would you?" laughed the politician. "I think perhaps you may some day."

The minor social conventions, which, after all, are possibly the major ones, were consistently ignored by Shelby.

"Not at home?" he repeated after Ruth's maid. "I guess you're mistaken. I saw Miss Temple at the window as I drove in the gate. Just look around a bit, and you'll find her."

He walked calmly past the bewildered girl to the drawing-room. In the centre of the apartment stood Ruth, her cheeks waving crimson, like a poppy field astir.

"Angry?" said the man.

Ruth waited till the open-mouthed maid had retreated down the hall.

"I'm furious," she answered, and looked the part.

"Think I'm a boor?"

She could not trust herself to reply. Had he dared smile then, she would have swept by him, but he was wholly grave.

"I'll tell you what you're thinking," he said quietly. "You are thinking that I have fallen short of your notion of me. You listened the other night at the court-house and thought kindly things. Then you were told by my enemies that I had used in part what was not my own. You were vexed, for it impeached your judgment of character. Then I failed of my appointment, and did you a more grievous wrong—I piqued your woman's vanity."

Ruth gasped.

"Your effrontery is—is fascinating."

Shelby's eyes hinted a smile. She had said what she thought.

"I shall not defend myself to you against the charges of the *Whig*," he went on. "I doubt even if I shall answer them publicly. Greater men than I have had their names blackened in a campaign, and deemed silence the wisest answer. People don't ascribe many virtues to the politician, but even he occasionally turns the other cheek. As for my tardiness to-day—well, I could have avoided it."

"You admit it?" blazed Ruth.

"Yes. I had my choice."

"And you chose—" The shabby figure she had seen descend from Shelby's office visualized itself sharply.

"Yes—poor devil—I chose Kiska."

Her mood veered, and she whirled impulsively toward him, all womanliness and contrition.

"Forgive me. How could I know? I thought—I thought—"

"That it was some heeler with a vote to sell?"

Her face betrayed her.

"Forgive me," she repeated. "You would have done wrong to turn him away because of me. I know of your noble deed—who does not? I am proud of you, and wished to tell you so. I wanted to see you for this—to praise your heroism. I've been your friend in that—that other thing. I could see how the crowd, the exhilaration, the sense of mastery, might lure one on. I looked at it dispassionately—with a friend's eyes. I was loyal till I thought you held my friendship lightly, and put politics before it. I own my mistake—my injustice."

Shelby had not dreamed of vindication so sweeping, and, with a word of modest disclaimer, led the talk to pacific commonplace. It was too late for the promised drive, and indeed neither of them thought of it again till the door had shut between them.

In leaving, the man's glance was arrested by an object on the piano.

"What is that called?" he asked abruptly.

"The cast? That is my Victory—the famous Victory of Samothrace, which suggested the poem everybody's reading. It's my despair. I've failed at drawing it for years. The original is in the Louvre, and towers gloriously over a staircase. I can shut my eyes and see it perfectly."

"Pretty old?" ventured Shelby.

"Oh, yes; it's an antique. See how ruffian Time has dealt with it."

The man walked slowly round the goddess, surveying her from every side.

"A day or two ago," he said simply, "I saw that image in a house, and, in my ignorance, thought a servant had broken it. I wondered why the people didn't pitch it out."

His tone went straight to her sympathy.

"Many are strangers in the kingdom of Art," she returned gently. "Most of us must come to it like little children."

Shelby was silent for a moment. Then he said:—

"In Bernard Graves's opinion I am aesthetically dead—I believe those were his words."

The girl started.

"I never repeated them," she protested.

"What," laughed Shelby, grimly, "has he told you that, too? He's evidently fond of the phrase. Perhaps he is right. Yet I hope not. I'd rather think I'm merely unborn. I am not a voluntary Ishmaelite. I simply haven't had the chance to learn."

CHAPTER IX

A fault recognized, it was Ruth's nature to be lavish of atonement, and by way of further expiation she consented a day or two later to make one of a driving party of Mrs. Hilliard's to hear Shelby speak in a village located "down north," as the local vernacular had it, near the shore of Lake Ontario. Ruth cared little for Mrs. Hilliard. She saw her through feminine eyes, and Mrs. Hilliard was not popular with women. But Shelby had privily told her of the project and begged her to accept.

"I had planned to rent the Tuscarora House tallyho and go with some eclat," the lady lamented at the eleventh hour, "but the way people have disappointed me is positively harrowing. There was Bernard Graves—I pinned my childlike faith on him; but he sent regrets. And Mr. and Mrs. Bowers. Wouldn't you think that they, of all people, would wish to go? But no; Mrs. Bowers said it did her rheumatic shoulder no good to traipse around nights,—that was her expression,—and Mr. Bowers actually told me that he was too busy organizing political meetings to want to attend them. Isn't he droll? Then Mr. Hewett had a sermon to prepare; and Dr. Crandall had a case of diphtheria to watch; and Volney Sprague—well, I really did not dare ask him, he was so horrid in his paper about Mr. Shelby's splendid speech. So one and all they began to make excuses, as the Bible says, till it has simmered down to you, dear

Mark Lee Luther

Ruth, and Joe, and Mr. Shelby, and me."

"Oh," said Ruth, with misgiving.

"A sort of survival of the fittest, don't you know, as some-body or other says. Was it Shakespeare? He really seems to have written all the clever things."

"No," Ruth replied with gravity; "it wasn't Shakespeare."

"Really? I thought it sounded Shakespearian. Well, as I was telling you, it has come to a jolly little company of four in my surrey, which, after all, is perhaps nicer than a dozen in a tallyho, though of course it won't impress the voters as much."

Ruth's eyebrows arched.

"Is that the object of our going?"

"What an idea, my dear!" Nevertheless, she colored. "We'll start early enough for a fish supper at the Lakeview Inn," she rattled on. "You know how good their fish suppers are. And perhaps we shall have time to stop at the camp-meeting of those ridiculous Free Methodists which is in full swing at the grove behind the hotel. Joe says that it will be the last night of the camp, and equal to Barnum's Three Rings and Mammoth Hippodrome. Doesn't that sound just like Joe? I'm sure we can manage to see something of it. Mr. Shelby's meeting won't begin till eight-thirty and Eden Centre can't be ten minutes' drive from the grove."

She sowed without conception of the harvest. The pleasuring so idly planned, the religionists whose vagaries provoked her laughter, were in time to bulk huge in a clairvoyant light of revelation.

It fell a ripe autumn day with the haze mantling the orchards like the purple of a plum, a day in whose magic atmosphere even common things wore an air of poetry. The very canal was transfigured.

"There is a bit of Holland," said Ruth, as they crossed the waterway on the ragged hem of the town. "If this were Europe and the courthouse over there could triple its age and take another name, this bridge would swarm with the 'personally conducted' admiring the view. I don't wonder that artists are beginning to paint the canal."

"They say a house-boat party came through last week," Mrs. Hilliard remarked.

"Tied their scow near my place," put in her husband. "Had the hold all rigged up with a piano and curtains and rugs. Harum-scarum looking lot of men and women you wouldn't trust to paint a barn. They overran the quarries and made pictures of the Polacks."

"Bernard Graves met them," Ruth added. "They told him that Little Poland was a second Barbizon for peasant models, with an 'Angelus' or a 'Man with the Hoe' around every corner."

Joe Hilliard guffawed.

"Guess they meant the woman with the hoe; she's the agriculturalist in the Polack matrimonial team."

Shelby was discreetly backward in these quicksands which the quarry owner did not fear to tread, but the canal stirred his imagination, too, and in a characteristic way.

"It takes seven figures to express last year's tonnage down the Ditch to tidewater," he told them; "stone, lumber, food.

Why it dumped over three-quarters of a million tons of food alone into New York City's maw. Yet they say it's antiquated and can't compete with the railroads. What else has kept the railroads within bounds? Ask any Tuscarora shipper what happens yearly when navigation closes. Abandon it! We'll see. The canal counties swing a pretty vote in this state."

Hilliard laughed.

"Think you're addressing the Legislature, Ross?"

"I heard you address the Assembly once," Ruth said. "I was a Vassar girl then, visiting Albany friends. You spoke about the canals, and the other members stopped gossiping and writing letters to listen."

"The canal is a part of my religion," Shelby answered.

They crossed the ancient shore line of the lake, the Ridge, so-called,—successive highway of the Iroquois, the pioneer, the stage-coach, and the ubiquitous trolley,—and caught presently the distant shimmer of Ontario, sail-dotted, intensely blue. That first glimpse of the inland sea always stirred Ruth to the depths. It was not the romance of New France alone which it evoked—that picturesque procession of redmen, *coureurs de bois*, friars, Jesuits, soldiers of fortune, La Salle, Frontenac, the conquering English, the conqueror-conquering American—but the mystery of the vaster tidal sea toward which it drew, whose supremest witchery none may know save the yearning inland-born.

"Calm as a puddle to-day," said Joe. "You can almost hear the Canucks singing 'God Save the Queen.'"

Dusk had set in when they left the deserted piazzas of the summer hotel for the camp-meeting in the grove. The flare of torches wavered afar between the tree boles, and above the lapping of the waves walled a drear hymn.

Mrs. Hilliard skipped girlishly in the woodland path.

"They've begun, they've begun," she exulted. "We shall see the fun after all."

"It's too early for the meeting in the big tent," Shelby told Ruth; "but if you've never seen anything of the kind, the scene which goes before will be quite as curious."

Skirting a makeshift village of tiny tents and shanties they issued to a torch-lit clearing in the wood whose central object was the greater tent, which, frayed, weathered, and patched as it was, yet stood to these zealots of an iron creed as the chosen tabernacle of a very God. Its rough benches were empty now, but before its dingy portal swayed and groaned a rapt circle of men and women, hand in hand, in whose midst an old man with a prophet's head and a bigot's eye was gyrating like a dervish as he mouthed the hackneyed phrases of the sanctified. As the new-comers pressed among the bystanders hemming the inner circle of the faithful, the performer with a last frantic whirl dropped exhausted, and rolling down a slight declivity lay stark and deathlike at their feet, his white beard and hair strewn with russet leaves.

Ruth recoiled with a shudder. The swaying circle redoubled its incantations, and left him to his envied beatitude. Their indifference seemed inhuman to the girl, and she would have stooped to the prostrate figure but for Shelby's detaining hand.

"Merely the 'Power,' as they say," he whispered, adding cynically, "Epilepsy can be feigned, you know."

She desisted, and a new actor waltzed rhythmically into the

glare of light. Her short rotund body writing not unlike an Oriental dancer's, the Widow Weatherwax had assumed the centre of the ring. The sanctified were without sense of humor, but the unregenerate onlookers were not proof against the comic aspects of emotional religion, and from the dark outskirts rang a ribald laugh.

"Why doesn't that dreadful woman wear a corset?" demanded Mrs. Hilliard in a stage whisper of Ruth, whose face went suddenly aflame.

"The widow would make the fortune of any Midway, Ross," Joe Hilliard chuckled, digging Shelby in the ribs.

"Woe, woe, woe," chanted the widow, spurred to anathema by derision. "Woe upon scorners! Woe upon them that sit in the seats of scorners! 'Ye shut up the kingdom of heaven against men; for ye neither go in yourselves, neither suffer ye them that are entering to go in.'"

Scripture-quoting was reckoned among the fine arts in the widow's circle, and an applauding chorus of Praise Gods and Amens greeted her dexterous use of the beloved weapon. She rounded the chain once more in her grotesque dance; then, suddenly spying the little group of her neighbors peering through the girdle of the sanctified, she halted, directly fronting them, and, singling out Mrs. Hilliard, who was conspicuous in a red tailor-made gown, she transfixed her with her beady eyes.

"Woe, woe, woe," she wailed again, rocking to and fro. "Woe upon Babylon! 'Babylon the great is fallen, is fallen, and is become the habitation of devils, and the hold of every foul spirit, and a cage of every unclean and hateful bird!'"

The brethren thrilled at the well-understood allusion to the speaker's abiding-place, while the outsiders, scenting a veiled scurrility, craned to listen and to watch.

Secure of her audience, the widow paused as if waiting the descent of the prophetic afflatus. Then:—

"'And I heard another voice from heaven, saying, Come out of her, my people, that ye be not partakers of her sins, and that ye receive not of her plagues. For her sins have reached unto heaven, and God hath remembered her iniquities. Reward her even as she rewarded you, and double unto her double according to her works: in the cup which she hath filled fill to her double. How much she hath glorified herself, and lived deliciously, so much torment and sorrow give her: for she saith in her heart, I sit a queen, and am no widow, and shall see no sorrow. Therefore shall her plagues come in one day, death, and mourning, and famine; and she shall be utterly burned with fire.'"

Ruth vacillated between fascination and disgust. The flickering torches, the soughing wind, the lapping waves, the old, old words, lent the denunciation a solemnity which transcended the bizarre mouthpiece. She shook off the impression, however, and asked Shelby to take her away.

"Yes; it's time to leave for the rally," he acquiesced. "I'll speak to the Hilliards."

As they turned, they saw that Mrs. Hilliard's eyes were riveted on the widow's in an hypnotic stare. In shrill singsong the woman was declaiming:—

"'So he carried me away in the spirit into the wilderness: and I saw a woman sit upon a scarlet beast, full of names of blasphemy, having seven heads and ten horns. And the woman was arrayed in purple and scarlet color, and decked with gold and precious stones and pearls, having a golden cup in her hand full of abominations—'"

Whereupon Mrs. Hilliard suddenly stopped her ears and grovelled on her knees full in the light of the torches, her shoulders quivering with hysterical sobs. There was a ripple of sensation at the prominence of the convert, and triumphant peals of "Saved by His precious blood," "Saved by the Lamb," "Look to Him, sister, look to Him," and the like. Then big Joe Hilliard stolidly thrust himself into the ring, and, raising the stricken woman, bore her away into the outer darkness. Apart from the crowd, Hilliard shook his wife with rough kindness.

"Wake up, girl," he said. "Nightmare's over. I guess you need a dose of camomile."

In the inky outskirts she presently threw off the obvious marks of her hysteria, but by little signs another woman might read, Ruth saw hours afterward that the spell possessed her still. Its gloom seemed to overcast the entire evening. Either through insufficient advertising, or the crass stupidity of the enfranchised of Eden Centre, who thought less of their political enlightenment than the noisy saving of their souls, Shelby's meeting proved a pitiful fiasco. Hardly a score had gathered in the low-ceiled schoolhouse, fetid with reeking kerosene lamps and wilting humanity; and of this beggarly handful two-thirds were women. Shelby assumed a cheerful front, declaring that a small audience so assembled was deserving of his best, but hewing to this line was another matter. Womankind are proverbially indifferent to politics; and a stouter resolution than his would have flagged in the presence of that preoccupied feminine two-thirds, whose eyes were centred on Mrs. Hilliard's tailor-made gown and Ruth Temple's fall hat. Used as he was to easy victory, this first disappointment of his campaign seemed bodeful of evil days to come.

CHAPTER X

Yet when mischief speedily befell, it wore so curious a guise that Shelby missed its import and laughed it aside for a random fling of jocund Fate. It began with a publisher's announcement of a volume containing the collected poems of the author of the admired, imitated, parodied, and derided ode on the "Victory of Samothrace," anonymous no longer, but the avowed offspring of Bernard Graves. Dazed, incredulous, and slow to do him honor, the prophet's own country advanced a theory of mistaken identity. But reluctant New Babylon had soon to recognize the young man's vogue. Through its supposed advocacy of woman suffrage the poem had all but founded a cult, and the disclosure of its true author, after months of guesswork and silly-season gush, bounced and ricochetted among the newspapers with astonishing ado. With the *Whig* in the forefront the local press began to echo the gossiping paragraphs and character sketches which, true, half true, and of whole cloth, padded the lean columns of a mediocre literary season, and New Babylon had faith. The last doubting Thomas yielded when it became necessary to convey the celebrity's mail to his home in a special bag; not even the ensuing plague of special correspondents, biographical dictionary solicitors, photographers, and worshipping pilgrims so stirred the local imagination; this surely was fame!

To Ruth Temple, who by some sorcery guessed his secret

before its public revelation, Graves went with his laurels thick upon him.

"How does it feel to be a celebrity?" he said, meeting her volley of questions collectively. "Much like a breakfast cereal, a patent medicine, or a soap. Byron said that the first thing which sounded like fame to him was the tidings that he was read on the banks of the Ohio. It's different nowadays. The first taste usually comes from seeing your name placarded on a dead wall between some equally distinguished rolled oats and a new five-cent cigar. Personally I think I first saw the 'gypsy' face to face when the Hon. Seneca Bowers told me that save 'Betsey and I Are Out' he had read no poem but mine in twenty years. That was my 'Ohio,' though of course Mrs. Hilliard's request for an author's reading at the Culture Club was an annunciation in itself. Am I becoming fabulously rich from my royalties? Alas! no; I must buy too many presentation copies for people who fancy that I obtain gratis really more than I know what to do with. Shall I write for the stage? I could as easily write a cook book. Do I give my autograph? Always, if a stamped envelope is enclosed. One of our hardest-working presidents daily set apart a time for autographs; why then should a popular writer pretend that it bores him? He is secretly tickled, and probably collects autographs himself."

Ruth laughed, but denied that he had exhausted her questions.

"Why did you withhold your name from your masterpiece?" she asked.

"Partly because it was my masterpiece,—it would be false modesty to deny that I know it,—and I had some notion of digging a pit for the critics. But the main reason was to confound my Uncle Peter."

"I didn't know you had an uncle."

"I haven't in the flesh. 'Uncle Peter' is generic—a polite lumping together of my chronic fault-finders within the family and without. You know him. Both masculine and feminine, he's eternally an old woman. Everybody knows Uncle Peter, the first to censure and the last to praise. Now, as I've been his especial tidbit and awful example for years, I had to school myself to the thought of snatching the daily morsel of gossip from his mouth. The murder out, Uncle Peter's grief is pitiful. How much sharper than a serpent's tooth is a prophecy of evil unfulfilled! It's not that he considers I've gone to work, incorrigible vagabond that I am; it's the fact that my intolerable idling has produced money which sets his teeth on edge—money, the golden calf of Uncle Peter's narrow idolatrous soul."

Ruth had no liking for his moments of acid mockery.

"Don't let Uncle Peter overshadow your friends," she warned.

"I'll not," promised the man. "And you—by what witchery of friendship did you find me out?" He shifted his seat, seeking her eyes. "Ruth, was it love?"

She did not answer immediately.

"Be my wife, Ruth," he said.

"It was not love," she replied simply.

It was one of the oddities of his temperament that at this moment he saw himself objectively. What a subdued neutral tinted thing was life! By all the canons of romance it was now his cue for perfervid speech.

"What then?" he asked quietly.

"Liking—a real liking."

"Will it grow warmer?"

"I cannot tell."

"I will teach you to love me," he declared, his artistic self nudging him meanwhile that he had dropped into the worn formula of the ages.

Ruth did not deny him the attempt, and he undertook a lesson on the spot, pointing out that they saw life through similar eyes; that art, music, literature spoke with a common voice; that if true marriage were perfect companionship, the auguries were not uncertain in their happy omen; so on till he wearied her with argument.

"All those things refine love," she put in at last, a little wistfully; "they are not its essence. A man may be a barbarian and yet lovable."

He desisted at that, and presently went away. Out of doors her words clothed themselves with a personal application. Shelby—lovable barbarian!—was entering the gate.

Of what immediately followed neither man retained a clear recollection. It was a clash of temperaments hopelessly at odds, in which the spoken word weighed little beside the mute antipathy jaundicing the mind. Yet the word played no small part in the sequel. Graves assured Shelby that he should spare no effort to compass his defeat; while Shelby in his turn suggested that the zest of the campaign would be doubled if Graves were only his ridiculous opponent.

Puzzling how the quarrel could have begun and hurried to

its climax so swiftly, Bernard Graves swung up the street heedless of his steps. Then the bland colonial facade of the public library confronted him like a smirking face and, as his vagrant fancy trifled with the conceit, its lips opened to emit two chattering girls.

"I was the tenth on the waiting-list," said one.

He saw that she spoke of his own volume which she held in a triumphant embrace with a box of caramels, and was filled with a nauseated disgust for his handiwork. Retracing his steps he climbed to the *Whig* office, and finding Sprague at his desk, he swept a pile of exchanges from a chair and drew it to the editor's elbow.

"Volney," he asked, "does this talk of an independent movement against Ross Shelby amount to anything?"

Sprague's eye lit.

"It's gathering headway every minute," he declared. "We require just one thing—a candidate of prominence and backbone."

Graves reached past the paste-pot to capture a fugitive match.

"What do you say to me?"

"What do I say!" Unwinding his long legs from his chair rounds the editor dealt his friend a clap between the shoulders which sent his cigarette spinning to the floor. "I say you're a trump."

Sprague had not a little in common with the type in the political cosmos which is contemptuously styled cloistered. Of New England stock, like most of Tuscarora, he had been born of a later migration than the pioneers', and was hence less tempered by New York influences for good or ill. Begotten a generation earlier, he would have tended transcendental pigs at Brook Farm. His earliest political recollections were associated with heated quotations from Garrison and Wendell Phillips, and the sharpest-etched memory of his childhood had to do with a runaway slave harbored in his father's garret. As a man he was given to printing Emersonian nuggets in the editorial columns of the *Whig*, his favorite sentiment being, "Hitch your wagon to a star," whose practical application led him over highways which knew not macadam. He now perceived nothing grotesque in Bernard Graves's proposal, nor did it astonish him. From his office window he had chanced to overlook the stormy meeting of the suitors, but he gave Graves no hint.

"With any other candidate I can think of," he declared, "this movement would merely signify the protest of a self-respecting minority; with you, the author of the famous Samothrace ode,—gad! I think it augurs victory by a handsome majority."

Graves colored.

"I had forgotten the ode," he confessed. "Couldn't we eliminate that from the campaign?"

"Eliminate it! Why, boy, it's half your platform."

"Is it?" said the novice, drearily. "Oh, very well. I thought I should like to run on the moral issue. Shelby is corrupt, and the other party is certain to name some creature who would out-Shelby Shelby if he got the chance. That seems to me issue enough for a third candidate without dragging in my verses. I'm sick of them."

"Do you find your royalties a nuisance?"

"Don't be banal, Volney. You understand me. I don't want to be the one-sided artist merely; I want to do things as well as write about them, and I want the provinces separate."

Sprague laughed paternally.

"If I'm not to be banal, neither must you be impracticable. It's the ode that makes you available and enables you to do things, and there can be no question of dividing your personality as King Louis something-or-other tried to do. You have placed yourself in my hands. Very good. I assure you that I can nominate you. You should therefore defer to my judgment. You owe me that."

"Of course."

"Yes; well, then. Congressman Graves that is to be, here is the situation in a nutshell: In Tuscarora Shelby has gained ground because of the Kiska affair. Little Poland has his lithograph in every window. Elsewhere in the Demijohn I've reason to know that he's in exceedingly bad odor, and that a third ticket would draw no end of support from thinking voters who like Shelby little, but the other party less. At present, you see, it's frying-pan or fire for them." The editor paused to charge a discolored corn-cob pipe. "Now your coming changes all that," he continued, tilting back in the wreathing smoke. "I tell you it warms my heart to think of you opposing Shelby; it's a draught of Falernian, no less. It's logically, it's romantically, fitting that you who unmasked his plagiarism should battle with him at the polls. Moreover, your discovery puts such a feather in your cap at the outset. You've proved your political acuteness; you've won your spurs. It's town talk that the credit is yours,—I acknowledge it whenever asked,—and now that you are to enter the field, I'll blazon it to the four winds."

"If the world takes it as placidly as New Babylon, it will do us little good."

"Ah, but the world isn't so stupid," retorted Sprague, beginning to rummage his chaotic desk. "There, sir," he went on, dragging a bundle of newspaper clippings to the surface, "there is the world's opinion of the exposure. Rochester, Buffalo, Albany, Utica, Syracuse, Troy—you'll find the comments of every important city in the state voiced by reputable journals; New York—why, New York gave it three editorials, not one of them less than two sticks. No utterance of the *Whig* ever attracted such attention. I tell you, man, that, your poem aside, your advent in politics with this thing to your credit makes you a figure of state importance; with the ode—gad, sir, your canvass is of national concern."

"It sounds like a dream of Colonel Mulberry Sellers's," laughed Graves, but he warmed to the editor's mood. "You're sure I can have the nomination? We're flying in the face of the Boss and all his works."

Sprague flung out his thin hands impatiently.

"I have told you that it rests with me."

The tyro dropped an acute, if indiscreet, observation.

"It seems to me," said he, "that you are something of a boss yourself."

"Every cause must have a leader. I have been the consistent head and front of the protest against Shelbyism, and the independent movement is of my creating. Why shouldn't I name the candidate?"

Bernard Graves retreated hastily from this ticklish corner, and put forward a vague supposition that there would have to be "caucuses, conventions, and things."

"Independent nominations are made by certificate."

"Oh," said the young man, meekly, "I see;" which was disingenuous. He silently debated whether this meant a species of letter of recommendation, but was shy of asking.

Sprague mercifully enlightened him.

"I've the law right here," he went on, tapping a calf-bound manual which Graves eyed with profound respect. "An independent nomination for Congress requires at least a thousand signers who must be electors of the district. We've ample time; it's a good three weeks before we need file our certificate with the Secretary of State, and a fortnight would answer to secure the minimum. But we'll not content ourselves with the minimum; the greater our list of signers, the stronger our argument in the campaign. Voters are gregarious, you know."

"I've noticed the importance of bell-wethers," Graves remarked dryly.

"Oh, but don't asperse the intelligence of the flock," deprecated the reformer quickly. "I've been thought to idealize The People; perhaps I do, but it is good for a man to keep sweet his faith in humanity. There's a saying of Emerson's that fits the case if I could remember it." He scoured his memory absently for an interval. "Well, no matter. It occurs to me that we'll need an emblem for our ticket. The law requires us to select some device. The eagles, ballot-boxes, roosters, stars, and the like have all been preempted, and aren't strikingly significant anyhow. We want something telling—a graphic symbol of our aim. You are a man of imagination; what is your notion?"

The man of imagination considered, and the editor's excess of nervous force spent itself in idle forays about his desk, one of which brought forth a foot-rule; whirling in the eager fingers, it proved an inspiration.

"Why not—" Graves began; "no, not that—a square, a carpenter's square. It symbolizes everything we stand for."

"Bravo! It's a slogan to win with. Square issues, square dealing, square men! We'll placard every fence and barn door in the district. A woodcut will cost next to nothing, and I'll run the posters off right here on the premises."

The suggestion bruised Graves's sensibilities.

"Is that necessary?" he protested mildly. "I'd really prefer to leave all that sort of vandalism to the other side; it's so philistine, you know."

BOOK II

CHAPTER I

Volney Sprague's flaming posters in black and red menaced Shelby from the selvage of the district to the threshold of his door. The State Committee had despatched him on a brief stumping tour, embracing a handful of canal counties, a section of the grape belt, and certain strategic points in the Southern Tier, and he had kept in fairly regular communication with Bowers; but while that leader's letters were usually as terse and meaty as Caesar's campaign jottings in Gaul, they somehow failed to impress the candidate with the actual condition of his political fences. It was therefore with the shock of almost complete surprise that he entered his proper bailiwick to find Bernard Graves's opposition regarded seriously. Saloons, cigar stores, street corners, the billiard room of the Tuscarora House, all his familiar haunts, buzzed with the vote-getting possibilities of an independent ticket in a community where regularity had become well-nigh a fetich.

Bowers was rudderless and irritable.

"I advised you to conciliate young Graves," he fretted. "And what have you done? Stroked him the wrong way ever since. I hope it's a lesson to you to keep politics and petticoats apart."

Shelby jeered at his inconsistency.

"You were good enough to suggest that I make up to the woman in the case."

"Not in the thick of a campaign."

Shelby's optimism was not easily dashed and he laid an energetic shoulder to the lagging wheel. His associate's rebound from depression was less elastic, and the candidate's thoughts furrowed a channel they had frequently taken of late. It was plain to him that the older man was no longer equal to the requirements of his leadership. Sound in judgment, shrewd in the reading of men, vigorous in action as he once had been, and on occasion could be still, he was nevertheless of an earlier and more leisured school of politics than the present lively generation which knew not Joseph. They knew other things—the youngsters—strange methods of the city ward; and the philosophic observers, who on all sides think they descry evidence of the corruption of the country by the city, would have glibly explained to the Hon. Seneca Bowers the causes of his inefficiency. He had come to rely more and more on his sprightly deputy, till now, virtual county leader and his party's candidate, Shelby, double-weighted, prepared to wage the battle of his life.

The demands upon his time were incessant. He would rise in his unlovely room at the Tuscarora House, leaden from insufficient sleep, to be buttonholed before he breakfasted— sometimes, even before he dressed; this man must be placated, that threatened, the other convinced by reason; another must be visited in sickness, another found work, for yet another must gratuitous lawyering be done—all this with jovial front and a camel's capacity for drink. This was his domesticity, amidst which must be sandwiched conferences and journeyings in Tuscarora County and the other counties of his district, and speeches on behalf of the party outside the Demijohn, entailed by too successful stumping in the past. Capping all was the perverse closet-reformer, Sprague, and his figurehead, Graves.

Shelby was a believer in short campaigns, and the time left the independents for attack was brief. They retrieved the handicap by added vigor, and subjected his every public act to merciless scrutiny. Sprague formulated the case against him in an early issue of the *Whig*:—

"We are asked," he wrote, "to publish our specific reasons for rejecting this candidate. We gladly comply. The counts of his indictment are many; we select five:—

"We refuse to support a candidate of any party whatsoever whose nomination issues from dishonest primaries. It is notorious that the caucuses preliminary to this man's nomination were packed. Can you gainsay it, Mr. Shelby?

"We refuse to support a candidate, be his nomination never so spotless, who degrades himself and the office to which he aspires by the theft of another's intellectual property. Can you deny your plagiarism, Mr. Shelby?

"We refuse to support a candidate, be his nomination irreproachable, his sense of mine and thine otherwise undulled, whose legislative record is tainted by traffickings peculiar to the Black Horse Cavalry—wanton blackmailers of corporate rights. It is of common knowledge that this man introduced in the last session a bill aimed at the legitimate profits of a great surface railway system, which he withdrew for no reason of public record. Can you make affidavit that the subsequent sale of a block of that same railway's stock by your business associate was without relevance, Mr. Shelby?

"We refuse to support a candidate, be his nomination

unimpeachable, his intellectual honesty unchallenged, his legislative record without stain, who, posing as the champion of our canals, nevertheless lends himself, through connivance at fraudulent contracts and the appointment of needless officials, to the squandering of the moneys set apart for their use. We invite you to disprove your complicity in the wasting of the state's millions, Mr. Shelby.

"We refuse, lastly, to support a candidate, be his nomination as unsullied as his personal integrity, and his legislative career as free from 'strikes' as his advocacy of our pirate-infested waterways is disinterested, who is yet so slavishly the henchman of his party machine that no measure it may propose is too unsavory to enlist his Dugald Dalgetty loyalty. By your closed lips you countenance the land-jobbing steal which your great state Boss failed by the merest fluke to saddle upon the River and Harbor Bill passed by the last Congress, and purposes to press anew;— dare you vote against your owner, Mr. Shelby?"

To all of which, reiterated and emphasized in pamphlet, broadside, poster, and stump speech, Shelby said publicly never a word, professing himself a believer in the policy of dignified silence. He touched the matter after an impersonal fashion with Bowers, however, as they read the onslaught.

"Give me the liquor habit, the tobacco habit, the opium habit, singly or all together," said he, "but preserve me from the vice of rhetoric."

Bowers had not this fine detachment.

"I don't wish to nose into your private concerns, Ross," he began, with visible embarrassment, "but this third count implicates me. I'd like to ask whether that stock I sold for you in Wall Street last winter was yours by—by—"

"By bona fide purchase?" whipped in Shelby. "Yes, sir; out and out. Do you think me as big a fool as this dream-chaser pretends I am?"

"No, no."

"Nobody should know better than you why that bill was introduced. You brought it to me from the Boss. Those railway people forgot that their party can't run campaigns on wind, and in his own way he jogged their memory. I saw that. As for the stock—your skirts are clear. You merely sold in a rising market what I bought in a falling one. If my position gave me a speculative advantage, it's my own business—nobody else's—not even the Hon. Seneca Bowers's."

The county leader's working features did not resemble General Grant's. In that unhappy moment he experienced the pangs of unhonored parenthood.

Presently he put out his hand.

"I'm sorry I offended you, Ross. I supposed myself too seasoned a campaigner to mind mud-slinging."

Shelby laughed apologies away and they parted friends. On the threshold it occurred to Bowers to ask:—

"Who is this Dalgetty fellow Sprague mentions? I never heard of him in politics."

"Nor I. Some ward heeler he thinks I resemble, I guess."

"He'd have made his point stronger by taking somebody that the plain people know. That's something mugwumps never learn."

Mark Lee Luther

"And there's another thing they don't grasp," Shelby added. "One personal talk with the average voter will outweigh enough high-toned editorials to sink a ship. When the reformer begins to rub shoulders in all sorts of places with all sorts of men his halo won't be so luminous; perhaps he won't call himself a reformer at all—just politician, perhaps; but he'll saw wood."

CHAPTER II

As a matter of fact, the independent candidate did give the shoulder-rubbing process a trial. Within the by no means contracted limits of Volney Sprague's paper-and-ink horizon the flurry of the attack on Shelby threw its ripples far, but Graves shortly damped the editor's professional delight by the remark that he had been assured of no man's vote because of it.

"There's the pity of our lack of time," frowned Sprague. "An educational campaign can hardly be too long. Many a demagogue has failed of election because we vote in November and not in dog-days."

"You'll have to admit that you've merely revamped old material. It's no news that Shelby has packed caucuses, stolen speeches, blackmailed corporations, jobbed canal contracts, and grovelled to the Boss."

"True," admitted Sprague, ruefully.

"We need the concrete to convince. Take this canal scandal: we've seen contracts go to Shelby's adherents on unbalanced bids, and the Ditch swarms with his useless inspectors at four dollars a day; but can you bring wrong-doing home to him?"

"To prove the Champion of Canals' complicity—what a master stroke!"

The morning after he popped into the young man's study, to the lasting detriment of a triolet.

"We can prove it," he exclaimed. "Gad! We can prove it!"

Graves regretfully dropped a blotter over his manuscript and advanced a chair.

"I've suspected that there were men in this town who could lay Shelby by the heels, were they to tell all they knew. The problem was to draw them."

"You can't expect his understrappers to quarrel with their bread and butter."

"No; that has been the stone of stumbling precisely, but we've got around it. In this blessed case, Shelby himself did the quarrelling, and thereby delivered himself into our hands."

Bernard Graves sat up.

"What have you found out?"

"I've found a man who seems to know of Shelby's crookedness, and is willing to tell what he knows."

"Well?"

"Jap Hinchey."

Graves's face lengthened.

"That beast," said he.

"Did you expect a Sir Galahad for such a service?"

"What would the word of such a man avail?"

"As much as any informer's; it isn't a chivalrous office."

"Nor is ours in employing it, to my thinking; informer and reformer sound perilously near alike. Still, as you delicately imply, we're not Knights of the Round Table. What has the sot had to say to you?"

"Well, the fact is he hasn't told me anything specific," Sprague had to admit. "The matter is still under negotiation, as one may say. Jasper is coy."

"Oh!"

The lukewarm monosyllable voiced disillusionment. With a partial return to the academic calm of his normal life Bernard Graves candidly told himself that the actual basis of his resentment against Shelby was trivial; that the editor's outlook on politics was Quixotic, not to say Micawberesque; and that his own wisdom in venturing for such a cause, with such a pilot, on such uncharted seas, was questionable to a degree.

Sprague was not devoid of intuition.

"I'm not rainbow-hunting this time," he put in quickly. "The fellow knows something interesting, and he's ready to out with it. He was employed in the Eureka quarries during the canal improvement, and saw things, he says, that we would like to hear."

"You talked with him?"

"Yes; he accosted me in a side street late last night."

"If he's anxious to inform and reform, why doesn't he? I don't like the look of it. What does he want?"

"You."

"He wants me?"

"He said he would speak plainly with you."

Graves's revulsion was fairly physical.

"You manage it, Volney," he entreated. "You will know how."

Sprague shook his head.

"He was positive on that point. It must be you or nobody."

"I doubt if it's worth while."

The editor lost patience.

"It was you who reminded me that we lacked the concrete. Now I offer it to you."

"But in such a shape!"

"Can you quibble over that—and in politics?"

"No one who knows Jap Hinchey's character would believe him under oath."

Sprague's reply was astute.

"I'm thinking of those who don't know him," said he. "The district is wide."

"And an affidavit is an affidavit?" His smile was sardonic. "Very well. I'll see him. What is Jap's At Home?"

"You will find him fishing on the dock behind his shanty, probably. I'd follow this thing up promptly, Bernard."

"Yes," promised the candidate, listlessly. "I will."

Alone, he fingered his manuscript, read it drearily, and of a sudden tore it into little bits, the mood which gendered it gone beyond recall. The sordid necessity of seeing Hinchey taught him afresh the folly of his dabbling in politics at all, and his whole being revolted against the contact with humanity in the raw which even mugwumpery seemed to entail. Left to himself, Sprague might have headed his own John Brown raid into the established order of things; led it with brilliancy perhaps, in any case with honest zeal. Yet the root of his discontent struck rather deeper than Jasper Hinchey and the cold waterish zone of reform; Ruth had her part in it. He somehow reasoned that his course merited her approval and encouragement; it had met with banter. So gyved, lagged the hope of the independents to his task.

Few towns, however small, lack their moral plague-spot, and Graves's errand bent him toward New Babylon's, a web of alleys styled the Flats, spun behind the business centre among the docks and rotting warehouses of a vanished commerce. The Flats had its business too—groggeries and a music hall where "sacred concerts" were given on Sunday nights and men had been stabbed on pay-day; groggeries, the music hall—and worse. The young man threaded gingerly into its dingy precincts, and by dint of a handful of Italian, picked up in a Roman winter's sojourn to be oddly practised on a local washerwoman sousing gay garments in the amber fluid of the Erie Canal, he singled out the Hinchey hovel from the squalid score it resembled. Before the sagging threshold tumbled a many-complexioned brood

Mark Lee Luther

of children,—they seemed a very dozen,—and in the doorway, with arms akimbo and hands on massive hips, gaped Jap's mulatto wife, for of such measure was the man. Graves crossed the alley, suppressing such of his five senses as he could shift without, and ascertained that the degenerate Jasper, true to prophecy, was fishing from the dock in the rear.

"Good afternoon," said the caller, affably, he thought.

Jasper grunted without lifting his eyes from his float.

"What do you catch here?" pursued the candidate, beaming good-fellowship.

The line suddenly drew taut, and a muddy fish whipped through the sunshine within a scant inch of Graves's nose.

"Bullheads," answered the laconic Hinchey.

The visitor was disconcerted.

"You—er—eat them?" he remarked blankly, eyeing first the beery-looking water and then the ugly fish.

"Naw," sneered Jap. "I'm foundin' 'n 'quarium." He tossed the bullhead into a pail, and, spying a piccaninny scudding round a corner, called: "Here, you chocolate drop, take this yer fish ter yer mammy. Two mor,' 'n' I'll hev 'nuff fer supper. Set down," he added to his guest.

"Thanks," said Bernard, hunting vainly for a clean spot on the string-piece. He lit a cigarette as a sanitary precaution, and bethought him to offer one to Hinchey.

"None o' them coffin-nails fer me," declined the Spartan. "I smokes men's terbacker."

Graves gave him a cigar which he chanced to have about him.

"I don't seem to have a match left," he observed, fumbling in his pockets.

Jasper Hinchey calmly relieved him of his cigarette, lit his cigar with it, and restored the costly importation, malodorous of fish. At the earliest opportunity Graves dropped it in the canal, a transaction duly noted by Jap.

"I've been told you have something to say to me," the young man said briskly, his social obligations seeming fully paid, and his eagerness to be gone swamping diplomacy.

Jasper rebaited his hook, impaling the wriggling earthworm with a solicitude worthy of comparison with Isaac Walton's refined martyrdom of frogs.

"Yes," he drawled; "I kind o' 'magine I hev."

Bernard curbed his impatience while Jap spat with deadly aim at an eddying chip.

"S'pose you know I've knocked round in pol'tics some?"

The young man said that he did. He thought "knocked" a felicitous word. Jasper Hinchey's public services had been heavy-fisted, relating chiefly to voting blocks of drunken Poles and Italians in warmly contested town elections.

"I've helped 'lect mor'n one feller t' office in my day. Take Ross Shelby now: both times he run fer th' 'Sembly I worked like a nailer. 'Cause why? He done right by me. Why I luved that cuss like—like—" he hesitated for a simile—"like my own son," he added, with the passing of one of his brood, and forthwith whacked the youngster for overturning the bait can. "Jes' like my own son. An' so I should still ef he hedn't done me dirt; ef he'd ben square. Now, you're square."

"I try to be," returned Bernard, ravished by the tribute. "That's my platform in this campaign, you know."

"Yes; jes' so. An' I rather 'magine I'll vote yer way."

"Thank you."

"Pro-vi-ded," Jasper added, "pro-vi-ded we c'n 'range things."

"Arrange things?"

Jasper's eyes wandered musingly over his interlocutor's face.

"'Range things, I sez, an' I sez it again."

He abandoned something of his drawl. "I 'magine I c'd tell sumpin ef I tuk a notion."

Graves brooked his tone with difficulty.

"I shouldn't be here if I didn't think so too," he answered coolly.

"Jes' so," agreed Jasper, absorbed in a sinker. "I c'd tell sumpin erbout a party thet I 'magine you'd cock yer ear t' hear."

"Shelby?"

"I 'magine I didn't jes' quite say. No, I 'magine not."

"If you will exercise your imagination less, Mr. Hinchey,

and say plainly what you have to say, I shall be obliged," retorted Bernard, exasperated by his shiftiness.

Jasper was unmoved.

"Easy t' see *you* ain't ben in pol'tics long. Wall, whut I've got t' say is this: I used t' work fer this party off 'n' on,—this party whose name I ain't a-mentionin'. He wuz in pol'tics too. Likewise run a quarry an' s'm'other things t' num'rous t' mention. 'Twas in the quarry I worked, mostly erbout 'lection time. Cur'ous, ain't it, whut good pay a feller'll git fer light work erbout 'lection time? Wall, this year I ain't hed proper treatment. This party 'lows money is tight, an' he's filled his quarry up with dagoes, damned dagoes." He paused to scowl over the shanties of his immediate neighbors and at the industrious washerwoman up the dock. "Wouldn't it make you sick th' way furrin labor's a-crowdin' out th' true 'Merican? I jes' despise dagoes."

Graves was too disgusted to reply. He recollected having heard a negro speak contemptuously of Jews, but this case seemed yet more extreme.

"Wall," pursued the true American, "I wuz with this party a spell when th' state tuk a notion t' sink a few s'perfluous millyuns in this ole ditch."

The listener became all attention.

"Queer doin's I seen long erbout then. Contractors is a scand'lous lot. Many's the load o' dirt I seen hauled out thet easy, whut th' state paid fer ez blasted rock. My, yes. But my party wuzn't workin' at contractin'; he wuz workin' at contractors, an' he knew 'em, lock, stock, and bar'l. He jes' owned th' whole blim pack. Thet's where his rake-off come in. 'Twant all dirt them daisies tuk out. There wuz as fustclass sandstun ez my party ever shipped f'm his quarry, an' f'm his quarry docks it went."

"You mean that this man connived with the contractors to misappropriate state property?"

"I 'magine I do."

"And your party is Shelby?"

"Never said no sech thing."

"It's what you imply clearly enough. Now, if you wish to help us, as you told Mr. Sprague, you must say precisely who and what you mean, and swear to it before Mr. Sprague, who is a notary public."

Jasper straightened.

"Fer nothin'?" His tone was inimitable.

Bernard Graves looked him coldly in the eye.

"We're not bribing people."

The loafer raised his hulking body and leered over him; the young man got upon his feet, half expecting assault.

"Anything we can do for you in a legitimate way, we will do," he added steadily.

"I want t' know."

"You can find me at Mr. Sprague's office any morning between ten and twelve."

Jasper Hinchey surveyed him with scorn as he turned to go. Fumbling in his rags, he extracted a greasy card.

"P'r'aps you'd buy a twenty-five cent ticket fer th' Jolly Rovers' picnic," he insinuated. "Mebbe it's not too stiff fer yer purse. They say ez how 'tis well lined, Mr. Graves."

"Do you know that the Penal Code makes soliciting a candidate to buy tickets a misdemeanor?"

Hinchey smirked.

"A party whut I know buys 'em without askin'," said he.

Jasper Hinchey did not call at the *Whig* office any morning between ten o'clock and twelve. It developed that he was engaged in some not too arduous labor at the quarries of the Eureka Sandstone Company.

CHAPTER III

Had the fantastic bolt of the Sprague clique been left to its own courses, Shelby would have borrowed no further trouble, but a fortuitous matter of radishes and ice-water suddenly put the quarrel on an altogether different level. About the hour when Bernard Graves hobnobbed with Jasper Hinchey, the third factor in the Demijohn District's political muddle sat down to dinner in a neighboring city. "Chuck" O'Rourke was fond of his dinner. A childhood of squalid poverty had taught him the joy of a square meal. The story of the years linking the famished boy to the pudgy red-faced man of the restaurant is unessential,—an everyday story, sordid, and barren of romance. The present knew him for a prosperous contractor and politician whose most conspicuous public service had been the adroit fashioning of Tuscarora County's minority party into a compact organization, to which the majority party found it expedient to cast an occasional sop of patronage. He had lived and thrived in an atmosphere of deals. Only within the fortnight had he aspired to hold office, since his party had for years lacked the fighting chance which the revolt against Shelby created. Tempted at last, he abruptly resolved to enter the congressional race himself, and this same day had effected the last dicker with other county leaders which would insure his naming in to-morrow's convention.

The day had gone unwontedly sultry, with a sudden

flushing of autumn with dog-day heat, and his active morning had been fraught with physical discomfort. He had consumed quantities of beer and whiskey in his rounds, and had looked upon the wine when it was red. His heavy fall suit was a weariness, and as he entered the restaurant he loosed his checked waistcoat, unveiling a row of diamond shirt studs which galvanized the languid waiters to buoyant life. He was escorted with pomp and circumstance to a seat in the shadiest window, swept by the torrid breath of an electric fan.

O'Rourke gulped a glassful of ice-water as he studied the menu card, and motioned for more. Two other glassfuls went the way of the first, and the negro refilled the carafe. The man pulled angrily at his limp collar and discussed his order. Vacillating for a time between broiled lobster and porterhouse steak with mushrooms, he cut the matter short by taking both, and buttressed the main structure of the meal with side dishes of banana fritters and griddle-cakes. He decided that peach short-cake and tutti-frutti ice cream would stop the gap for desert [Transcriber's note: dessert?], and expressed a preference for "fizz" as he scanned the wine list. With a happy afterthought he recalled the fleeting waiter and ordered him to fetch a cocktail as an appetizer.

The ice-water carafe was within easy reach, and, pending the coming of the cocktail, it lowered steadily. Hard by, also, stood a dish of radishes, out of season, but succulent. He cleared the dish, and meditated assault on its fellow at the table adjoining. However, the brave advance of the lobster, the porterhouse, and the champagne bucket diverted him, and he tucked a napkin under his flabby chin with a genial smile. Then the smile shrivelled; waiters, porterhouse, lobster, champagne, winked out in utter blackness, and Chuck O'Rourke slid heavily to the floor.

The dead man's associates met the emergency with a sharp

move. The following morning Shelby caught a persistent rumor that the convention, wanting its slated candidate, proposed to indorse the candidacy of Bernard Graves; which same thing, after a moving tribute to the fallen leader, the convention with cheerful promptness did.

The Hon. Seneca Bowers was unnerved. He had had to cope with no such outrageous problem in the whole of his honorable career, and in a state of mind bordering panic he packed his grip and posted to New York for a conference with the Boss, leaving Shelby to temporize as best he might. Nor was Shelby inactive. The O'Rourke crowd had been placated in small matters times out of mind, and he went about the present task in the usual way, directing one of his people to inquire what they wanted. These hitherto insatiate gentlemen replied that they wanted nothing, adding pleasantly that they were well content with what they had. The possibility of a victory in a gerrymandered district, however won, was without price. Shelby appreciated their point of view and addressed himself to measures more feasible. If he could not shake their allegiance to Graves, he might succeed in preventing Graves from taking up with them, and the agencies for influencing public opinion which he could control began accordingly to ridicule the idea of a reform candidate's accepting such an indorsement.

Graves refused to be drawn, and for forty-eight hours held his peace with the aplomb of a veteran. Then Bowers came back.

"Has he accepted?" The words were out before he could take Shelby's hand.

"Not yet."

"Thank heaven. Tell me what you've done."

Shelby recapitulated.

"That's right," approved his senior. "There's nothing more to be done with Chuck O'Rourke's bandits just now. Graves is the man to consider. Is he still mum?"

"As a cigar sign. How does the Boss take it?"

"Urbanely, as always. He's silkier every time I see him." Bowers's memory lingered upon the soft-spoken interview with the great state leader.

"Well?" Shelby jogged him crisply.

"He knows all about Graves—as he knows about everybody. Says he has met the scholar in politics before. Do you remember how he took care of that kid-gloved aggregation which tried to run him out of business a year or so ago? He dumped this distinguished kicker into the cabinet, had another made a plenipotentiary, foisted off number three into some windy commission on the other side of the planet, and so on down the list. They said it seemed to be in the air that harmony should prevail."

Shelby laughed.

"The Boss is the smoothest made," he owned. "What does he advise in this case?"

Bowers leaned forward importantly.

"What do you think the young man would say to an author's job—some French or Italian consulate?"

"I'll tell you what I say: if the Boss advised that, he's growing senile."

"I didn't say he advised it. He merely suggested that literary people bit at that kind of bait. As a matter of fact, he didn't advise anything. He said if we couldn't fix things with the O'Rourke crowd, that the situation would have to develop a bit."

"Queer sort of talk," Shelby commented. "I wonder what he wants?" He puzzled over it a moment. "Well, whatever develops, don't talk consulate to Bernard Graves. The Boss is a pastmaster at side-tracking soreheads, but there's a point involved in this case that he doesn't grasp. Disappointed lovers are probably out of his line."

Bowers shifted his cigar to reply, but thought better of it. His hold on the wheel was weakening, and he remarked to his wife that night that this should be his last active campaign. Shelby entertained a similar opinion.

When the two men met on the morrow the situation had indeed developed. Persuaded against his own judgment by Volney Sprague, Bernard Graves had consented to assume the mantle of Chuck O'Rourke, deceased. To the repressed amusement of his new allies, he stipulated that the employment of questionable methods should be left to the common foe, and that they must accept him absolutely unpledged.

Shelby ran a gauntlet of chaff to his law office that afternoon, and found Bowers awaiting him in bilious mood. He was hazing the rooms with gusts of tobacco smoke, a sign of nervousness in so deliberate a smoker. They nodded curtly without words, and Shelby ran perfunctorily through his mail. Presently he raised his eyes and met Bowers's gloomy scrutiny lowering through the fog.

"You look like a hired mourner," he remarked, swirling the smoke.

"I feel like a real one."

"Well, don't wear your weeds so conspicuously. The enemy will imagine they have us scared."

Bowers swore listlessly.

"They have."

"Don't include me. I've a little sand left, I hope."

"It's the most serious fight we've ever had in the district. It's so unexpected. And I can't see how we are to blame. The organization backed your nomination cordially. We couldn't foresee that Volney Sprague would make trouble, any more than we could know that O'Rourke would gorge himself to apoplexy. And who, for the love of heaven, would have thought Bernard Graves would step into Chuck O'Rourke's shoes! I've been in politics for thirty years, Ross, with my fair share of good luck and bad, but I've never been up against the equal of this. It's—it's—" He broke off in despair of adequate characterization.

"Brace up, brace up. You need a brandy and soda."

"I've had two."

"Then take a glass of milk," rallied Shelby; "paregoric, boneset tea, anything. I'm ashamed of you."

Bowers smiled wanly.

"You're a younger man, Ross. You can rebound. I can't any more. I'm too old. I—I've lost confidence in myself."

"I haven't lost confidence in myself," ejaculated Shelby. "No such alliance of thugs and goody-goods shall down me. I'm in this game to stay and to win."

His stout words in some degree bolstered the discouraged veteran, and they turned presently to a discussion of ways and means. The outlook was not cheering. The fusion of the opposition had fallen at a time when the funds collected to meet the exigencies of an ordinary campaign had been mainly expended.

"The State Committee must help," declared Shelby. "There's no valid reason why they shouldn't. The corporations have given them everything they asked this year."

"I sounded the Boss. He was not encouraging."

"Damn him," said Shelby, "what does he want?" That question would recur.

"We have raised everything locally that our people will stand, and you may say that of the Demijohn generally. If there's more to be got, it must come from those most concerned."

"You mean me, I suppose?"

"It's your political future that's at stake."

Shelby drummed his desk. By and by, taking his checkbook, he began to run through the stubs, jotting figures on a pad.

"I've spent three thousand dollars already," he said at last. "Three thousand legitimate dollars. I've never footed it up before, and it's rather staggering. Of course, the big items—the assessments of the local committee and the other county committees—I had kept in mind. What I have not realized was the constant drain of small amounts for this and that,—printing, lithographs, bands, flag-raisings, you know what. And treats—why, I spent over seventy-five dollars in bar money alone the day of the Pioneers' picnic, while the County Fair meant the price of a good horse. It's a good thing for me that the torchlight idiocy has gone out. Still, the 'Shelby Base-ball Club' is as big a nuisance. Three thousand legitimate dollars," he repeated. "We now come to the illegitimate."

The older man winced. Shelby was too frank for him at times. While he recognized that vote-buying was of occasion necessary for party success, he made it his boast between his conscience and himself that he had never directly taken part in it. So now he hemmed, and merely said:—

"We're fighting a mercenary foe."

Shelby bent for an instant to his figures. Then, with offhand abruptness:—

"There's something I never told you. When I went into this campaign I mortgaged my real estate holdings here in town. I tell you now because I must negotiate a loan on my share in the Eureka, and of course you are the man to approach."

Bowers started.

"Is it that bad, Ross?"

"Yes; it's that bad. Money's the argument now."

"Suppose—suppose you lose?"

Shelby considered the possibility.

"Then I'm ruined. But I shan't lose. I shall win."

There was less buoyancy when Bowers had left; more studying of the check-book, much reflection and calculation. Money, money, money; the thought hounded him.

Down in the Temple carriage drive the worried man could see a boy holding a mettlesome saddle horse, caparisoned for a woman's use. In fair weather it stood there at this hour every day. To-day it was suggestive. Shelby sprang to his telephone.

CHAPTER IV

With the stable boy's assurance that within ten minutes his horse would stand at the curb, Shelby locked his door against surprise, and, with an eye on the Temple driveway, made a rapid change to his riding clothes, which he was accustomed to keep by him for emergencies. As he finished, Ruth, lissome in her black habit, cantered daintily out with a laughing nod to Volney Sprague, who was watching her from the *Whig* office over the way. His clerk was absent serving papers in Etruria, and, hanging a mendacious "Back-in-1-Hour" sign on his outer door, Shelby leaped down the stair.

In the public eye he grew more sedate, and trotted soberly out of the business district in a direction contrary to that taken by his neighbor. Then, of a sudden, he shamed John Gilpin with a right-about, and, circling by side streets and quiet lanes the course he had just covered, galloped countryward in pursuit. The manoeuvre was not new to him. He had employed it on occasion to hoodwink Mrs. Grundy for Mrs. Hilliard's sake, scrupulously meeting and leaving the lady outside the corporation limits, a ruse which deceived nobody save the deceivers. Nor was it effective now. Ruth passed Mrs. Bowers's argus-eyed bay window, as did Shelby, and Mrs. Grundy had her speculative pickings of the event.

Mark Lee Luther

Ruth spied pursuit where the turnpike elbowed sharply from the outskirts. For a demure girl her smile was mischievous. Walking her wiry little pony till the footfalls of Shelby's chestnut cob beat the 'pike a scant hundred yards behind, she flicked her animal ever so lightly with her riding crop. The man saw a puff of dust, a twinkle of little hoofs, and a lithe figure outlined for an instant against the autumn sky as it sped over a hill and far away. The cob labored to the crest and pondered his defeat. A half-mile down the unkempt old toll road, where the goldenrod dropped stately bows to the purple aster, and Bouncing Bet viewed their livelong philandering with scorn, was the impertinent runt—walking! Down thundered the cob. No evasion now. Two hundred yards, one fifty, one hundred yards, seventy-five, sixty, even fifty—and again the pursued was spirited away in a cloud.

Shelby bore it thrice, and raised his voice. Ruth's surprise was a delightful thing to see.

"I've tried these three miles to overtake you," he scolded. "You must have heard me."

Ruth surveyed the smoking cob.

"We did hear a noise. My pony is so restive."

"The little beast looks as demure as yourself. I believe you knew it was I."

Ruth's glance swept a neighboring field.

"Have you ever associated cabbages with beauty?" she asked. "Just look at that reach of blue-green."

Shelby admired obediently. Then, the occasion seeming to demand a certain finesse, he said:—

"There's a man out this way I must look up—a kind of farmer, drover, and jockey rolled in one. He influences a bunch of votes. It's very pleasant to find you riding the same way. I'm glad we met—that is—if you—"

Her smile stopped his limping improvisation in mid-career.

"You needn't invent anything more," she said. "You're not good at it."

"There really is such a man," he defended, with a contented laugh; "but he can wait. I'd like to be quit of the political grind for a while. May I rest?"

"Yes; you may come," Ruth decided.

His appeal struck a womanly chord.

October was spendthrift of its pigments. Every isolated copse was a mimic forest fire, each bivouacked corn-field a russet foil, the air a heady wine. Shelby thrilled with dumb pastorals and a vague longing to do and speak in keeping with the spirit of the scene. A tuft of oxeye daisies in the shelter of a ruinous worm fence attracted him, and he reined the cob from the highway to fetch them. To his bewilderment Ruth's face shadowed at the gift.

"Poor things—what made you?" she lamented. "I've watched them there for a fortnight. What clumsy florist could have grouped them with the tall grasses so exquisitely, and set the little red vine clambering over all in the fence corner, so satiny and lichen-gray?"

Shelby was mystified.

"I thought that they would look smart in your belt—that all women wanted to pick flowers when they saw them—" he stammered. "I'm afraid I know little of women's ways."

Her laugh was a caress.

"Don't put my rudeness upon the sex," she said. "It's because I dabble in paints and things that I thought of these flowers first as a picture. But I assure you I'm just as much given to plundering them to set off my hair and dress as any daughter of Eve," wherewith she placed his offering, as he would have it, in her belt. He seemed to her always a kind of shorn Samson when afield from politics, and now, as she had often done, she drew him to speak of what he knew best.

"I used to think you cared little about such things," he told her presently. "The average woman doesn't care greatly. If she had the ballot, she'd probably vote for the handsomest man—if the candidate was a man."

"I'm afraid I should," owned Ruth. "For instance, I never could vote for a candidate with mutton-chop whiskers. And fancy having to decide between two women!"

"Vote-buying would have a scope which staggers the imagination."

The comment set her thoughts running on the accusations of corruption which were bandied from lip to lip during this campaign.

"Are many votes really bought?" she asked.

"Yes, many," Shelby answered frankly. "I shouldn't care to have you quote me, but I'll admit that I've sometimes bought them myself."

She was dumfounded at his candor, and half regretted it.

"Is it—is it quite necessary?"

"I think it is—sometimes. And so it will be till the reformers show the practical politician a better system, or human nature changes its spots. Indiana was bought for Lincoln in '64. It would take an unpractical man, even an unpatriotic man, to deny that the crisis did not justify the step."

"Every candidate is not a Lincoln."

"Nor every year a '64. Timid people compound with their conscience by calling that Indiana affair a war measure. But we're talking of our own state, whose political name has justly or unjustly become a hissing among the nations. I don't deny there's some reason for it. We are big, with big opportunities for corruption, and the tradition of sharp practice is of long standing. We bribed, intimidated, and filibustered in swaddling clothes, and stole a governorship as early as 1791. The tricks of to-day have all gone stale with handling, for the patriots we honor were politicians too."

"That is a novel point of view for me," Ruth admitted. "It's so easy to think the old time the best time." This was the pleader of the court-house rally, and she forgot the gaucheries and limitations of a moment since.

"All in all, the Catilines meet their Ciceros," said Shelby; "the Tildens undo the Tweeds. General Jackson once said he was not a politician, but if he were, he should be a New York politician. You see the state is an eternal riddle— 'pivotal,' as the saying goes—the mother of parties, the devotee of none; and there lies half its fascination for the politician—I might say for the statesman. What passes for mere politics here might well figure as statesmanship elsewhere. We don't call our commonwealth the Empire State for naught; its interests are indeed imperial, and it is no mean office to shape its destinies. It is the man in politics who does this, whether you will or no. A free government requires parties, parties require politicians—in last analysis the mouthpiece of the sovereign people. I dare say you're wondering what all these generalities have to do with vote-buying in Tuscarora. I'll tell you. It's true that not every candidate is a Lincoln, that not a few men are personally unworthy of the offices they hold or seek; but this also is true, that many an unworthy man is worthy of election, even by bribery,—I say it deliberately,—because of his party's sake, for that party's success may signify the country's salvation. You have, of course, heard sad things said of me. You will hear more, and I shall not run around among my friends to deny them. Worthy or unworthy, I merge my personality in that of my party, in whose ultimate patriotism I have enduring faith."

Ruth was no logician.

"I don't believe you unworthy," she said.

"That's better than a hundred votes," laughed the man, vastly pleased. "Let me promise you something. If I'm elected to Congress, I will do and say everything a new member can to wipe out the tariff on objects of art."

It was her turn for mystification; if he had his shallows, he also had his depths.

Shelby did not ask if she were pleased; he saw it.

"You wouldn't have thought it of a practical politician—one of the 'aesthetically dead,'" he smiled. "Yet it is the politician you should seek to interest in these things. He'll see their value if he's taught. You opened my eyes—did it in a social way, which is the best way. It's through his social side, be it in barroom or drawing-room, that the politician is most easily reached, for he's a human being. Reformers don't see that; they aim at the intellect direct. You didn't dream, in talking about art to me now and then, that you were doing a possible public service. That's the key-note of woman's best influence in politics, I've come to believe—unconscious argument, not speechmaking. You have influenced me more than I can tell. I've grown. You have broadened my horizon. Will you make it broader? I ask you to marry me."

It was a little moment before she took his meaning, so much did his blunt proposal seem a part of the staccato chat of politics from which it issued.

"I cannot," she said at last.

"Why?"

It seemed ridiculous to speak of the affections to this businesslike creature who apparently counted them not worth mentioning; so she answered that they were unsuited to one another.

Shelby shook his head emphatically.

"I can't agree with you. Are you engaged to marry any one else?"

Ruth colored under his cross-examination, but replied that she was not.

"We'll let the question lie fallow for a time," Shelby arranged. "Think it over impartially."

She tried to bid him put the thing wholly out of mind, but he adjourned discussion as summarily as he might a committee meeting, and spoke of other topics.

It was sundown when they neared the town, returning by way of Little Poland and the successive quarries bordering the canal. Shelby dropped a careless glance at the docks and yards of his own company, now quiet with the day's work done. Then he looked again. Outlined against the sky a man climbed to the tow-path and walked away. Shelby recognized Bernard Graves.

"Ride on slowly," he directed. "I'll join you in a minute. There's something needs looking after in the Eureka."

CHAPTER V

The intruder wheeled at the hoof-beats and waited. Purpling with rage, Shelby thrust the cob's nozzle fairly in Graves's face.

"You're a damned spy," he taunted.

Graves went pale, but his jaw set.

"You know better, Shelby," he answered, without passion. "I am here openly. I came before the quarry shut down for the night, as your men will tell you."

"You're a spy," repeated Shelby, fingering his whip. "Come how or when, you're a spy. I know your back-door tactics. You sly into other men's private business, as you're trying to sly into politics."

"I care nothing for any private business of yours which doesn't besmirch your public character."

"Besmirch!" Shelby pounced upon the word. "I know your kidney—you pure souls who shirk jury duty and whine down taxes."

Graves backed from the nervous whip.

"I want no words with you," he said.

"I dare say; but you'll have them." He reined the cob to block Graves's further retreat, forcing him well upon the string-piece of the dock. "You're here to smell out canal scandals," he charged. "You want to know what became of the marketable stone that was taken from the canal prism. You'll get your wish right here and now. I took that stone, my pattern of civic virtue; sold it, my pink of reformers. You needn't have screwed Jap Hinchey for that knowledge. I would have told you the truth any time, and much good may it do you. Are you ass enough to believe that the contractors went outside their specifications to dispose of the spoils banks to my company? They had their warrant from Albany in black and white. Every act was within the law."

"The more shame upon Albany and the law; it is the letter of the law which shelters you."

Shelby rasped a laugh.

"I know something of the spirit of laws."

"I doubt not. You've helped make enough disreputable legislation to qualify an expert."

"What right has a dilettante like you to sit in judgment?" he demanded, the other's barb rankling none the less that he had invited it. "You have no notion of just political expediency; no notion even of politics with which you meddle. Politics isn't book knowledge; it's flesh and blood fact. Party fealty means nothing to you. You've not voted a straight ticket twice in your life."

"I know where that shoe pinches," retorted Graves. "You mean I've consistently neglected to vote for you. Somehow I never could swallow your assumption of divine right to hold office all the time."

Shelby's fingers knotted round his whip-handle.

"I'd like to trounce you," he menaced. "It's a hiding you need."

"For presuming to run against you? Let me make it plain that I'm not to be intimidated by you or any of your creatures."

"I'd like to trounce you," repeated Shelby, hoarsely, beside himself with the gadfly inquisition of the past few days. "I'm sick of your pharisaical ways. I bottom your lofty motives well enough. Jealousy goaded you into politics. You're a reformer because the heiress wanted none of you. If Ruth Temple—"

Graves wrenched the whip from Shelby's grasp, and struck with all his might. The warded blow spent itself on the pommel of the saddle.

"Stung, eh?" Shelby leaped from his stirrups and closed with him. The cob took fright at the reeling men and pounded off up the tow-path toward the town.

Then another horse loomed of a sudden from out the dusk, and Ruth herself rode straight upon them, enforcing a separation.

"How dare you drag my name into a low political quarrel— either of you?" No one answered her. "Give *me* the whip." Shelby, who had regained it, obeyed without a word. Ruth flung it far into the canal. "Now if you will be brutes, use brutes' weapons." Wherewith she turned an indignant back and galloped an exit from the scene as spirited as her entrance.

"You knew she was there," accused Graves.

"I left her in the road, damn you. I couldn't know she had seen."

Standing on the dock's sheer edge, they glowered into one another's eyes through the fading twilight, the great steam cranes behind flinging out giant arms over the stone heaps, the black water below glancing with fitful gleams of steel and copper from the sunset's last saffron afterglow. The yellow headlight of a low-lying grain boat stole nearer, unheeded till the straining mules toiled by.

"I don't know what keeps me from—"

Shelby's lips were tardy of framing what his heart lusted.

"Fear, perhaps."

"If you think that, then—"

A rain of oaths from the driver warned them too late of the trailing tow-line. They tripped together, and in an embrace of self-preservation together fell into the cool still waters which ever draw unruffled, though their banks smoulder with passion and political intrigue from the Niagara to the Hudson.

Shelby rose first, half-strangled, and laid hold upon the wall. Still cursing fluently, the driver pulled him to the string-piece, and both men peered out over the watery blackness, now cut with a widening shaft of light from the boat's lantern. Graves seemed to have vanished utterly, and Shelby made the banks echo with his name, but the canal returned no answer. The man was now as ready to save as a moment since he had been ready to destroy, but before he could slip again into the water, the boat glided past, discovering Graves in dim silhouette against the gray timbers, swimming at ease.

With a parting curse, indicative of relief, the driver set off down the tow-path after his mules, while Shelby waited on the brink till the boat went by, intending aid if the swimmer's strength should fail. But Graves was of no mind to cause him the lifting of a finger, and to the watcher's bewilderment cut directly behind the great rudder into the swirling wake, headed for the heel-path, which he attained with a dozen vigorous strokes, and clambering the sloping embankment, disappeared in a clump of willows.

The autumn frosts nip Tuscarora betimes, but Shelby sat staring in his sodden clothes, till he fathomed his rival's motive, and chattered forth a laugh. Then he hurried across the dock to the little tin-roofed office of the Eureka. He was without a key, but he rummaged a pick from one of the neighboring sheds, forced the staple of the padlock, and, popping into the oven warmth of the cabin, mended the fire in the tiny sheet-iron stove. His first precaution was to drain his pocket flask, which had somehow come through unscathed, and, as he peeled away his clinging garments in the flickering light, he telephoned the Tuscarora House for a change of clothing. In the reflective half-hour before the coming of the messenger he felt a genuine regret that Graves had gone his own way. The affair had dropped already into humorous perspective, and it seemed to him that, had they stood side by side in this cabin, every barrier must have fallen and the outcome been wholly good.

Nature's reaction from the too tense hours of that crowded day was at its utmost swing as he gained his hotel room and smoothed the roughness of his quarry toilet. The familiar chamber revolted him; its warring colors jarred; the nymphs of his favorite picture were devoid of blandishment. Nor did his cronies of below stairs attract, and the liquor he had taken left him no appetite for solid food. He craved nothing so much as rest and human sympathy.

Mrs. Hilliard was at home.

"You never fail when I need you," she said, as Shelby couched his jaded body in the cosy library before an open fire. "Joe is always out, of course. I don't mind that—now. Milicent too is gone to-night,—a children's party. I've been lonely—depressed. Since you came—ah, well, see for yourself what I am."

A maudlin self-pity, born of alcohol, dimmed Shelby's eyes.

"It's like a home to me," he confessed, his voice uncertain. "It's like a home."

"And some call you hard!" Mrs. Hilliard extended both plump hands to him. "How they misjudge you."

"Everybody misjudges me, Cora," Shelby declared, not backward in manual demonstration himself; "everybody but you."

The lady released herself adroitly, and fluttered the music at a piano just beyond the half-drawn portiere of the adjoining room.

"Shall I play?" she asked.

Shelby nodded like a sultan from his cushions.

"Ragtime," he directed. "Something with a tune." The other woman had surfeited him with classicalities.

He built air castles as he watched and listened; fabrics furnished after the manner of the Hilliard home and peopled by two kindred souls. If this insidious luxury were his—the warmth, ease, leisure, Cora! He considered the turn of her neck, her profile, the famous shoulders, now clothed yet not concealed. She was handsome still; ripe, but not over-ripe, ambitious, capable. They were singularly congenial, he and she. He could have blundered worse than in marrying her, had not burly Joe forestalled. *He*—inappreciative hulk!—was no fit mate for her. She needed sympathy, cooeperation, the fellowship of her mind's true complement: in fine, himself. If the other woman should not—if Joe—! He clipped the revery of its conclusion.

In that evening's long intimacy—how long or how intimate neither realized till afterward—the man bared his financial necessity.

"God knows why I blab this," he ended. "I've told nobody else the whole truth, not even Bowers."

She lagged short of his meaning at first.

"But you'll have plenty in time," she said. "There will be your congressional salary and all the new opportunities."

"Without money I may never draw that salary."

"You don't mean you'll fail! You don't mean that, Ross?"

He bowed gravely.

"But it's impossible. Why, everybody will vote for you—almost everybody. Joe alone will give you two hundred votes."

"It will require more than Little Poland's good-will to elect me," he smiled grimly.

"You must *buy* votes?"

"Yes."

"And you have nothing?"

"At this moment I haven't enough ready cash to give me a decent burial."

"Don't speak like that." She rose impulsively, and unlocked a cabinet in the chimneypiece. "Here is a little—not much—a hundred dollars perhaps. I want you to take it; it's mine—some of my allowance. I want to give it to the party. And there's more. I've a mortgage—my very own. You shall have that too—for the party."

Shelby leaped to his feet as she thrust the bills in his hands.

"My God, Cora," he cried, "I can't take this—your pin money!"

She caught the notes from his protesting fingers and forced them into his nearest pocket.

"You shall," she pleaded; "you shall—for the party."

He seized her hands and bent to meet her eyes.

"Cora, Cora," he whispered hoarsely, "you're not doing this for the party! It's not for the party! It's for me, Cora, for me—"

"Such a nice party—party—" A fragment of Milicent's treble good nights drifted in from the sidewalk like an echo.

CHAPTER VI

Shelby waked from a restless night to confront a restless day, in truth, an anxious week. Two things he set about instanter; he wrote a manly letter of apology to Ruth, and he returned Mrs. Hilliard's money. All day long he parried and laughed down fatuous comment on his supposed cropper into the canal, for the cob had returned to his manger and founded a theory that his master let gossip accept as true. He dissembled with greater ease as the hours lapsed, finding reasons why the inner history of the incident would remain secret; neither Ruth nor Bernard Graves was likely to tell—he certainly should not. In the evening it was bruited that Graves was sick, and the morrow's *Whig* diagnosed his malady as influenza. Shelby thanked his practical stars that the ducking had had no such issue for him. By the second evening he was doubly thankful, for the press despatches were ticking out to whom it might concern that the distinguished author of the ode on the "Victory of Samothrace" and other poems lay low with pneumonia.

In common with hundreds, Shelby sent a message of regret, which, like its fellow-hundreds, nobody at the Graves cottage found time to read. Many of these notes and telegrams, however, found their way into the *Whig*, but Shelby hunted its despised columns in vain for his own. This seemed to him and to Bowers a deliberate attempt by Sprague to stamp him as unfeeling,—to coin party

Mark Lee Luther

capital,—and with the notion of righting himself in the public eye Shelby determined upon a personal call at the house. By a piece of good fortune, as unexpected as it was welcome, he was received by Ruth, who had volunteered to lighten the burden of the sick man's mother in ways like this. She was unembarrassed, courteous, even kind in a formal fashion, telling him in subdued accents what he knew she must know he knew already from the newspapers. The patient's case discussed from every point of view, the caller burned to forward his own concerns, to renew his apologies, to make his peace; but he could find no opening, and shortly went away. Yet his silence did him better service than speech. Ruth mistook his unrest for contrition, and pitied him.

As Graves's disease neared its crisis, with hurried summoning of consulting physicians and rumors of a resort to oxygen, Shelby found it impossible to avoid an occasional glance into an immediate future in which Graves figured merely as a memory; but whatever his speculations, he was decently chary of voicing them. Some of his party associates were more outspoken, and the opinion was advanced over the Tuscarora House bar that, the loss to literature aside, the young man's taking-off could not but simplify the political situation. The Hon. Seneca Bowers, being of the old school, quaintly declined both speculation and discussion.

The day of the crisis Shelby saw Dr. Crandall step from his phaeton to his little sham Greek temple of an office at the foot of his lawn, and followed him. The bluff physician greeted him with a scowl.

"Well, sir?" he jerked out, fumbling and smelling among his bottles.

"I wanted news of Graves."

"I doubt not."

The words of themselves were innocuous, but the doctor's hammering emphasis was formidable.

"I resent your tone," protested Shelby.

"And I, sir, resent your inquiry."

"You must have received many like it. However, you may keep your bulletins. Those of the consulting physicians are probably more reliable."

With this shaft he turned, but Dr. Crandall was beforehand and closed the door.

"Not yet, sir, not yet," he said grimly. "I have a bulletin for you, deem its worth what you will. And I have more. I must administer some nasty medicine. My patient will recover, sir, and no thanks to you."

"I don't know what you mean."

"Yes, you do."

"You accuse me of lying—"

"Bah, sir, stop your ruffling. Now for your physic. At the instance of my lifelong friend, Seneca Bowers, I consented against my better judgment to preside last month at your ratification meeting, and so lent you, as I may say, my public indorsement. I shall not publicly stultify myself by repudiating that action, but my vote, thank Heaven, I never pledged. I warn you, sir, that, as sure as I see the sun rise on election day, I shall cast my ballot for your opponent, or my name's not Crandall."

"Very well," sneered Shelby, coolly. "If your political allegiance follows your fee, there's no more to be said."

"I am stoically indifferent to your slanderous imputation," fumed the doctor, his manner a very Judas to his words; "but I assure you there is more to be said, and that I purpose to say it. I have yet to tell you that you are a blackguard, sir, a violent blackguard, whose proper level is the ward cesspools of the metropolis where crime and politics stalk hand in hand. Medical science will save the man you would have done to death."

Shelby passed the vituperation, puzzling how much the irate doctor knew.

"Is your patient's delirium contagious?" he asked.

"Ha!" cried the doctor. "You do take my meaning."

"It's clear enough that you are hinting at foul play on the flimsiest of evidence."

"Evidence, evidence! I want no surer evidence of your intent than poor Bernard's wanderings; there's method, sir, even in delirium. If I wished further proof, the fact that you too were in the canal that night would suffice."

"Fevered maunderings and a coincidence!" Shelby laughed him in the face, too contemptuous to set him right. "Keep your vote, you pompous ignoramus," he jeered, and left him sputtering.

Worsting the choleric physician in argument was a mere matter of keeping one's own temper, and Shelby took no pride in his victory. It was a relief to know that he knew so little, but the possibility remained that, in the weakness of convalescence, Bernard might let fall details more damaging than Dr. Crandall's tissue of half-knowledge and inference. Ruth and pneumonia eliminated, the quarrel might have become public property and welcome, with a likely chance of its working to his advantage; but, alas, he himself had dragged Ruth into it past all elimination, and now Bernard's sickness had whipped up a sea of maudlin sympathy which exposure might easily precipitate in a political tidal wave.

From this day forth, event crowded event. The news from the sick-room was the signal for renewed activity all along the line of battle, and the spectre of his great need haunted Shelby with added terrors. Bernard Graves's allies, apt disciples of the late Chuck O'Rourke as they were, jumped at the shining possibilities laid open by their candidate's condition, and, abetted financially by their State Committee, set a pace in corruption unprecedented in the checkered history of the Demijohn. Volney Sprague was powerless. The freebooters listened sedately to his protests and redoubled their offending, well aware that in their candidate's chamber politics could have yet no place. Far from the turmoil, the celebrity ate the jellies of his idolaters, and spent his waking hours in the impractical companionship of a certain Shelley and one John Keats.

The beset leaders strained the machine's every cog to meet the emergency. Out from a corner of the Chairman of the County Committee's safe came a pudgy manuscript book which few eyes ever saw,—a book made up of voters' names, their party, and at times their price set down in strange symbols which the initiated might translate into terms of dollars and cents. Probably every county committee in the Demijohn Congressional District could show the like. There was earnest thumbing of these volumes, with changing of symbols to fit changed conditions, and the call went out for money. Little came. The State Committee was deaf to argument or entreaty, and the Demijohn seemed drained. Shelby and Bowers personally did what they could.

For reputation's sake, the old leader went down deep into his pocket, while Shelby tossed into the breach everything he realized from his mortgaged quarry interest which long outstanding debts did not require. Nor were these latter inconsiderable. Involved in innumerable schemes which sapped his capital without prospect of ready dividends, it seemed to him that every land syndicate, stock company, insurance policy, what not, of them all was demanding instant propitiation. Brave it out with Bowers as he might, Shelby walked none the less in the shadow of a mighty fear; and had not Mrs. Hilliard left town for her annual autumn round of the shops of New York, he could have gone to her prepared to accept her supremest charity.

In his blackest hour the distracted man encountered the Widow Weatherwax. Since her sibylline performances at the camp-meeting he had seen little of her, the fascination of will-making being temporarily eclipsed by a local temperance crusade led by Mr. Hewett, which enlisted the full energy of her not inconsiderable powers for conscience-guided meddling. The parson had deemed the time ripe for a war on the groggeries of the Flats, with the outcome that most bar-rooms of the town, including that of the Tuscarora House, were found to be violating the Sunday closing law. In the legal unpleasantness which followed, Shelby's name figured as attorney for the hotel proprietor, one of the lawyer's regular clients. It was a purely formal service, without moral implication of any sort, but it bared Shelby's whole legislative record on the liquor question to pin-prick attack, and cost him, as he now learned from her shocked lips, the invaluable political support of the widow.

Buttonholed while crossing the court-house lawn, and backed into a corner between the county clerk's office and the jail, Shelby had to listen with what patience he might to her denunciation of what she called his vile concord with Belial.

"Yes, yes, Mrs. Weatherwax," he wedged in finally; "but we can't all think alike. Now if you were a liquor dealer's wife, you would sing another song."

The widow shuddered.

"Me!" Another shudder. "Me marry a saloon keeper! Me!— a W.C.T.U. and a I.O.G.T.!"

Shelby grinned.

"They say I.O.G.T. means 'I Often Get Tight.'" Somehow he could not resist the ancient rural fling.

"You know well 'nuff 'tain't," retorted the widow, indignantly. "It's the Inderpendant Order ov Good Templars, and I'm an orf'cer with regalyer. It's purple, and has gold lace."

"I'm amazed at your wearing such fripperies," teased the man; "but you must look simply ravishing."

The widow was bomb-proof against humorous attack. Drawing herself to her full height, as she might clad in full regalia of purple and gold, she mouthed:—

"'I loath, abhor, my very soul with strong disgust is stirred, when e're I see, or hear, or tell ov the dark bev'rage ov hell.'"

The dumpy little figure, swelling like a pouter pigeon's, was so irresistibly ludicrous that Shelby forgot his troubles and threw back his head in a gust of laughter.

"Think it's funny, I s'pose." Her face was vinegar. "'Tain't to be expected a boy brung up in a distillery 'ud know better."

Shelby sobered.

"Confine yourself to facts, please," he interposed. "My grandfather's entirely respectable distilling business was closed out before I was born."

"'Twa'n't b'fore your pa was made a drunkard, Ross Shelby."

He went red with impotent anger.

"By God!" he swore. "If—if you were a man—"

"There you go a-swearin' at a poor weak female."

"Let me pass," he choked. "Let me pass. I don't know what I may say to you."

She stepped aside.

"Go," she said, with a fat little gesture. "Mebbe you've got pressin' business. Mebbe you want to write billy-doos to Mrs. Hilliard. Mebbe them opery glasses needs dustin' off s'more."

He fled lest she say worse.

Clearly William Irons had been wax in the widow's hands, and on his auburn head would have fallen the accumulated spleen of weeks had not the youth met his employer at the office door with a telegram whose portentous message engulfed all lesser cares.

CHAPTER VII

Shelby read, pondered, and finally roused from his preoccupation to meet the bovine stare of his clerk.

"Railway guide, William," he ordered sharply.

"Yep."

"And call up the station agent. Have him wire for a lower berth on the Lehigh to-night."

William Irons waited.

"Go on, go on," called the politician, crossly, glancing up from his time-table. "Have you foundered halfway?"

"Nope. You didn't say where to."

"New York, New York."

"Yep," said William, placidly. "What train?"

Shelby left off staring at his blotter for an instant, to fling him the information. William Irons rubbed one long leg against its fellow as he leaned to the telephone and ruminated the mystery of this impending flight into what was for him the great unknown. This air of suppressed excitement had never attended Shelby's departures.

"Goin' to use it yourself?" he inquired.

"Is the station agent aching to know?"

"Nope," returned William, frankly. "He didn't ask."

"Then you needn't. Now get Mr. Bowers's residence, and ask if he is there."

"Got him," announced the clerk presently, as if he had trapped a rat, and stood expectantly aside. To his disappointment Shelby merely made an immediate appointment at the Bowers's home. More bitter still, he took the message with him.

"Lightning has struck," Shelby greeted the old man ten minutes later, handing him the telegram. "I've been ordered down to the Boss. This means make or break."

The Hon. Seneca Bowers unslung his glasses and slowly read the summons.

"I guess it had to come," he commented.

"Oh, yes. Things have reached lowest ebb. In fact, they're so low that you must put up my car fare."

Bowers assented readily.

"Whatever you need you shall have, Ross. You must go in good style."

Shelby pocketed the sum which he thought would meet his travelling expenses and listened to his friend's rather dolorous words of encouragement.

"I think he'll do right by you," Bowers concluded feebly. "I think he'll do right."

Shelby jerked a grim smile.

"The Boss always does right—when it pays."

In the smoking-room of the Pullman that night the traveller was accosted by an unctuous person who looked like a race-track tout. He would have described himself as a man "interested" in legislation; he had been described by other people as a lobbyist, but that was in the days before the machine absorbed the lobby.

"And how does the Hon. Calvin Ross Shelby find himself?" beamed the new-comer, dropping into a seat alongside. "Busy days in Tuscarora, eh?"

"Yes; busy days, Krantz," assented the harassed man, concealing his annoyance under a cordial greeting. If ever he had needed a quiet hour it was now, and he had sought the smoking-compartment because with a carful of women and children it seemed to promise solitude.

"Shall miss you around Albany this winter," Krantz said feelingly, exploring the pockets of his horsey waistcoat for a cigar. "We always got along so well together."

Shelby was silent under this moving reminiscence.

"I'll have some of my Washington friends look you up," pursued the man. "They're good fellows, all of 'em."

"Thanks," said Shelby, without enthusiasm. "Better wait till I'm elected."

"My dear sir, can you doubt? Your resplendent gonfalon, if I may so express myself, has ever been Victory's chosen perch."

"I've pulled a majority hitherto."

"And you will, you will. In fact"—his voice fell—"we think it such a foregone conclusion that one of my friends who is looking over the prospective House wants to make your acquaintance. You're sure to jibe. He's interested in the unlucky River and Harbor scheme."

"Oh."

Krantz looked out at him from underneath his saurian lids, and blew a smoke ring toward the rococo ceiling.

"Through an option or two I'm rather interested myself," he continued smoothly. "I'd like to see every good man indorse a good thing. I haven't been told what your opinion is." Getting no answer, he added: "Of course we expect to pull the thing off in this winter's session. If not, then the fight goes into your House. Between ourselves, just where do you stand?"

"You don't need to be told that it's a gigantic job."

Krantz's benevolent features expressed blandest regret.

"Now isn't it a pity that misconception should be so widespread?" he exclaimed, apparently to the writhing ornaments of the ceiling. "Isn't it a pity? But it's so often true! Take that street railway bill of yours last winter: how that enlightened measure was denounced!"

Shelby scowled.

"We're talking of Washington."

"They've a lot in common, Albany and Washington."

"I don't want them to have for me."

Krantz laughed.

"How reform does drop its gentle influence round! Has the fusion movement in Tuscarora converted you?"

"No," Shelby answered. "I've grown."

Krantz looked bewildered, laughed a little, and asked point-blank, "Shall you come out against us?"

"You'll know in Washington."

"If elected," qualified the man.

"Naturally."

Krantz rang up the porter to ask if his berth were ready, rose, yawned, and shed a benevolent smile.

"From things they're beginning to say about Tuscarora down at headquarters," he remarked impersonally, "I venture to predict that we'll know within twenty-four hours. Good night."

The River and Harbor bogy wove the pattern of Shelby's troubled dreams. In a way, he had grown, as he liked to think, and by this touchstone he knew it best. Whatever his practice, his quickened ideals were loftier than of old, and across the future's broader field, should it be his to till, the man was honestly ambitious to trace a straighter furrow than his ploughshare had ever turned. But his past and the insistent present seemed to hamper every forward step. It was an open secret that the disciplining of the man he hoped to succeed had issued directly from his refusal to stand with his colleagues in this question, and Shelby in his heart approved his course. He did not anticipate that he should meet a like dilemma; the winter session of the old House would doubtless settle the matter, as Krantz had said; but Volney Sprague had harped upon his possible action so incessantly that he could easily see why the organization might wonder at his silence. Was the time for speech, then, so near as this creature warned?

Yet he took a certain comfort in Krantz's companionship in the morning, as from the crowded ferry he watched the city's sky line detach itself from the mist. Notwithstanding his legislative career, New York was almost an unknown country, and this battlemented mystery overawed him like a frowning bastion. It challenged the alien to do and dare, but it quenched his individuality. Krantz, obviously, was hardened to its lesson. He elbowed the jostling pack in the ferry slip as one of them, called the elevated road the "L," and was otherwise enviably sophisticated. Shelby imitated at a distance, but the hall mark of the outsider was too deep for ready erasure. He would persistently apologize to people with whom he collided, and surrender his car seat to standing women.

He had mentioned a Madison Square hotel as his destination, and on Krantz's saying that he meant to stop there briefly, too, it fell out that they approached the room clerk together, and that Krantz registered for both. So it chanced that, unknown to himself, the candidate was entered with a fine flourish as the Hon. Calvin Ross Shelby. The two men breakfasted together, and Krantz presently went about his business, leaving Shelby in some quandary how he should employ the interval before the hour appointed by the great leader for their meeting. For a time he loitered in a window overlooking the restful oasis of the square, a place of fountains and pleasant leafage, dominated by a graceful tower which served as footstool for a shining goddess on tiptoe to greet the morning. His eyes were not long bent upon the goddess,—he did not "live with the gods,"—nor yet upon the greenness, since he had lived all his days with shrubs and trees; he watched the commingling ride of Broadway and Fifth Avenue, watched till it dizzied and saddened him. What did he count here?

Presently he returned to the desk with an inquiry concerning his room. There had been a shift of clerks since his arrival, and the newcomer asked his name, his impassive scrutiny travelling from the man to the signature, and from the signature back to the man. A youngish person, looking the successful broker or lawyer, who had been chatting with the clerk, saw the movement and imitated it as Shelby walked away.

"And you said there were no celebrities," he bantered.

The clerk shrugged listlessly.

"The 'Hon. Calvin Ross Shelby,'" read the reporter. "There ought to be a story in a man who has the nerve to subscribe himself like that in a New York hotel. What do you know about his pathetic case?"

"Stranger to me," the bored one unbent to say.

The questioner spied a fellow-reporter whose specialty was politics.

"Billy," he demanded, pointing to the register, "who is the Hon. Calvin Ross Shelby?"

"Candidate for Congress in the Demijohn District," returned the political expert, promptly, smiling at the signature. "Rather picturesque fight the honorable is having.

He's bucking a fusion opposition headed by the author of that popular poem about a statue. Where is he? I want to see him. There's nothing else doing here."

They pursued the stranger down the corridor, overhauling him at the entrance of the cafe.

"The Hon. Calvin Ross Shelby, I believe," said the political reporter, lifting his hat, and naming the newspaper he represented. His companion, who looked like a broker, but whose present mission was to screw copy out of hotel arrivals, followed his example, and the group was almost immediately increased by three more well-dressed cosmopolitans with ingratiating manners and a scent for news.

Five New York reporters hanging on his words! To achieve this giddy pinnacle on the heels of calling himself an atom seemed to Shelby almost to pass belief. Somehow he rallied.

"Gentlemen," he beamed, "I'm glad to see you. Have a drink."

No liquor distilled could add to Shelby's intoxication. It was not reporting, this swift interchange of trenchant thought between men of the world; or if reporting, a sublimated sort, free of note-books and the disconcerting trademarks of the guild as he had known it elsewhere.

"I can't understand the hostility felt by some public men for the press," he remarked, thumbs in armholes, coat lapels thrown benignly back. "Our relations, I take it, should be confidential."

Practice followed precept, and in that delightful atmosphere Shelby's confidences flowered like young May. Tuscarora County was put through its paces for a gaping world; Clinton's Ditch—"well-spring of New York's commercial supremacy, gentlemen"—shown in rosiest apotheosis; the Empire State pedestalled imperially among the nations. Nor could his versatility be bounded by politics alone. The inevitable allusion to Bernard Graves's poem involved literature, and to stand, as he did, under the same roof with the nymphs who had long bodied forth his pictorial ideal, was to invite a public avowal of his proposed championship of free art. He was lured the farther into this quagmire by the guileless questioning of one of his listeners, who lingered in obvious fascination after his fellows had departed, and, in happy ignorance that the cherubic youth was the son of an artist of distinction, and himself no mean critic of things artistic, Shelby voiced opinions more vigorous than discreet.

"There was a time," he confessed apropos of the nymphs, "when I thought those ladies the best ever. Young eyes won't hesitate between a plump Venus and a lean Madonna."

"And now?"

"Well, I haven't altogether renounced the world, the flesh, and the devil, but my taste has changed. A good animal picture fetches me,—something like Rosa What's-her-name's 'Horse Fair' you've got up-town in Central Park. I call that big art."

"Big art; that's the word," agreed the cherub, shaking hands. "It measures 197 x 93 1/2," he murmured to his cigarette.

CHAPTER VIII

The Boss was an awesome figure to up-state politicians, and Shelby approached his place of business with a trepidation not wholly owing to his tangled fortunes. It was his first visit. There had been meetings between them at Saratoga conventions, and more times than a few he had furthered the leader's indirect ends in the Albany committee-rooms and on the floor of the Assembly; but greater than Shelby had found it impossible to penetrate the great man's inner circle at Saratoga, and their subterranean dealings in Albany and elsewhere had usually been transacted by way of Bowers. The Boss's methods were circuitous, cog fitting smoothly to cog till the remote agent rather than himself seemed the prime mover. Only in emergencies was he direct.

His apparent aloofness multiplied his power. He held no office; he made no speeches; he had no obvious axe to grind. He seemed to count politics his diversion, not his business, and emphasized this attitude by a strict supervision of the huge commercial enterprise whose head he was. He arrived in this company's offices punctually at ten o'clock, and here he was readily accessible throughout the working day, a figure as politically unprofessional as one could imagine. Yet politically he was as absolute as a boss ever is. At once the most abused, hated, dreaded, liked, and respected man in the state, fables without number clustered round his elusive personality. One account would paint him a church deacon, frock-coated, smug; another with cloven hoof. He was said to be a Hedonist, a Marcus Aurelius; a glutton, an ascetic; a satyr, a pattern of domestic virtue; an illiterate Philistine, a collector of book plates and first editions. A legend, widely current, ran that he played chief bacchanalian at dinners whose vaudeville accompaniments were too gross for a bill of particulars; while another, equally plausible, had it that he lunched daily on a red-cheeked apple raised on the farm which had cradled his undistinguished infancy. He was popularly known as Old Silky.

Shelby's card barely preceded him into the Boss's presence. It was not a sumptuous throne-room; an austere chamber rather, one might without exaggeration say a roomy cell, with puritanic chairs and khaki-colored regiments of letter files. There were two concessions to a softer scheme of life,—a lounge and a bowl of red chrysanthemums, both with associations. On the lounge, which parenthetically had lesser though not less interesting memories, a President-to-be had sat a suppliant, while the bowl, always flower-heaped, recalled an hour when a tempestuous petticoat, his protege, had swept straight from operatic triumphs to shower roses at his feet. This ruddy bowl lit a broad, low desk from which now advanced a gray-haired man of a certain shy friendliness and modulated tones.

"This is right obliging of you," he said over the hand-clasp. "Don't tell me you've already lunched?"

Shelby had, but dissembled, his tone dropping in unconscious imitation of the leader's. Every apprehension forgotten, he yielded instantly to the charm of his unassuming friendliness.

"Then you must honor me. Five minutes with these papers and I'll be with you." He turned to a pile of type-written letters awaiting his signature, his whole demeanor a graceful protest against this retarding of their pleasure. "Here are the afternoon papers if you care to look them over; they come upon us before the ink is dry on the morning's batch. No, no; not that uncomfortable chair, Mr. Shelby. Take the lounge, I beg of you. Stand on no ceremony here. This is Liberty Hall."

Somebody should write the philosophy of chairs. One may retain convictions in furniture which is palpably vertebrate; lapped in billowing upholstery it is a moot question; and like many a caller's before him, Shelby's brain tissue became a jelly of flattered complacency. It sufficed merely to simmer in a sense of equality with the silver-haired gentleman at the desk. The Boss! He had heard that the great man loathed the homely title his leadership entailed. It was not pretty; but its rough forceful Americanism had never struck Shelby as inept till this moment. Applied to this suave yet virile creature it fell grotesquely short, missing the key-note of his supremacy. Set back some centuries, this Boss would have been his Eminence the Cardinal.

It may be doubted had the Boss actually worn the red hat whether a procession of liveried messengers could have impressed Shelby more than did a small desk telephone half concealed by the chrysanthemums. Its bell tinkled incessantly, and with infinite patience the leader interrupted his work again and again to answer it, seeming from Shelby's vantage point to murmur secret messages into the petals of the flowers. The dismembered half of a telephone conversation is not ordinarily illuminating, and the Boss's words in themselves said little. How tremendously much they might connote, the visitor as a business man and a politician thoroughly appreciated, and his imagination did the occasion something more than justice. Desk telephones were unknown in the simpler Tuscarora world.

Thus the five minutes were lengthened out to ten, and then with apologies to a quarter of an hour. Shelby's eyes dropped to the newspapers on his knee and fastened on a headline—

"SHELBY AND THE DEMIJOHN."

It required a second reading. The absorbing present had for the moment sponged the morning's happenings from his thoughts. To remember explained without cheapening the sensation. He was used to a relative prominence in the rural press, but neither this nor the talk with the reporters had prepared him for inch-high capitals on the first page of a metropolitan newspaper. What New Yorkers thought of this particular newspaper was a detail.

SHELBY AND THE DEMIJOHN.

A Sidelight on the Storm Centre of
the Most Picturesque Political
Fight in the Empire State.

The Opponent of the Author of the Ode on the
Victory of Samothrace talks of his Rival
for Congressional Honors and his Book.

MR. SHELBY'S VIGOROUS VIEWS ON THE
ISSUES OF THE CAMPAIGN.

There followed a well-spiced "story" in which Shelby, with his diction chastened and his colloquialisms omitted save where they lent a racy strength, was made to say the things the reporter concluded he ought to have said—it was a party organ—and to sparkle after a fashion which actually attained by few in the presence of the interviewer. Even at his weakest he was caused to shine. A kindly platitude he had let fall anent Graves's book astonished him as he met it again; the merest crust upon the waters, under the reporter's manipulation, it returned to him a filling loaf:—

"But," said Mr. Shelby, "is the production of literature, however delightful, the fittest school for official life? This, I conceive, is the whole issue between me and this gifted youth whose illness I deplore."

It would have been well had he stopped here; but he turned to the other papers. There was no repetition of the first page glory, his eulogist's contemporaries entertaining other ideas of space; but he found his name in most of them.

"MR. GRAVES'S OPPONENT HERE"

"That virtuous spellbinder of county fairs, the "Hon." C. R. Shelby, reached the city to-day arm in arm with the notorious Jake Krantz. The character of this aspirant for congressional preferment in the so-called Demijohn District may be readily judged by the company he keeps."

Shelby needed no plainer signpost than the style to warn him that he had fallen foul of the caustic journal which had flayed his plagiarism. He stole a glance toward the desk, wondering whether the Boss had read these things. Then he ran hastily through the scurrilous perversion of his words. Could nothing curb this tyranny?

Yet a greater indignity was in store. His cup brimmed at the discovery that in the cherub also he had cherished a viper. His mortification was too keen for the perusal of more than an occasional phrase: "Art's New Patron"—"The Champion of Canals couches a lance against the tariff on art"—"his naive canons of criticism"—"judges a picture by its area of canvas—the bigger the better."

"Scoundrels!" he suddenly rapped out, crumpling the papers

in his disgust.

"I beg your pardon?" said the Boss, gently, peering over the chrysanthemums.

"I beg yours. These—these reporters have misrepresented me."

"Dear me! Do you mind that? You shouldn't. One has to be Jekyll or Hyde. There's no happy medium. But luckily the public takes care of that. Trust the public to guess, Mr. Shelby, that you're neither an art critic nor an ass. And don't be rough on the reporters," he added, getting up. "They work hard for a living, poor boys. Caricature is the press's peculiar tribute to the significant."

Outside the door of the private office Shelby's face suddenly froze. Several newspaper men had gathered to question the Boss, and among them the victim recognized one of his detractors. The impulse was strong to snub, but taught by the leader's example, he smiled instead and dropped a friendly nod.

"Seeking whom you may devour, gentlemen?" inquired the Boss. "So am I. It's past my lunch hour, you know."

With a dozen words he outlined the matter over which they were exercised, called one and another by name, shunted an inconvenient question, told a little story, and had slipped out of the building with Shelby before the pupil realized that the interview had fairly begun.

"I like the boys," he declared. "They slate me, but we're good friends."

The incident impressed Shelby only less than the desk telephone, and the walk to luncheon intensified his respect.

The Boss explained that he ate at a mid-air club rather remote from his place of business because it compelled a chestful of fresh air; and Shelby underwent the unique experience of promenading busiest Broadway with a man to whom people bowed on every hand. The Boss took it all as equably as the country lawyer might his morning salutations between his office and the Tuscarora House; but to Shelby, from Trinity to St. Paul's, and from the City Hall to the granite sky-scraper, whose elevator shot them story after story to the roof, was a splendid triumphal progress. It was a democratic people's homage to power.

The big green and white club dining room in the sky took up the wondrous tale. Greetings everywhere, and jovial beckonings to join this group and that. At the great man's instance, however, they were placed at a table for two, whose outlook seemed to the stranger to embrace the kingdoms of the earth. Life, pulsing life, as far as the embarrassed eye could carry; life in the mazy streets below; life in the forking estuary's tide; life, eager red-blooded life, to the crest of the horizon's hills! Nerve ganglion of a continent, market-place of a world! Shelby swept the panorama again and again as his host gave his quiet orders to the waiter, tracing the Hudson from the shipping-crowded bay till its blueness melted in the haze beyond which lay the commonwealth, the empire, whose political destinies seemed to rest in the hollow of this man's hand. It drugged the senses to attempt to gauge his power.

The Boss was speaking of Tuscarora and the Demijohn. Out of painful experience he had come to believe that the truest privacy is the privacy of the crowd, and indeed the mounting chaff and chatter of the lunch hour insured isolation most complete. He was speaking of Tuscarora and the Demijohn, and it had begun over the salad, apropos of Bowers.

"His political usefulness is at an end," said the leader. "There was nothing tangible to be got from him at our last conference, and I determined to send for you."

Shelby essayed a middle course between expectation and regret.

"He says it's his last campaign, poor old chap."

"Yes," concurred the Boss, without sentiment; "we talked it over. It was our opinion that the organization requires younger blood—in fine, your own."

"Mine?" The query was perfunctory.

"You logically succeed—on a condition."

"A condition?"

"Your election to Congress."

After a moment Shelby said:—

"It's an incentive to work."

"It's the least you've to work for, if you will permit me to say so."

"I don't understand."

The Boss was silent while the servant changed the course. Then he searched the younger man's eyes.

"Let me point out what your election may mean," he went on. "It has been an unusual contest. Mr. Graves's candidacy has interested an audience which is fairly national in its scope. If victor, you will take your seat a marked man, equipped with a prestige uncommon to newcomers in Washington. You will have defeated a celebrity, and you will stand accredited one of the party leaders of your state."

Shelby's eyes widened.

"One of the leaders?"

"I mean that I like you."

While the waiter brought the finger bowls the significance of the simple words burned into Shelby's brain. The two men lit cigars and waited; Shelby's was gnawed to shapelessness. Left to themselves again, the Boss said softly:—

"Two years from this fall the governorship should go to your section."

Shelby's color mantled and ebbed, leaving him white.

"Our choice,"—the Boss's purring note sank—"our choice, if my poor opinion should carry weight with the convention, our choice will be you."

Before Shelby could force a broken word of acknowledgment from his dry throat the Boss had plunged into a keen analysis of the situation in the Demijohn. Local statistics, finances, patronage, men's names, habits, and characteristics, the minutest details, were at his finger-tips, and the conclusion of the whole matter drove home like a sledge.

"Your election hangs on money; on your election hangs your future."

"I've spent every cent," returned Shelby, with slow distinctness.

"Yes; I know," was the quiet rejoinder. "I have hoped that the State Committee would do something. The circumstances are, as you say, unusual."

The Boss leaned across the table with a smile.

"Why mince matters, my dear fellow? You shall have any sum you ask if you will assure us of one thing. You have left your friends in doubt as to your attitude toward the River and Harbor unpleasantness. Not even Bowers could enlighten us. Now as far as the enemy is concerned, it doesn't matter, but it does matter to the organization. The project was abused beyond all reason—though that is neither here nor there. Whatever the captious may call it, the thing has become an organization measure, and as such a test of loyalty. Are you loyal?"

Shelby turned his drawn face toward the window. Truly he had been brought up into a high place and shown the kingdoms of the earth.

"Yes," he answered; "I'm loyal."

CHAPTER IX

In leaving his party headquarters up-town two hours later, Shelby trod air. Accustomed to eschew a too nice scrutiny of means if the end seemed meet, he merged every doubt and queasiness in the recurring tide of hope. Everything ministered to his profound content—the great leader's parting assurances, the flattering reception at headquarters which followed, the leap from need to affluence. It was another atmosphere, another sun, another city.

The afternoon gayety of the streets was wholly to his mood. One need not be an atom here. To concede a little, to dare a little—that was the Open Sesame. He held his head sturdily erect. He looked the impudent city in the face, its equal. With the sense of equality budded a tolerant liking, a Go-to-Old-Ant-Hill frame of mind, with admixture of charity. He must study the Ant Hill, find out its interests and its needs, since from the chrysalis of the country legislator was shortly to evolve the statesman whose constituency was the state. The thought was broadening—surely he had grown!—and fertile of large sweeping views of things and men. Why be petty? A human signboard advertising Bernard Graves's volume for ninety-eight cents, with the privilege of return, evoked no unkind thought against his rival; and from this loftier plane he could see even the morning's rencounter with the reporters in an indulgent light. He bought later editions of the afternoon papers that he might rehearse the episode from his new point of view, and was disappointed to find that where some fresh sensation had not crowded him from print altogether, he was dismissed to out-of-the way corners which nobody read. Yet this, too, he met with a statesman's broad philosophy.

"Lady in hansom wants to speak with you, sir."

Shelby had drifted into the shopping district with some vague notion of visiting a wax-works museum, dear to the rural heart, and was loitering among the novelty fakirs who lined the crowded thoroughfare. He turned to confront the liveried carriage attendant of one of the great department stores, who, indicating a cab at the curb, repeated his message. With the hansom's doors thrown wide to display her gown, sat Mrs. Hilliard, smiling.

The man strode to her side and caught her outstretched hand.

"Cora," he exclaimed, in undertone, "you're the handsomest woman on the street!"

If there had been anything more remote from his purpose than this meeting, it was this speech. He knew of her presence in the city, he knew her address; but from prudential motives he did not precisely formulate he had determined not to go to her.

"Get in," she murmured, her pleasing color heightening. "We mustn't block the way."

Such superior tact in the face of urban conditions impressed him,—he would have stood gossiping, as in New Babylon's sluggish streets,—and almost without volition he obeyed.

"The Avenue," directed Mrs. Hilliard.

"Which?" asked cabby, his florid face filling the trap.

"Fifth, of course," said the lady, with annoyance.

It has been remarked that Mrs. Hilliard aimed to be cosmopolitan, and it is pertinent to add that one of the chiefest delights of this, her annual pilgrimage, was to ride the livelong day in hansom cabs. People in the sort of fiction she was fondest of "called a hansom" at least once a chapter.

"You never came to see me," she accused, as they drove on.

"You can't know how busy I've been." This was well within the truth, as was his further statement that he knew no good could come of calling at the Waldorf at this hour. "You have proved that I should have missed you."

"But your card wouldn't. It would have had its silent message. Do you realize that we haven't met since—"

"We've met now," he interposed hastily; "and I'm another man."

"Don't tell me the old one's wholly gone."

"Never fear. I forget nothing. I appreciate what you wanted to do for me—what you have done; but the necessity is past, thank God! The load is lifted—there's money to burn—I'm free, free!"

"Dear friend," said Mrs. Hilliard. "You make me so happy."

"And I've been honored," he exulted. "I lunched to-day with our great leader—and, Cora, whatever they say against him, he is indeed great—and he was more than kind." It was near his lips to hint of the rosy future, but he spoke instead of a lesser, though nearer prize, which the day had assured. "He believes in me, and he has asked me to return home by the governor's own special train!"

"I knew it, I knew it. I was sure that they would appreciate you at the last. I've seen the papers, too, and I'm so proud. I want the people at home to know that the big outside world is awake to your importance. Even New York journalism pays its tribute."

"Did you—er—read all the papers? One has to be Jekyll or Hyde, you know," he added, appropriating the Boss's illustration without compunction. "Some of them were—facetious."

"Indeed I did not. I only skimmed the horrid ones; but the others I read through and through, and sent them home. I threw the spiteful ones away. They were jealous of your success."

He smiled a little at this.

"Not rabidly jealous, I guess."

"The governor's train!" She made him as elaborate an obeisance as the hansom's contracted limits would permit. "And yet you condescend to take the air with humble me."

He laughed joyously.

"I feel like a boy with a holiday," he confessed. "I'm free—free!" He kindled at her suggestion that they make it a holiday in truth, and repeating, "I'm free," gave himself to the spectacle of the street.

Mrs. Hilliard suddenly remembered to be cosmopolitan, and bringing her lorgnon into action, returned stare for stare as their driver threaded his dexterous way through the clattering, glittering maze of four o'clock Fifth Avenue.

With bewildering facility, she named the owners of the great houses—usually striking amiss, though Shelby could not know—and from some little experience with New York horse shows, could recognize an occasional carriage occupant. Her adaptability abashed him, setting her mysteriously apart from the woman whose past had been so intimately linked with his, and not until they tacked across the plaza into the wooded entrance of the park, which somehow suggested Tuscarora, did he pluck up the old sense of comradeship. There were still glittering equipages in plenty, and at every turn benches black with sightseers, for the day was a bit of summer gone astray; but this and that bright-liveried copse or shining pond or meadow cropped by sheep evoked the familiar setting of their other rides without effacing the city towering beyond.

"I guess you were born for this kind of thing, Cora," he broke the silence.

The woman gave a flattered little laugh which tapered to a sigh.

"You, too, were meant for something wider than Tuscarora," she returned; "and you will get it,—get it here, perhaps. The great New Yorkers are usually country-born, you know. You'll find your niche—no small one; find it and fill it; while I—? Ah, well; this isn't the talk for your holiday."

He brushed her sleeve with a light pressure.

"Make it your holiday, too. Let yourself go."

"Our holiday, then," she assented; "no past, no future, just here and now."

Copying nature's lead, the character of the park changed by and by; the way rose from a sun-shot ravine and wound a wooded hill full of forest scents and subdued surf-like echoings of the city's roar. Strange rock upheavals with writhing strata flanked the by-paths, a mystery and an invitation, and the man and woman left their hansom to shuffle, a pair of children, in the fallen leaves. A squirrel, tame to familiarity, pushed his nut-begging little nose fairly into their fingers.

"How perfectly Edenic," murmured Mrs. Hilliard. "I feel as if there wasn't another human being besides you on earth."

Paradise before the Fall had its dinner problem to discuss, as witness the apple affair, and so presently had Shelby and Mrs. Hilliard. But it was the man, not Eve, who put the idea forward as the fitting climax of a memorable day, as perhaps did Father Adam, though she it was who ran the garden's resources through, and decided which to choose. The talk had ranged from Sherry's and Delmonico's to Chinatown and the Ghetto, when Mrs. Hilliard recollected a place ideally suited to the occasion.

"It's on Riverside Drive, and overlooks the Hudson," she explained. "I've heard Ruth Temple speak of it, though I can't remember the name. The driver will know; it's historic."

The driver did know, and whipped them smartly out of a park exit where the heights fell abruptly away and the elevated railroad far overhead twisted a wriggling S into Harlem's sixth story. Then the land again rose sheer on gray curtains of masonry, splashed red with October ivy, lifting city on city. A cathedral's beginnings, looking a ruin, now cut sharply against the sky, neighboring a hospital with the facade of a chateau. Then they skirted a pink and gray university grouped about a dome, and a great man's tomb which might have been a Titan's pepper-box, flourishing presently between files of waiting hansoms and automobiles to their destination.

The restaurant was crowded, but they luckily succeeded to a just vacated table by a northern window which swept the valley. A sunset of myriad tints and opalescent fires made molten copper of the river and a carnival float of every craft.

"We have it clear to-night," said their waiter, as if the establishment somehow deserved the credit. "You'd not think that big cliff to the left was opposite Yonkers. That's Fort Washington nearer on the right. A fight came off there up on the heights, you know. Washington had to look on from the Palisades and see the Hessians bayonet his troops. They say he wept."

Mrs. Hilliard considered him through her lorgnon, but the man was busy with the napery and escaped punishment.

"The house is pretty famous, too," he went on. "Joseph Bonaparte lived here for a while, you know, and when Fulton tried his steamboat—"

"Yes," interrupted Mrs. Hilliard, icily, "we know."

"Beg pardon," returned the servant, taking the order slip. "Out of town people generally like to be told."

"It's no use, Cora," rallied Shelby, at the first opportunity. "You're handicapped. You'll never pass for a native while I'm along." He divined that she was vexed, and shifted instantly. "Thank you for bringing me here. After this day of ours we couldn't have picked a finer sundown."

"Sundown—and the end."

Shelby threw her a glance, and beckoning the waiter, added champagne to his order.

"We'll not let the celebration peter out in the dumps," he declared.

She demurred faintly. She was unused to wine with her meals, she said; Joe had old-fashioned ideas about women and wine, and so on; but in the end they shared the bottle equally, and the holiday took a new lease of life. Night set in before they finished. The river went black and mysterious, the shipping lights winked forth like glow-worms, and the illuminated walking beam of a ferry-boat minced a fantastic progress from shore to shore. The sometime home of the ex-King of Spain flowered within and without with electricity, and life simplified itself to cakes and ale.

From the steps they watched their hansom detach itself from the long line of yellow-eyed monsters waiting in the outer gloom.

"It must end now," sighed Mrs. Hilliard. "There's the theatre,—why not? New York is so big."

"I must not."

"Nothing heavy. Say burlesque or vaudeville?"

"If I dared—"

Shelby put her in the hansom and gave the driver the name of a music hall. The lights of the theatrical district charmed the last prudent doubt away.

There was a moment's embarrassment at the ticket-office. The little theatre they had chosen enjoyed a considerable vogue, and the man at the window could offer nothing less than a box. Shelby was staggered, but recalling his affluence, flirted a bill through the opening and neglected to count his change. Not until the usher had brought them to their box did Mrs. Hilliard comprehend the situation. She whispered, "Oh, Ross!" hesitated an instant, then entering, laid aside her wraps under the opera glass inquisition invited by her blond hair.

"How could you?" she murmured, as the house darkened.

"I wouldn't back down before that ticket-seller with you there behind looking so handsome and swell."

"We should never have come."

Shelby caught her fingers in a reassuring squeeze.

"Don't you worry," he enjoined. "This isn't the Grand Opera House of New Babylon."

Perceiving that other men smoked, Shelby lit a cigar, and as the plotless play began to unfold its tuneful fooling Mrs. Hilliard forgot to be apprehensive. She observed in the audience another woman with blond hair sipping something from a glass, and wondered if she were missing an opportunity to be cosmopolitan. If so, she deemed it the part of wisdom to remain provincial, for it had not escaped her notice that since dinner her mental processes had undergone some subtle change. For one thing, her sense of humor had quickened. Joe had often maintained she had none. If Joe could see her now! No; that was not her meaning precisely; but at any rate, it had quickened. How every antic of the comedians appealed to her! The excessively tall and the excessively short Germans who talked into one another's teeth; the young person who sang coon songs in a fashion not negro, but all her own; the giant with a boutonniere which a midget mounted a step-ladder to spray; the famous plump beauty whom Shelby whispered she resembled—all the merry-andrew company won her laughter and applause.

Once Shelby laid a restraining hand upon her arm, but she laughed the more. When the curtain fell on the first act and the lights went up, she was laughing still. She wondered why New Yorkers stared so. Perhaps they, like Shelby, who had oddly shrunk into the shadows of the box, thought she resembled the plump beauty for whom cigars were named. She stared back at them collectively, for somehow they seemed to wear one face. It was a thin, clean-shaven face, with keen eyes behind glittering glasses; a familiar face—the face of the editor of the *Tuscarora County Whig*.

CHAPTER X

"You had better walk to the hotel," Shelby suggested. With the darkening of the theatre for the second act he had piloted his companion to the street. "It's but a little way."

It proved a great way as he contrived it. Striking across town to one of the quieter avenues they paced block after block in the teeth of a wind which smacked of salt. At length Shelby brought their steps to a right about and headed for their destination, just short of which his charge abruptly halted with an hysterical in-take of breath.

"Not yet," she protested. "I can't go in yet. I must think it out here with you. I daren't alone. I'm afraid of something—of myself—I don't know what—"

The man bent a critical glance upon her.

"No; I guess you're not quite fit," he decided. "On we go."

"It's awful! He, of all people!"

"Bad mess."

"He could ruin me."

Shelby readily pictured a few ruins of his own, but

chivalrously refrained from their presentment. His predicament occurred to her, however.

"And he could defeat you—"

"Never mind me."

"I can't stop minding; it's too late. I've minded so long—too long and too much. I've put you before Joe—before Milicent even. I've—"

"Don't say anything you'll be sorry for," he interposed, turning into a side street. "You're on your nerves—flat on your nerves."

She promptly proved his assertion by slipping without warning from his side. They had chanced abreast of a rambling little church tucked with its trees and shrubbery and greensward amidst buildings which dwarfed its tower to a pretty toy. Some droll giant might have plucked it out of Trollope and set it here to throw off its atmosphere like a fragrance from rectory to chantry. Its lich-gate held an image before which Mrs. Hilliard melted in a welter of devotion.

"Tommyrot," fumed her guide, nonplussed at this new vagary.

Ignored, Shelby braced himself patiently against a pillar in the dusky recess while the penitent knelt and pattered in deeps of contrition which the ministrations of her low-church rector in New Babylon had never plumbed. But patience vanished at the sound of footsteps up the street.

"Quit it, that's a good girl," he begged, reconnoitring.

Despite the lively devil's deputy at elbow the appeal wavered on.

"It's a policeman coming. He'll think—" Shelby broke off his conjecture to utter some banality about the moon, to drown her invocation. Wayside prayers were no more a novelty than wayside curses in this region, and the officer rolled indifferently by. "Now go back to your hotel, and get to bed," pleaded the man, gasping like a criminal with a reprieve. "Things will look brighter in the morning. I'll be in to see you before my train leaves."

Her devotions at an end, she issued docilely to the pavement, saying, "You can't know the comfort."

"It's a pity it isn't contagious," commented Shelby, grimly; but before they quitted the shadows for the lights of Fifth Avenue he added gently that he begrudged her nothing.

Directly he saw the elevator whisk her to her room, the man posted back to the music hall in search of Volney Sprague. What he should say to him was not clear, but see him he must. Out of the jumble of his thoughts that idea beset him like an obsession. The audience had begun to trickle into Broadway, and as the stream broadened to fill the doorway he was hard put to it to scan every face, but he persisted till the last loiterer had left. Then an attendant told him that the place had yet another exit upon another street, which, beyond all doubt, the editor had used.

Baffled, but not without resource, he turned again to the newspapers and rummaged the lists of hotel arrivals for Sprague's unnoteworthy name. Naturally too obscure for mention! Yet in the same breath it started out at him from miscellaneous political gossip as one of the day's callers at the headquarters of a local revolt against the machine. Shelby construed the visit as a still hunt for funds, and, in the light of his own financial rebound, meant to have his chuckle from it, should he ever unhorse the worry by which he was hag-rid. Consulting a city directory, he set forth on a fagging tramp from hotel to hotel—a quest barren of result for the excellent reason that Sprague, according to his custom, had registered at the Reform Club.

Late to bed, and after persistent sheep-counting, much later to sleep, Shelby woke with the morning far advanced and the hour of his departure near. It was necessary to eke out his wardrobe with a purchase or two against the journey with the governor, and between his shopping and his breakfast, the deliberate talk he had meant to have with Mrs. Hilliard bade fair to dwindle to a handshake. As the morning brought no grounds for optimism, he was not altogether sorry that the interview must be short; indeed, by daylight his own necessity seemed the more pressing; but he faced his obligations, and prepared himself for the role of Sturdy Oak to Mrs. Hilliard's Clinging Vine. His astonishment, therefore, was doubly great when he learned that the Vine had developed a backbone of its own, and left the hotel, bag and baggage, upward of an hour ago.

Being a practical man, Shelby promptly made friends with the baggage agent, who recalled that the "blond lady's" belongings had been forwarded to the Grand Central Station,—Shelby's own destination,—whose waiting-hall the perplexed candidate was shortly scouring in pursuit. The sequel was unexpected. He did not find Mrs. Hilliard, but he did stumble fairly into the arms of Volney Sprague.

Startled, but outwardly self-assured, he half offered his hand.

The editor gave him a perfunctory good morning, but his own right hand made no movement to free itself from the magazine whose leaves he had been turning at the news-stand.

Shelby slid his extended fingers forward haphazard to a learned periodical, which fell open to a discussion of cuneiform inscriptions.

"Are you bound for Tuscarora, too?" he inquired.

"I'm going home."

"Which train?"

Sprague named his train after a leisured moment's study of an illustration.

"That's my own—or will be, rather, till Albany, where our car gets its own engine. I'm in for a day or two's campaigning with his Excellency; rear end speeches, and that sort of thing, you know."

The editor was unimpressed.

"If you care to drop in, I'll introduce you to the governor."

"Thanks, no. We've met."

Shelby's color mounted under repeated rebuff, and his self-respect was nil; but a sincere desire to shield the woman whose folly he had abetted, rose beside the spectre of defeat to drive him on.

"See here, Sprague," he said abruptly; "that was an awkward thing last night—"

"To see me?"

"The general look of it," came laboriously. "You understand

I—she—"

"Excuse *me*," put in the editor, dropping his magazine and backing off.

Shelby anchored him by a lapel.

"We've got to have this out. I want you to understand that she was unwell—despondent—malaria, you know—and resorted to—"

"Laughing gas is your plausible defence."

Shelby went brick-red.

"Be a gentleman," he said.

"Gad!" Sprague quenched a wry smile. "And from you! What are you after?"

"Are you going to use this?"

Volney Sprague started, glared, and fell to violent polishing of his eye-glasses.

"After all," Shelby blundered on, "she has been your friend—entertained you—the club and all that—and you couldn't—"

"Did she send you to me?" broke in Sprague, fiercely.

"She? No. I'm responsible. I thought perhaps you—it's been a bitter political fight—you might be tempted—I admit it is a temptation—to make capital—"

"Gad!" The editor spat out his favorite ejaculation as if it were a toad.

Mark Lee Luther

"We ought to spare her—to spare a woman."

"Don't, don't, don't," protested Sprague. "Can't you see—can't you see that no decent man—no; you couldn't see that. Use a thing of this sort? Faugh!" He swung on his heel and plunged through a nearby doorway to the open air.

The result was tangible, but he had paid for it with the most abasing quarter-hour of his life, and Shelby, too, craved another atmosphere. And he obtained it. The governor, his private secretary, one or two members of his staff, a state senator popularly known as "Handsome" Ludlow, and the newspaper correspondents who were to accompany the party, were clustered sociably in the observation compartment of the private car, and on Shelby's entrance every man jack of them got upon his legs to welcome him, as if the Boss had twitched them by unseen strings. His Excellency clapped him graciously on the shoulder, the staff officials and the secretary reflected and passed on the gubernatorial warmth, the senator pressed cigars, and the newspaper people, whose habit was to lump all personages as frail humanity, went through their introductions like the good fellows that they were. It was unlooked for, delightful, insidiously flattering—a plain intimation that he had become a star of greater magnitude.

"We're due to pull out in three minutes," the governor told him. "I was really worried about you."

In their several echoes the secretary and staff conveyed that they too had known alarm.

"Fact is, we bank on you to mesmerize the rural vote," put in Handsome Ludlow, jocosely. "You'll work your passage all right, all right."

The jest carried a covert truth. They did count on Shelby,

and Shelby did work his passage in sober earnest. The governor who sought reelection was a mediocrity of means—a barrel, as the phrase goes—whose function in campaigning was to draw checks, shed radiance on cheering crowds, and make way for speakers who had something to utter besides hems and haws. No one could be less fitted for the five-minute give-and-take talks from the rear platform than this amiable figurehead, and no one of his company was so much at home in it as Shelby, on whom the brunt swiftly fell. The senator, the staff officials, and even the poor governor were passable in the deliberate evening meetings for which they were billed in this town and that—though here, too, Shelby frequently snatched the honors; but the heady victory over the chaffing, brawling, even missile-throwing packs surging round the car wheels and up the steps, was always his and his alone. Suggested to fill an unexpected vacancy, he was quick to appreciate that chance, and the Boss had given him the opportunity of his life; and with an eye on another campaign two years hence, and with the heartening thought that by now the State Committee's dollars were implanting convictions throughout the Demijohn District's fertile soil, he put forth the impetuous best that was in him.

Nor was Shelby's best contemptible. The charge up the canal counties had not measured half its course before the increasing crowds, the space given his doings by the correspondents whose good graces he seduously [Transcriber's note: sedulously?] cultivated, the deference of his Excellency and his chameleon staff, all told him that the glory of what the party organs courteously styled the "governor's brilliant dash" was his and not the governor's.

"What we didn't count on," observed Handsome Ludlow, with a touch of envy, "was campaigning with a whirlwind."

CHAPTER XI

So Shelby came in triumph to his own people, the governor at his chariot wheel, and fought the last stubborn week of his campaign. His mail was now burdened with invitations to speak, but he made few speeches.

"The voter a speech will influence has made up his mind," he said to Bowers. "The heart-to-heart talk is the trump card of the eleventh hour."

To play this card required a prodigious amount of travelling about the district; and between these activities and the speaking engagements he was in promise bound to fulfil, Shelby saw little or nothing of New Babylon till midnight of Saturday, which was the virtual end of the canvass. Seen again, as he viewed it now, the town would look raw and provincial despite patriotic throes of self-deception. On moonlit nights the New Babylon Electric Light and Power Company hoarded its energies, and an inky pall accordingly lay over the muddy streets which the pale melon rind in the clouded zenith did nothing to dissipate. The contrast between this niggardliness and the midnight brilliance of up-town Broadway was inevitable, and the jolting Tuscarora House free 'bus came readily into unflattering comparison with a certain rubber-tired hansom cab. Naturally midnight, a jaded body, and the Tuscarora House free 'bus might well jaundice any scene; but the returning native recognized these as accidents merely in the phenomenon of his changed vision.

The hotel bar-room was boisterous with the usual Saturday night gathering of the set which in its innocence supposed itself fast, and the maturer poker crowd, Shelby's own cronies, was in protracted session elsewhere in the building; but he managed to evade them all and lock himself in his ugly room. For some sophisticated weeks he had suspected the household gods here assembled to have feet of clay. Now he knew it; but with the feeling that the place was a temporary husk at best, he avoided a too particular inventory of the pseudo-marble clock, the vases of pampas grass, the album, and the garish pictures against their background of pink roses blushing in a terra-cotta field, and ran drowsily over the little pile of accumulated mail.

With one exception he found a politician's budget, and the exception brushed its fellows imperiously aside. It was a tinted intriguing thing, faintly odorous of patchouli; its contents without date, superscription, or signature, though for the reader the scent was Mrs. Hilliard writ large; a single straggling line of characterless script.

"Why," it inquired, "have you forsaken me?"

The man yawned.

He awoke refreshed and lay in snug indolence listening to the rival sextons pealing first bell for Sunday service. Whatever their doctrinal disputes, the churches of New Babylon made a shift for concord when it came to bell-ringing, whose stately performance was regarded by no less a theological expert than the Widow Weatherwax as "spiritoolly edifyin' and condoocive to grace." Drifting between cat-naps Shelby usually found it a fillip to the fancy. He would detect infant damnation and argument for sprinkling in the deep boom of the Presbyterian bell, and instant dissent in the querulous note of the Baptist, whose echo droned "i-m-m-e-r-s-i-o-n" to infinity. This was the cue for a jaunty flaunting of apostolic succession on the part of the Episcopalian sexton, only to be himself reminded by the First Methodist that there were bishops and bishops. So on, assertion, rejoinder, surrejoinder, and rebuttal, till the dispassionate philosopher in the pillows wearied of his conceit and directed his thoughts toward breakfast.

From breakfast Shelby ordinarily turned to the sporting columns of the Sunday papers, but today he found his thoughts reverting to church-going as a not unpleasant sedative after the storm and stress of his campaign. Reasons multiplied: it would be a sop to the prejudices of no small body of the voting population; an act of tolerance worthy of a mind open to broad horizons; a lightning-rod for supernatural approval of his cause; and a simple means of falling in with Ruth Temple, since by a happy coincidence Ruth Temple and a large block of the church-going vote worshipped under the same spire. Some little time later, therefore, Shelby was ushered to a prominent seat in the midst of a decorous flurry of excitement which stirred the Presbyterian congregation from choir-loft to rearmost pew. Unknown to the visitor, the Rev. Mr. Hewett was scheduled to preach on the ethical issues involved in the present election.

The minister entered the pulpit almost immediately and laid eyes upon Shelby as he announced the opening hymn, coloring at the discovery. His voice wavered perceptibly in the earlier parts of the service as the absorbed congregation noted; but by sermon time he had conquered his nervousness, and with set jaw thundered out his text from Jeremiah: "Why trimmest thou thy way?" With this entering wedge the parson clove into an analysis of practical politics which did not stick at instancing corruption near at hand, and whose climax was a bitter denunciation of ignoble leadership and the doubly ignoble laxity of the indifferent led. It was as pointed an attack on local conditions as he could frame without complications with his deacons, who were politically of divers minds, and the fusion managers might have used its final exhortation to "vote your conscience" as their own ammunition, without altering a word.

Shelby sat under it all like a graven image, careless of the raking fire of eyes from every point, sang "America" with unction at the close, and advancing with the benediction to the pulpit stair, congratulated the bewildered clergyman on his "effort," and before he could conceive, much less deliver, a coherent reply, slipped down a side aisle and greeted Ruth.

"Vigorous, but intemperate," said he, "and typically ministerial. The right road and the wrong road in politics don't abound in sign-posts, and pretty frequently both carry grist to the same mill."

The riddle of his character piqued Ruth at that moment as it never had, and before they separated he obtained permission to call upon her after tea—a privilege which he interpreted as license to present himself betimes and stay to an unconscionable hour. Yet he talked fluently and well, and went out at length into the night tingling with the consciousness of having touched fingers with the higher life of his cherished aspirations. By the token of Ruth's interest, moreover, he took hope that he had not been found wanting where he was most ambitious to excel. It was a thing to lay to heart, an epochal page in his history which sleep alone could fitly round. Nevertheless, a disturbing impression of something essential left undone haunted the borderland of dreams to remain formless till morning, when his pocket handkerchief jerked a note odorous of patchouli to his bedroom floor.

It was annoying. Of course Mrs. Hilliard had a certain claim, and had he been less occupied on his return from stumping the state with the governor he would have gone to her. By rights he should have made the effort to see her after receiving this message—yesterday, in fact; yesterday the golden. He would have gone, too, if—frankly, if the stature of the man he had become had less exacting ideals of womanly perfection. To the grown man of broadened horizon Mrs. Hilliard had come indubitably to seem a bore. Still, she had her claim.

"I'll drop in after election," he decided, and laid his hand to the day's work.

It proved a long, hard pull, made up of details petty enough in themselves, but considerable in their relation to the whole scheme of his defence. However, he reached its end cheery in the belief that the sun of Tuesday would light no Waterloo.

"I'll win," he said to Bowers. "By no walkover, I admit; but I'll win."

"M-yes; I guess, but by the narrowest margin the Demijohn ever gave. The slightest flurry might snow us under."

"I'd stake my head on it."

"Some who have betted less than that have hedged."

"Who?" exclaimed the candidate, quickly.

"Tuscarora House sports—I won't mention names—but poker friends of yours."

"Sandy lot, they are," broke out Shelby, contemptuously. "I hope you counteracted the effect."

"I instructed some of our people to cover everything they would put up," Bowers answered dryly. "You know I don't bet myself."

Shelby guffawed and clapped him on the shoulder.

"Same way you don't stoop to buy the purchasable? Lord! If the Tuscarora floaters only knew their Santa Claus!"

But Bowers merely coughed.

Tickled with his joke at the expense of his associate whose handling of the State Committee's saving aid had been masterly, Shelby went to his evening meal in a humor which even a second note from Mrs. Hilliard could not damp. In scent, brevity, and chirography it was the counterpart of the first, telling him that the nameless writer was wretched, and begging him to come to her. The appeal found him in a softened mood. Viewed at the close of an irksome day, Mrs. Hilliard's society had attractions which his hypercritical mind of the morning hours slighted; and while her message in itself left his withers unwrung, he concluded that it was perhaps as well to break gently with "poor Cora" now, as later, when possibly greater growth and broader horizons might create barriers yet more awkward. Under a show of letter-writing, accordingly, he lingered in the hotel office till he was certain that Joe Hilliard had joined his boon companions of the billiard room, when he let himself quietly out of doors and made his way to the quarry owner's home.

"I was afraid you might come, and then that you mightn't," the woman whispered, in the obscurity of the hall. "Joe had a headache, and said at first that he wouldn't go out to-night; but he went."

"Yes; I know. Servants out?"

"Oh, yes."

"And Milicent?" he pursued, scorning hypocrisy.

"I let her go away for the night. The poor child needed a change."

As they left the hall he discovered that she was in evening dress—the black gown glittering with jet beads and bugles which she had introduced at the first autumn meeting of the Culture Club. He held her hand high, and turned her slowly round after the manner of the dance.

"Did you do that for me?" he asked, his face lighting.

She nodded.

"I wore it the night of your nomination, and I put it on to-night to bring you luck at the polls. Was it silly of me?"

"Not if somebody else doesn't see."

"Joe'll not see. I shall have gone to my room before he comes. I'll not keep you long. It's enough that you've proved you cared to come. It's a crumb of comfort in my wretchedness."

"You know I've been on the jump," he returned, adding dryly, "You don't look as wretched as your note led me to expect."

"You can't know."

"Not till I'm told."

"The scene there's been, I mean."

"Scene? What scene?"

"With Joe—about you—New York—everything."

"There wasn't need for a word. Nobody's blabbed. I saw to that. I went to Sprague in New York."

"I told Joe," she confessed. "You didn't come that morning—and I was frightened. I thought if stories were to get to him, I'd best be the one to tell them. So I left at once."

"If you had only waited."

"If you had only got word to me."

They fell into explanation of their several movements, from which Shelby, white-faced, suddenly cut loose, saying:—

"What does he know? For God's sake, what does he know? What did you tell?"

"Oh, that I met you, had dinner, went to the theatre—"

"Then why—"

"I'm coming to that. While we were away somebody—Mrs. Weatherwax, I suppose—filled Joe full of malicious town gossip about our—our friendship—and he was terrible. Oh, you can't know, you can't know!"

"But me—me!" cried Shelby, clutching her by the arms. "What about me? Is he down on me? His votes,—his two hundred votes, you know,—they could defeat me—ruin me! Tell me—tell me—"

"No, no; it's not you he blames; not you, Ross. It's I. He

thinks I'm a fool—the brute! He calls me a fool!"

"Thank God! Thank God!" ejaculated the man, laughing wildly in his revulsion of relief.

"But I—I am miserable," sobbed the woman, and clung to him when he would have released her. "You will go to your triumph and your future,—what have I left now?"

Shelby swayed unsteadily with his burden, his eyes on the perfect shoulders whose curves played and quivered with the labored breath. He recalled a fragment of poetry—something about "morbid . . . faultless shoulder-blades," which he had overheard Bernard Graves quote to Volney Sprague as Mrs. Hilliard passed at the club. Morbid had seemed an inept word then, but he began to spy out a certain fitness. The house was too still by far—dangerously still; the stillness of espionage. With a flash of intuition he lifted his eyes, and in the doorway met Joe Hilliard. Almost at the same instant the woman in her trumpery saw him too.

"Joe!" she called, in an incredulous, husky whisper. "Joe!"

He loomed there in the dusk like a rock, and with a frightened whimper she tottered and clung to him as she had clung to Shelby.

"I'm not a bad woman, Joe," she babbled. "I'm not a bad woman."

"No one has accused you," replied her husband, putting her gently away.

"Nor am I what you doubtless think," stammered Shelby. "It's all a mistake, Joe; a big mistake. It can be explained—it can be explained—"

Hilliard doubled and relaxed a mighty fist.

"No; not under this roof," he said quietly. "Go!"

CHAPTER XII

The scandal derived its impetus from the vulgar circumstance that the Hilliard washing went to line on Tuesday (Monday having dawned lowering and ended stormy), thereby exposing more family linen than could possibly have been foreseen, since the day laundress and Mrs. Hilliard's housemaid were bound in friendship by a common appetite for gossip and for tea. Monday's unfinished labors despatched, these familiars laid their heads together over a pannikin of their favorite brew, and the laundress, poising her saucer with the elegance which was the envy of her circle, ventured the opinion that the housemaid was holding in reserve a palate-tickling morsel concerning the missus; whereupon the housemaid cloaked herself afresh with mystery and "suspicioned" that she could tell things if she were one of those odious persons who carried tales, which of course she was not.

Blowing and sipping with the calm which is the handmaiden of true elegance, the laundress conceded both propositions, and edged forward the suggestion that talebearing and confidence between intimates were horses of dissimilar color. This was readily admitted by the housemaid with its corollary that anything intrusted in confidence to the bosom of the laundress was as good as locked in the mute confines of the tomb. With these time-honored preliminaries the crisis above stairs as seen from below stairs was promptly bared to the scalpel.

"Whin he come home lasht night He was here," the housemaid imparted in a whisper.

The laundress hurdled the ambiguous pronouns like a thoroughbred.

"Is it th' trut' ye're tellin' me?" she demanded, forgetting her graces, and grounding her saucer with a clatter.

"Cross me hear-rt," said the housemaid, enjoying her sensation.

"Ye'll excuse me intherruptin'—"

"Ye're no intherruptin'. 'Tis th' ind iv th' shtory."

"But phat did th' good ma-an say?"

As the faithful soul did not know, she remarked that there were some things which a lady in her delicate position could not confide even to a bosom friend. She hinted, however, that in the light of what she had told the laundress a week ago of the family jar occasioned by Her meeting Him in New York, the present state of things was easy to conjecture.

But the laundress thirsted for details.

"Was his dayparture suddin like?" she asked.

Feeling that the force of her narrative might suffer from the admission that she had only entered the house by a side door after she had met Him walking rapidly away from the front, the housemaid answered merely by moving sighs. The laundress reasoned from past experience that the font had gone dry, and suddenly remembered that she was promised to help with the Bowers's heavy ironing. This was at a quarter before nine o'clock.

At ten minutes past nine o'clock the laundress remarked across the ironing-board to Mrs. Bowers that if she were one of those odious persons who carried tales, which of course she was not, she could expose the carryings-on of somebody living not a hundred miles away to a tune which would bring the blush to New Babylon's outraged cheek. Mrs. Bowers made haste to answer that she was of principle firmly opposed to gossip; but as an intelligent woman, she recognized that certain things require ventilation for the good of the community, and was accustomed in such emergencies to send personal reluctance to the rear. The tale of how He coming unexpectedly home found Him with Her was then put through its paces with such skilful jockeying that not one in ten would know it for the same dobbin so lately brought limping to the light.

As now set forth, He had fathomed Her and Him with more shrewdness than the world had given him credit for possessing—poor man!—and had been hoodwinked by their transparent devices for meeting at the golf links and on lonely country roads no more than had Mrs. Bowers or any other person of equal virtue and capacity. He had seen, and he had warned. Then, stolen sweets becoming perilous near home, the culprits had taken their several ways to New York,—most fit choice for such a pilgrimage! This too was fathomed and forgiven. O unwise clemency! O base requital! Violence upon discovery? No doubt. Loaded pistol constantly in the house since the last burglar scare. At this Mrs. Bowers recollected shots in the night; Seneca had said "Campaign fireworks"; but she knew better; shots, of course. Dreadful thing to happen at one's very door. An immediate separation naturally. By all the laws of righteousness she should not be given the custody of the child.

In affairs requiring ventilation for the common good Mrs. Bowers could conceive of no instrument so sure as the Widow Weatherwax, who providentially dropped in to borrow flour at the precise moment Mrs. Bowers had decided that if she ever meant to run over and copy the widow's unequalled recipe for floating island, this was the time to do it. Quite in the same breath with her greetings, therefore, Mrs. Bowers intimated that were she one of those odious persons who carried tales, which of course she was not, she could astonish the widow with a chronicle of happenings not remote in time or scene. But when told, the widow was not astonished.

"I've knowed she wuz a Scarlet Woman since the last night ov the camp-meetin' at Eden Centre," she explained. "It come to me when I see her a-standin' outside the circle, and it was borne in on me to testify b'fore the brethren."

In this, its third edition, the tale gained picturesqueness and circumstantial weight. To the New York episode the widow contributed the imaginative touch of a baffled detective, while Mrs. Bowers's shots in the stilly night passed into the province of undisputed fact. The circumstance that the widow had only that morning seen the destroyer of homes walking abroad unmaimed, was but touching evidence that the husband had been too grief-crazed to send a bullet to the mark. The widow almost remembered that the destroyer had limped; therefore the injured man must have resorted to natural weapons. Doubtless the beginning of proceedings for an absolute divorce hung fire only because this was a legal holiday.

As the clock in the town hall struck ten the good women parted company, and the now able-bodied scandal careered bravely into the world. Tinctured by personal equation, the respective variants of Mrs. Bowers and Mrs. Weatherwax had minor differences in the dramatic grouping of detail, but they were variants, nevertheless, and adhered in all essentials to the notable fabric these ladies had joined forces to erect.

Early in the morning the Hon. Seneca Bowers returned to his home for a warmer overcoat, and met the petrifying version of his wife. His first thought was of its bearing on the election.

"True or untrue, Eliza," he declared, energetically, "this servant's chatter must go no farther."

"But if he's a bad man—" began Mrs. Bowers, uneasily.

"I'm not concerned with his morals; it's the party I'm thinking of. Not one soul must you tell—understand that clearly—not one soul."

"I—I did tell one—just one."

"In God's name, who?" cried her husband.

"Don't swear, Seneca. And you a church member."

"Who? Who?"

"Mrs. W—W—" It was impossible to articulate that tongue-worrying name with her lord glaring at her so dreadfully.

The man blenched.

"Not old Weatherwax!"

"Y-yes."

Bowers's jaw hung flaccid. This phenomenon continuing,

Mrs. Bowers took alarm.

"You've not gone and had a stroke, have you?" she wavered timidly, feeling for his pulse.

Bowers revived with a grunt, and bolted for the door. His buggy wheel protested stridently as he cramped the vehicle at the horse-block, reassuring Mrs. Bowers that his natural force was not abated; and his flight down town affronted the ordinance against reckless driving which he himself had framed.

Shelby, unnaturally pale, but composed, was issuing from his office staircase, and joined him directly at the curb.

"Jump in," said Bowers, making room.

"No time now."

"But this is important—critical, in fact." Observing no sign of compliance. Bowers lowered head and voice, murmuring, "You know I'm no hand at carrying tales, Ross, but—"

"You won't have to," cut in Shelby. "I know."

"You know?"

"Baffled sleuth—discovery by husband—shots—kicked down steps—divorce case summons in the morning—you see the whole roorback has come my way."

"Roorback!" Bowers caught at the straw. "We can make a sweeping denial, then?"

"Whole hog or none." He smiled sarcastically into the face which had so suddenly gone bright. "The truth has been so far outstripped that you can't see it with a telescope. Get handbills printed denying the story, denounce it as a partisan trick, and sign the statement yourself as chairman of the County Committee. Have them distributed all over town, and station men—men, mind you, not boys—with a supply just outside electioneering limits at each polling place. If the yarn spreads elsewhere in the district, wire our people to take similar measures."

"Ross!" Bowers called him back. "I don't need to tell you how glad I am. I never believed it of you."

"Thanks for the vote of confidence," laughed Shelby; "but I'd rather you'd hurry the handbills."

He had a more urgent reason yet, for wishing Bowers to take himself off. A block or two up the street, where the trees began to interlace their denuded branches and the court-house common sparkled with frosty rime, he had seen the Widow Weatherwax accost Ruth Temple. The girl had stopped when addressed, but almost immediately walked on, as if to escape the little busybody who, nothing daunted, trotted at elbow for a rod or more. Then Ruth came down the slope alone, and was intercepted by Shelby at her gate.

"I must speak with you," he said abruptly. "My good name is being dragged in the dirt, and I must assure you—"

"No, no," Ruth interposed.

"I tell you I must. You have heard this calumny. I saw her stop you—the woman who is peddling it from door to door. I must speak—it's no time for mincing words—speak to you personally—Bowers will answer to my constituency—speak to you personally, I say, appeal to you to believe in me. You don't know what your belief in me has been—my inspiration, my safeguard. Don't take it away— it's vital; don't deprive me of all this on hearsay. Say you'll not. Give me a sign—"

"Go win in spite of it." In a single wave of generous impulse she had spoken, put out her hand, and slipped past him, flushing, through the gate.

"I can't fail now," he exulted, detaining her an instant. "And victory means so much. It means—listen: I'll tell you a thing I've breathed to no one else; success to-day means the governorship two years hence! It's been fairly promised me—the governorship! That's the great stake—part of it, rather; you're the rest; you who believe in me and bid me win. I've not changed my mind since the day we rode together. I told you to think over what I said, and I've given you time. I meant then to come to you on the night of my election—a victor—and so I shall. I couldn't know that I should have the executive mansion to offer you, but it's none too good. I'll come! I'll come!"

CHAPTER XIII

There was more solid ground than mere confidence in his destiny behind Shelby's bold front. The earliest mail delivery had shed a glimmer of hope in the shape of a midnight note from Mrs. Hilliard. He did not require her reminder that the voting strength of Little Poland was no longer to be counted in his column—he had thought and fought that out in the small hours; but he did need and pounced upon the statement that Little Poland's master would be out of town the greater part of election day. The scrawl ended with an appointment for a clandestine meeting at eleven o'clock, toward which he now bent his steps on leaving Ruth.

Mrs. Hilliard had named a cemetery on the immediate outskirts as the rendezvous—a choice on whose evil omen Shelby wasted no thought. In the heyday of their flirtation he and Mrs. Hilliard had made frequent use of it as a Platonic trysting-place, and he climbed the silent paths toward the summit of the mount, as it was styled in that level land, with no sentiment save approval of her wisdom in seizing upon the one spot in all New Babylon whose privacy was certain.

Mrs. Hilliard, shivering in the lee of a pretentious granite shaft which bore her family name, was more susceptible.

"Bleak—desolate," she chattered. "What an end for our Fools' Paradise. But where else could we escape their prying eyes?"

"You've heard what they're saying?"

She nodded listlessly.

"Who has not heard?" As they huddled in the shelter of the monument she brooded over the plain below wherein the canal, livid, yet unfrozen still, half girdled the town in a serpentine fold. Each chimney curled a light spiral into the nipping air. "Under every one a wagging tongue," she said. "It's known to every soul except one."

"You mean he's still in the dark?"

"He can't know yet. He took an early train to Centreport. It's some quarry business that could not wait. I remembered it last night—after—after you had gone; so I wrote. It was past two o'clock before I dared steal out to post the letter."

Shelby shrugged into the collar of his ulster.

"I don't deserve all this," he muttered.

"Don't say that. You've done things, too. You've stood for—things; something to pin faith to. You are—"

"I'm your good friend—remember that."

"Friend!"

He drew her farther into shelter, and tucked her furs about her throat.

"Now concentrate your mind," he enjoined, "and tell me

exactly the lay of the land. Did he communicate with the foreman at the quarry before he left?"

"Yes. I overheard him telephone Kiska before breakfast. He said he'd return at half-past three. There's no train to-day from Centreport till then."

"And there is no other till the polls close. He said nothing, then, about voting the hands before afternoon?"

"They're at work this morning."

"On election day! You're sure?"

"They're working half a day on full day's pay. Joe's hurrying some contract through. I don't understand it very well, but the stone has to be shipped before the canal freezes on account of—something—freight rates—"

"Never mind that. What did he say to Kiska about voting— that the men should be ready at such and such a time?"

"No, no; I know about that. Before anything happened it was arranged that the men should vote about four o'clock. He merely told Kiska he'd return at three-thirty."

"Good, good!" exclaimed Shelby, making ready for action. "Every naturalized mother's son in Little Poland shall vote for me before the train can even whistle. Now, you go home, Cora," he charged, "and drink something hot against this graveyard chill. Keep a stiff upper lip—that's my creed. Everything blows over in time. The scandal is so tall that it will topple of itself. Nobody will believe it after election."

"But Joe? Think of him when he learns what they're saying, and that you've outwitted him."

Shelby grinned.

"That's the situation's one humorous phase," said he. "The two things will neutralize one another's effect,—like Kilkenny cats, you know. He'll not dare raise a row about the votes for fear of lending color to the scandal."

But Mrs. Hilliard, whose sense of humor was sluggish this morning, rejoined bitterly;—

"The row will fall to me."

"He needn't know your part in this—the matter of the votes; and as for the other thing—well, after all, he is your husband, hard and fast, and you'd best try and patch things up."

She straightened, flashing him a stony look, and he braced himself for a hurricane; but to his equal discomfiture she went down beside the shaft in a passionate fit of weeping.

"I should be under here," she sobbed; "I should be under here."

Shelby, tingling to be gone, shifted from foot to foot, and offered some blundering solace which she put away.

"You've ceased to care," she accused.

He protested, adding indiscreetly that she had done too much for him for that.

"You've filled the place he should have filled!"

Shelby was silent, goaded to torture by the lapse of precious minutes.

"There's only blackness ahead!"

"Don't take the dark view," entreated Shelby, groping desperately for a bright one. "The man can't live always—so much older than you—and then—your life's your own—"

The bowed figure shuddered.

"It's a dreadful thing to do—but I've thought that, too. I can't help it. You—you are the real one—the real one—" She waited.

"Yes." It was screwed from him.

"The real one—and if—I know I don't need your promise —but if—"

"Yes, yes; of course if—"

Neither of them would name the contingency. Shelby contrived a leave-taking, and bounded down the terraced slopes. It was quite noon when he reached the Tuscarora House, but without a thought of food, he got his horse and buggy from the livery, speeding the harnessing with his own hands, and whipped away for Little Poland.

On reaching the Hilliard quarries he confronted unexpected obstacles. The men had quitted work and scattered to their homes, and Kiska was to be discovered neither in nor around the little office. However, the Polish lad in temporary charge, Kiska's own son, was not slow to recognize the original of the campaign lithograph which in his home enjoyed honors second only to a highly-colored Madonna, and went flying in search of his father. Shelby took instant advantage of his absence to telephone Bowers, whom he luckily located at his midday meal. He learned that the handbills had been sown broadcast with encouraging effect, and that the general opinion of the voting public leaned toward unbelief. Shelby told his whereabouts, and requested the prompt services of Jasper Hinchey and three or four kindred spirits, ringing off after certain mysterious, though concise, directions regarding a concert hall in the Flats, which he meant shortly to utilize.

He had barely hung up the receiver when a telegraph messenger from town brought a despatch for Kiska. Shelby's breath shortened at sight of the yellow envelope, but he mustered a specious unconcern, telling the boy that the foreman's return, though certain, was not within immediate prospect, and volunteered to receipt for the message himself—an offer readily embraced by the lad, who, without a glance, pocketed the book in which Shelby scrawled Kiska's own name, and fared away with a head aflame from the bonfires of the coming night.

The envelope was loosely gummed, and gave under gentle persuasion. Shelby threw a glance from either window of the narrow room, and drew the paper from its cover. It was from Hilliard at Centreport, and announced that he had missed his train. The reader's delight was qualified by the succeeding statement that he should come by the canal, and that the men were to be in readiness.

"He's hired a launch or tug," commented Shelby. "Horses aren't to be had to-day for rubies or fine gold."

He replaced the message, sealed the envelope, and flung it on the table, catching sight of Kiska, as he did so, striding along the canal bank toward the office. The big Pole burst into the room a moment later, his simple face aglow at the meeting, and sputtered broken excuses for keeping his preserver waiting. Shelby shook both his grimy hands, and smilingly supposed that Kiska had made up his mind how he should vote. Kiska's English was uncertain, but there was no misreading his gesticulation.

"And Little Poland?" insinuated the candidate, blandly.

"Leetle Poland ees ein beeg vote," Kiska eagerly assured him; "joost ein beeg vote for Meester Shelby. Whan you save me, Meester Heelyard he say eef anybody no want to vote for you, he can joost valk aus de qvarry."

"Very kind of him," said Shelby. "Now, since you all know your own minds, I'd take it as a favor if you would get to the polls at the earliest possible moment. The voting promises to be heavy toward the close, and I don't care to have my friends inconvenienced. By the way, Kiska," he broke off carelessly "there's a telegram for you over there. It came not ten minutes ago."

By dint of facial contortion Kiska puzzled out the meaning, and handed the message to Shelby, who gave it grave perusal.

"Ah," said he. "You see he's anxious about it, too. If there was any way of reaching him by wire, we could relieve his mind; as there is not, the wise course is to go ahead. His coming by boat is uncertain. It will be a nice little surprise for him to find that you've got the votes all in."

So it seemed to Kiska, and the business of rallying Little Poland to its civic duties was instantly got under way. Here, too, were obstacles. Having been told to present themselves at a later hour, the villagers were in all states of unreadiness; but by impressing this helper and that, doing the work of three men himself, and with the reenforcement of Jap Hinchey and his co-workers, whom Bowers hurried to the scene in a hired carriage whose bravery of varnish made mock of their rags, Kiska at last collected his compatriots. The rented vehicle was urged back at a gallop to Bowers and continued public usefulness, and the whole body of enfranchised Poles, under the escort of Kiska, Jap Hinchey, and his fellows, trudged off in groups of five and ten to New Babylon.

Little Poland lay within the same voting precinct as the Flats, and when Shelby had assured himself that the straggling column was finally in motion, he rode on in advance toward this quarter and the concert hall to which he had made mysterious reference in his telephoned directions to the Hon. Seneca Bowers. From the elevation of a canal bridge he searched the waterway for a sign of Hilliard's coming, pondering anxiously whether a pillar of smoke at the horizon's rim were his herald; but a glance at his watch reassured. The train which Hilliard had missed was barely due, and to cover the distance by boat meant an additional hour at least. Employing a street urchin to lead his horse to its stable, he struck out on foot for the Flats.

At the tawdry concert hall everything was as it should be, and in the brief interval before the arrival of the Poles he received inspiriting news from one of his workers. Money was flowing, buckets of it, but beyond doubt they held the longer purse. Their policy of offering high prices to the floaters at the outset had drained the disciples of the late Chuck O'Rourke before twelve o'clock, and patriots were now to be had at bargain rates. Some few conscientious souls who could not see their way to a Shelby vote had been induced to stay away from the polls altogether; and at least a dozen irreconcilables had been laid by the heels with bad whiskey before they had done protesting that not all the powers of darkness could deter them from casting an unsullied ballot under the emblem of the Square.

The Poles came hulking in, Shelby himself keeping tally at the door, and when Kiska had urged the last loiterer over the threshold, the key was turned. Drinks were sparingly circulated, and Kiska harangued the crowd briefly in Polish, hammering in Shelby's instructions for their conduct in the voting booths, and impressing them with the fact that good cheer in plenty would await them here on their return. Under the efficient supervision of Jasper Hinchey and his lieutenants they were now guided to the polling-place in squads of three or four, returning presently to unlimited refreshment and a surreptitious two-dollar bill—shining examples and incentives to such as had not yet voted to speed their going.

Yet with all their willingness, the affair consumed time, and twice Shelby went into the dusty wings of the stage to a window overlooking the canal, and strained to detect the panting of a laboring launch or tug. But the last quarryman voted, the polls closed, darkness fell, and Joe Hilliard was not yet come.

CHAPTER XIV

A pleasant local custom fell this night into abeyance. Years out of mind the adherents of the leading political parties had mingled sociably before a non-partisan bulletin board in the courthouse, much as hostile camps fraternize in the truce forerunning peace. But the old, simpler order of things had suffered more wrenches than one in this acrid congressional campaign, and the warring factions could unite only on the hibernian proposition that union was impossible. One party, therefore, made ready to gather in the accustomed place, the other in the Grand Opera House, while seceding remnants from both swelled the crowd in the street before the office of the *Whig*, which, with unlooked-for enterprise, had prepared to announce the returns by stereopticon.

At six o'clock Shelby broke his fast with a ravenous meal at the hotel, which Bowers shared, and three-quarters of an hour later the two men shouldered through the boisterous mob in the streets to Shelby's law office, where arrangements had been perfected to receive the returns by messenger and private wire. The *Whig* bulletin over the way had already massed a constituency extending to the Temple lawn, which, in default of definite news, it was edifying with views of foreign travel and cartoons bearing on the larger issues of the election. Within doors the telegraph operator was already installed at the ancient table which had graced the grand-paternal distillery, and William Irons was making good the tedium of a dreary day in the deserted office by goggling from the ticking instrument to a consignment of iced champagne just arrived from the Tuscarora House.

Shelby was in rare fettle.

"William, thou abstemious youth," he addressed the clerk, "I am tempted to empty one of these cold bottles down your scandalized neck and pack you off with another for the Widow Weatherwax!"

He had the youth carry the wine to the rear room and set out glasses against the coming of his friends, drinking a bumper meanwhile to William's good health and the sentiment Confusion to Fusion. Never a solitary wine-bibber, and William remaining recalcitrant, he returned to the outer office and demanded "no heeltaps" of the operator and Bowers. This accomplished to his taste, he crammed a greenback into the dazed clerk's fingers and dismissed him for the night with the injunction to buy and blow the biggest tin horn in New Babylon.

His intimates now began to drift in, and the toast of Confusion to Fusion enjoyed a wide popularity, the telegraph operator and the county chairman being the only ones permitted to flag in the exacting ceremonies which the occasion required.

"I'll do my hurrahing when the returns are in," said Bowers, and stripping to his shirt sleeves he took his station under a drop-light and made ready to figure the local result.

But the local returns were tardy. It developed early that throughout the Demijohn split tickets had prevailed to an unprecedented extent. Heretofore reliable localities ran after strange socialistic and prohibition gods, to avoid voting for either of the leading candidates; while Graves and Shelby both gained support in quarters where it would have been sheer fatuity to hope. The hurrying news from the country at large shamed the dribble at the threshold. Texas and Vermont, those stock commonplaces of election night humor, went Democratic and Republican by the usual majorities, and all signs pointed to a sweeping victory for Shelby's party in state and Union. And still Tuscarora and the Demijohn aped the Sphinx.

Men elsewhere became curious. Bowers received and passed silently to Shelby demands for a forecast from other county chairmen in the district; from leaders prominent in the state; from great metropolitan newspapers which were tabulating the congressional elections of the nation and studying the complexion of the future House.

"Claim the district, of course," directed Shelby. "Say we're deliberate, but true blue."

The drumming humble-bee [Transcriber's note: bumble-bee?] voice of the crowd below the windows watching Volney Sprague's bulletin suddenly lifted in a lion roar. Elation in that quarter was ominous, and Shelby drew a curtain. It appeared that a minor revolt against the Boss in New York City, with which the Tuscarora independents had felt themselves peculiarly in sympathy, had made good its claim for recognition. Shelby turned from the window with a laugh.

"Merely a little extra diplomacy for Old Silky," he said. "Within a twelvemonth each reformer will have a foreign mission."

A tactless friend embraced the occasion to wonder where the Boss would banish Bernard Graves should he chance to win; but even idle speculation on such a possibility was so distasteful to the company that the blunderer only retrieved his mistake by toasting Confusion to Fusion anew.

The returns from the laggard Demijohn presently thickened, and Shelby left his seat to pace the floor, while Bowers, with an unlighted cigar between his teeth, and looking very like Grant indeed, figured, discarded, and figured again as successive reports modified his calculations.

"Never saw its equal—never!" he grunted. "Here's our own town hanging fire till almost the last like some jay village in the Adirondacks. We've always prided ourselves on being prompt." He caught a flying sheet from the operator and groaned: "We *are* the last! By the Great Horn Spoon!" For Shelby's ear alone he muttered: "The last, Ross; New Babylon's the last, and the die by which you lose or win. Figure it yourself."

Shelby ran through his senior's calculations and nodded without speech. No one spoke now. Not a wine-glass tinkled. The room sensed a crisis. By telephone, special messenger, and the instrument at the table the belated story of New Babylon's vote pieced itself together under Bowers's pencil. The candidate hovered above him, intent on every stroke.

"Good God!" he whispered suddenly; "it hangs on the Flats!"

"Yes; it's the last precinct. They sent word that the thick-skulled Poles and the rest had made an awful mess of the ballots. Tom"—to one of the onlookers—"'phone the Flats again."

But on the instant the Flats embodied itself in the doorway in the person of a breathless messenger. Bowers's trembling fingers fumbled the paper and cast it fluttering toward the floor, but Shelby fastened on it in mid-air, read it, crumpled it, mechanically made it smooth again, and laid it gently on his desk. There came a second roar from the street, a medley of cheers, groans, hisses, and the blare of horns. Shelby again drew a curtain. On the *Whig's* screen was displayed a huge rooster with the legend: IT'S GRAVES!

Shelby caught a murmuring from the group behind him: vapid expressions of regret, scorching condolence, pitying oaths; then the voice of a newcomer, a newspaper correspondent, asking Bowers if they conceded their defeat.

He spun about, crying,—

"We concede nothing."

The reporter said that the returns as received indicated a slight majority for the fusion candidate.

"We dispute the returns."

"But, Ross,—" Bowers put in.

"We dispute the returns. Should the official count be adverse, we shall dispute that. In view of the methods employed by the allies of the independents, it becomes nothing less than a public duty to carry the contest to the floor of the House of Representatives."

"It will be a House of your political friends," remarked the correspondent, impersonally. "Shall I then quote you as claiming your election?"

"Most emphatically, yes. Quote me as confident of a verdict approving my public course and rebuking the slanderous attack on my private character."

"What's the use?" protested Bowers, as the reporter hurried off in quest of Bernard Graves. "It's too late to bluff."

"Use," echoed Shelby. "I tell you, man, there's a blunder in the returns. Look, man, look!" snatching up the report from the Flats. "Isn't that arrant nonsense on the face of it? The Flats, mind you; our own little pocket borough of the Flats! Don't talk to me about the Poles muddling things; those inspectors of election can give them cards for stupidity and take every trick. Let me 'phone the Flats."

And he was right. The inspectors of the belated precinct, conscious of unwonted delay, nervous from long weighing of defective ballots, harassed by incessant demands for their report, had capped the climax of their offending by announcing the result as favorable to Graves. The mistake was discovered and rectified within fifteen minutes of its commission. Shelby had carried the precinct, and with it the election by something less than two hundred votes.

Giddy with the reaction, the Hon. Seneca Bowers gulped glass after glass of champagne, toasting Confusion to Fusion like the veriest roisterer.

"And we abused the Poles," he said in self-reproach. "Ross, it was the Poles who saved the day."

Shelby was the one self-contained being in the room.

"Yes," he answered soberly, "it was the Poles."

With stern straightforwardness the *Whig* bulletin over the way had promptly set forth the corrected result, and the crowd, now swollen by more deserters from the tame gatherings in the little theatre and the court-house, was clamoring for a sight of the victor whom everybody knew was within hearing. Shelby's jubilant companions were puzzled at his reluctance to comply with the popular demand. He declined to show himself, however, till the arrival of a serenading brass band compelled an acknowledgment, when he stepped from a window to a little balcony and spoke a few grave words: he had never doubted their support, they had repaid his trust, he was grateful; as he had championed their lesser interests in the smaller field, so should he strive to further their greater concerns in the national lists to which he was to pass their chosen knight.

Within the law office preparations were rife for adjourning to the Tuscarora House as a less restricted arena for the celebration which the fitness of things demanded. Shelby begged them to go before him, promising to follow.

"I need a few minutes to myself, boys," he said. "It's been a strain, you know."

They caroused away. Bowers the most jocund bacchanal of all; the operator boxed over his instrument against harm and slipped out; and Shelby was left solitary with the litter and the lees. One by one he extinguished the lights, and in darkness, at length, halted at the window from which he had so often marked the goings and comings of Ruth Temple. The old house was brilliantly alight in its lower rooms; lit, he dared hope, in honor of his triumph and his anticipated return. He turned and left his office with elastic step.

Fumbling with the lock in the dim light of the hall, he was spied from below by a newsboy who came bounding up the stairs.

"Extry! Extry 'dition of th' *Whig*, Mr. Shelby," he called. "Read all about yer 'lection an' th' drowndin' accident!"

"Drowning accident!" Shelby started and seized a paper.

"Who is drowned?"

The lad did not know. He had not read beyond the headline which seemed to promise salability. But in the obscurity of the landing Shelby came upon the particulars swiftly enough. Skimming the brief despatch, here a sentence, there a sentence seared itself into his memory.

"Missed his train at Centreport—conscientious citizen, valuing his vote—hired a naphtha launch—collision—hampered by clothing—leaves a sorrowing widow—"

"Th' extry 'dition is two cents," reminded the urchin.

BOOK III

CHAPTER I

The executive mansion was strewn with the wreckage of the inaugural reception. A musky odor blent of plant life and massed humanity hung thickly throughout the spacious rooms and corridors; the bower of palms and flowery brightness at the foot of the great staircase, which had fended the orchestra, and incidentally barred an intrusive if sovereign people from the private apartments, was jostled and awry, its blossoms half despoiled; here lay a trampled glove, there a shining shred of braid, beyond an embarrassed cigar stump—dumb emblems of social Albany, gold-laced officialdom, and the unaristocratic unofficial ruck, whose mingled tide had beat upon the new governor's threshold in the late hours of the afternoon. A clock somewhere about the scene of devastation chimed midnight, and a man with attractive black eyes, who had been monopolizing his hostess upward of two hours, outstaying all other guests save one, now took his belated leave.

"Yes; I prophesy a brilliant season, Mrs. Shelby," he said. "With a woman of your talents in this house, Albany must at last awake."

Cora Shelby returned to one of the smaller reception rooms, where an open fire wrought changing shadows in the face of the Hon. Seneca Bowers.

"I think ex-Senator Ludlow is perfectly fascinating," she exclaimed. "Have you known him long?"

"All of ten years," returned Bowers, with a little tightening of the lips. "Most everybody in politics knows Handsome Ludlow."

"Ah, he is handsome. And so polished, too."

Bowers found the topic difficult, and changed it.

"What's your opinion of Ross's inauguration?" he asked. "I call it an A-1 success."

"It would have been a success," discriminated Cora, "a pronounced success, if Ross had approached it with a tithe of the spirit I urged. But no; simplicity, simplicity! You would have thought the affair a transfer of Methodist parsons. No military escort to the capitol, no decorations in the Assembly Chamber to speak of, no music, no anything that the occasion demanded."

"Fuss and feathers never did appeal to Ross," said the guest. "Besides, I guess he thought the last administration had splurged enough for two."

"Their fine plumage covered as slovenly housekeeping as I ever saw," interjected Mrs. Shelby, momentarily diverted from her husband's shortcomings. "I wish you might have seen what I have seen in out-of-the-way corners of this establishment. What the servants did for their wages I can't conceive. But, after all, those people had the right idea of upholding the dignity of the position. The ex-governor didn't decline an escort to the capitol when he took office. That puts me out of patience with Ross every time I think of it. Then, to cap the climax, he didn't even take a carriage; he walked!"

"Walked down with me," Bowers chuckled.

"And, by Jove, nobody knew him. One of the orderlies wanted to keep him out of the executive chamber."

Cora shuddered, and the old man bestirred his wits to soothe her outraged sensibilities.

"You must remember that he made his run on an economy platform," he reminded. "He believed it, too, every word. After all, you can't say that you've not had things your own way here at the mansion."

"It's a mercy I did. He would have had the house reception and the staff dinner equally prim if I hadn't put my foot down. I said no; be as puritanic as you please at the capitol, but the executive mansion concerns me; I'm governor here."

"Tolerably big commonwealth, too," commented Bowers, dryly. "Somehow it puts me in mind of what I thought palaces were like when I was a boy."

"Oh, yes; it's well enough, though the decorations aren't to my taste; but the location is very unfashionable—orphan asylums, hovels, saloons, and all that under one's very nose."

"I hadn't noticed the saloons."

"Well, there's a saloon at any rate. I saw it to-day from one of the south windows. The state was stupidly short-sighted to buy a house in this quarter. The executive mansion ought to stand in Quality Row."

"What's that?" asked Bowers.

Mark Lee Luther

"Not much to look at—just a block or two of houses near the capitol, not one of which could have cost more than my own place in New Babylon, for all that famous people have lived in them; but it's the cream of Albany."

"Everything else is skim milk, I suppose?"

Mrs. Shelby eluded the classification.

"Nearly all that's socially significant is grouped thereabouts," she pursued; "the cathedral, the Beverwyck Club, Canon North, and Mrs. Teunis Van Dam. The canon and Mrs. Van Dam are the keys to the social citadel, I assure you. Probably you noticed them on the platform at the Inauguration. Then, she helped me receive this afternoon, thanks to a bit of diplomacy."

Bowers absorbed these esoteric deliverances in meekness.

"It takes a woman to bottom such things," he said admiringly. "I guess you'll pass."

Cora herself harbored no doubts, but she disclaimed a single-handed victory.

"I shouldn't know all these things yet if it were not for the governor's military secretary, Colonel Schuyler Smith. Do you know him?"

"I'm not sure that I can place the colonel," ruminated Bowers. "Is he that blond young dandy whose sword got tangled in his legs?"

"Yes, poor dear! He's not used to wearing it yet. But he's a treasure. He's Mrs. Teunis Van Dam's grandson, you know, and like her is descended from all those delightful old Dutchmen who make such enviable ancestors, and have stained glass windows in the cathedral. He knows who is who, I assure you. Ex-Senator Ludlow does too, for that matter; though he doesn't care for Mrs. Van Dam's circle. He thinks it too stately and old regime. He goes with the younger set—Mrs. Tommy Kidder's—and he says Mrs. Tommy is quite my own style."

The governor entered the room in the midst of these matters and listened soberly. Shelby had taken on more years than his congressional service spanned. His dark hair had grayed at the temples; his old puffiness of jowl and dewlap had vanished; and the strong bone framework of his head showed for what it truly was. Tuscarora ancients, who remembered the pioneer, said that Shelby favored his grandfather.

Bowers turned to him with a laugh.

"It's a mighty good thing you've got a skilled pilot in these waters," he said.

"Yes, Cora knows her way around," returned her husband. "I dare say the world's a brighter place for this varnish, though I've noticed that when you scrape through it people average much alike. It's meant more to me to-day to have you here, old friend, than the notables. You gave me my start." He hesitated, glanced at his wife, and added: "But they were all welcome. Cora has come into her kingdom, and I wouldn't abate a single courtier."

"I've waited for my kingdom," she declared; "waited for it in sackcloth and ashes. You can't call Washington anything else for a congressman's wife. Her husband may get glory; she gets snubs. Now my turn has come, and I've plans galore. Milicent's debut is one of them. I'll bring her out with a ball when she has had enough of her finishing school. Ex-Senator Ludlow thinks it an inspiration."

The men exchanged a look.

"Handsome Ludlow isn't an ideal adviser for young girls," dropped Shelby, quietly.

"He's a victim of gossip; he told me so. You and I know too well what that means to countenance it. Besides, you're going to appoint him commissioner of something or other—I read it in yesterday's papers; but that's politics, I suppose."

Shelby gloomed in his corner, but made no answer.

Bowers essayed a diversion.

"I saw Bernard Graves's wife in the assembly chamber this morning," he remarked. "Seems to me she's looking rather peaked since her marriage."

"Ruth Graves here!" exclaimed Cora.

"I saw her too," said Shelby. "She congratulated me later in the executive chamber. She has been living in New York this winter. Graves is still lecturing around the country, telling how he wrote his poem and what it's all about."

"I presume she couldn't resist coming up to see how we would behave," Cora reflected, aloud.

"She is visiting Mrs. Van Dam," added the governor.

"Of all people!" Mrs. Shelby's wonder was unrestrained. "I do remember, though," she continued presently, "that she made friends here when she was in Vassar College. It's plain enough why Mrs. Van Dam has taken her up again. She wants to know all about us."

It was an easy step now to the conclusion that perhaps such an old friend really merited an invitation to the executive mansion.

The governor brushed his forehead with a weary gesture, drew a chair to Bowers's side, and unfolded a bundle of manuscript.

"I know it's late," he said apologetically, "but there's a bit of my message I'd like to read to you. There'll be no time in the morning if you're still bent on taking the early train to Tuscarora. I'd like your opinion whether it's what the plain people want."

Mrs. Shelby found the reading unspeakably juiceless and went yawning to bed. Nor did the governor detain Bowers long. A servant entering presently discovered Shelby before the grate alone.

"Don't wait up for me," he directed kindly. "I'll see to this fire, and remember not to blow out the gas."

The relic of the old regime restrained his surprise at these democratic doings, smiled decorously, and withdrew. Jocosity slipped out at his dignified heels. The man before the fire drank deep in self-communion, and his face was grave. For the first time that crowded day he could look his future in the face. Yet, evoked by a woman's handclasp in the long line which had filed by him as he stood in the executive chamber surrounded by his glittering staff, it was the past which most absorbed him. It struck him as a wanton caprice of fate that they should have been flung together that day. Ruth, whom he had promised a share in these honors; Ruth, whom he had boasted that he would return and claim; Ruth, whom he had put away because he must, because of a loftier standard which—grimmest irony of all!—she herself had unwittingly set up. He wondered—as he had wondered often in the years which had witnessed her marriage, his own, and his rise to power—whether she *had* waited that night; whether she *had* cared as he, apart from the red passion of the struggle, could perceive that he had cared.

A vagrant memory of the morning's inauguration intruded. The moment of his oath had been a time of solemn consecration for him, a laying on of hands unseen; the shades of his greatest predecessors stood round about; the genius of the state was in presence. Then came Cora and kissed him. Emotional souls in the gallery applauded the act, but the husband divined its prompting egoism and was cold.

CHAPTER II

Neither the public nor the honorable body to which it was directly addressed took the new governor's message stressing general retrenchment and the pruning of useless offices seriously. Nothing in the recent course of the party wooed faith in its promises to purge and live cleanly, and the accident of a huge majority in the late elections, owing to national issues, had set not a few mouths watering for fruits of victory which had lately dangled out of reach. The machine was perfected to its utmost, and the young year was held to signalize the full flowering of the Boss's topping supremacy. The great man was now master of the county committees of the metropolis and the greater cities; of the State Committee; of the Legislature, of the lieutenant-governor, and apparently of Shelby. The cartoons depicted the chief executive as a craven monarch yielding his sceptre to the leering power behind the throne; as a marionette twitched by obvious wires; as a muzzled dog, ticketed with the Boss's name.

Whereupon Shelby, in a quiet way, did an audacious thing. By an odd chance the first enactment of the Legislature which reached his desk affected Tuscarora County. It was a general measure concerning marsh lands, philanthropically worded and fathered by an assemblyman from an eastern county; but its special purpose, as Shelby fathomed, was to give certain Tuscarora people a selfish advantage in a locality as familiar to him as his hand. The Swamp, as Tuscarora called it, embodied his boyhood notion of primeval nature, the one spot untamed amidst tilled and retilled commonplaceness, the last fastness and abiding-place of the unknown. Rude corduroy roads threaded the wilderness in parts, and from this Red-Sea sort of passage the lad had peered and questioned in delicious fear. Even now the man had but to shut his eyes to recall it with the senses of the boy. Cowslip, wood violet, and Jack-in-the-pulpit bloomed again, the scent of mint was in his nostrils, fairy lakes lured amidst the ferns, and the way wound through lofty halls whose wonderful pillars set foot in emerald pools and sprang in vaulting hung high with wild grape. Once in those tender years he had skirted the spot by night when owls hooted, unnatural frogs boomed, will-o'-the-wisp stalked abroad, and Old Mystery held carnival; that breathless experience almost outdid the delights by day. All this issued from the phraseology of a bill—this, and something more. He held the measure a day or two and invited its sponsors, ostensible and real, to a conference. They were trained legislators, with whom he had served and fraternized, and in this matter furthered the interests of men in his native county who had backed him from the beginning of his career.

"Gentlemen," he said, regarding them quizzically, "this bill reminds me of a Tuscarora story." They laughed at the familiar beginning, and the governor laughed with them. "It's about a man who ran a grist-mill on a creek fed by a certain swamp, which I guess you know about. He was easygoing, the water was often too low for grinding, and the little mill had business for six, since there wasn't a rival within thirty miles. The pioneers came prepared to camp when they brought grist, and I suppose loafed around pitching quoits and cursing the mill trust by whatever name they called a monopoly then. One day along came a cute boy astride a mule with two bags of grain. He sized up the crowd ahead of him as he carried in his grist, and decided that if he waited his turn the country would grow up without him. The miller happened to be tinkering his water-wheel, so the boy got his bags into a dark corner unobserved, and with a handful of mill dust gave his work the finishing touch of ripe old age. I dare say you think he took the man in, but he didn't. 'Bub,' said the miller, 'I used to do that trick myself.'"

Shelby's old associates in log-rolling took the unmasking good-naturedly, but declined the amendment he suggested. He dismissed them with charming civility, jotted a laconic memorandum that the bill meditated a raid on public property for private gain, and with the calm of a gardener lopping a weed, withheld his signature.

It were hard to say whose smart was shrewder, the spoilsmen's who mourned the backsliding of a pal, or the professional reformers' who chewed the galling fact that not one of the elect, but a practical politician, had done this creditable thing. Both joined forces to fling clods. In the greater world, however, Shelby's simple act won swift approval. In the cartoonists' fancy the wires of the puppet-show had gone awry, the dog bit the heel at which it slunk, the usurper's knuckles were rapped by the sceptre he would have seized. The press teemed with anecdotes and personal gossip of the governor. Everything he did or said became of interest: his dress, his habits of work, his Tuscarora stories, his domestic life. An admirer on Long Island who bred bulldogs sent him a white pup trained to answer to the name of "Veto." Triplets in the valley of the Susquehanna were christened "Calvin," "Ross," and "Shelby," respectively.

During this time no word passed between Shelby and the Boss. The leader had not witnessed the inaugural cere-monies. Indeed, he had not attended the inauguration of a governor since his party regained control of the state. He and the governor-elect had lunched together frequently, however, and in concord discussed the forthcoming message and the party policy of the incoming Legislature. With two years of common work and intimacy behind them, they felt slight need of explanations. The machine as it stood was of their joint perfecting. Accordingly, the Boss viewed the cartoons with his habitual serenity, noted that a fund of good will was accruing to the party through the personal popularity of the new executive, and smilingly assured the reporters, who scented a quarrel, that Shelby was the right man in the right place. He found no thorn in a special message reminding the fortnight-old Legislature that, with the chief financial measures yet untouched, the bills already introduced called for the outlay of millions; nor did the speedy pruning of several sinecures, one of which was held by that tried veteran, Jacob Krantz, dash his cheery confidence. Krantz and the ousted were quietly found corporate business openings of glittering promise, and the campaign slogans were proved no mere catch-vote generalities.

Meanwhile the ancient city of Albany privily assorted its impressions of Shelby's wife, and awaited the dictum of Mrs. Teunis Van Dam. Although it was by deeds, rather than speech, that she made her judgments public, Mrs. Van Dam among her intimates did not deny herself the luxury of a stout opinion vigorously expressed.

"Mrs. Shelby's a fool," asserted the old lady in her positive way to Canon North, "but, after all, one of our own church people and the governor's wife."

"Either claim is weighty," smiled North; "tenderness for the family skeleton, respect for the state. United they're irresistible." For a social autocrat the canon took his position simply. Indeed he would have been rather astonished to learn that he was anything of the kind. "But the governor— he's genuine," he continued musingly; "I'm drawn to the man. He seems to me a power to be reckoned with—presidential timber, perhaps. Of course all our governors are heirs apparent by virtue of their office; but unlike so many of them, he isn't of a stature to be dwarfed by the suggestion. I think him rather Lincolnesque in a way, though I don't press the comparison. Perhaps it's merely his smile—have you noticed it?—the 'sad and melancholy smile on the lips of great men' that Amiel tells us is the badge of the misunderstood."

"Pshaw!" returned Mrs. Van Dam. "I've known two or three great men who wore sad smiles. When a disordered liver wasn't at the bottom of it 'twas the wife."

North gave over the argument.

"Nobody would impeach Shelby's liver," he laughed. "He's as robust as a patent medicine witness after taking."

"Oh, I don't accuse Mrs. Shelby," rejoined Mrs. Van Dam, quickly. "The governor's smile isn't the issue. One and one don't make one in the state of matrimony any more than elsewhere on the globe, and whether he and his wife agree or disagree doesn't interest me in the slightest. What does concern me is the important fact that the mistress of the executive mansion of the great state of New York appears not to know certain things she ought, chief among them the true character of ex-Senator Ludlow."

"I'm afraid it's true," owned the canon.

"Before Ruth Graves left I suggested that she intercede. She has tact, knows the Shelbys well, and had received an invitation to visit them. But she declined visit, intercession, and all. I'm sorry. Somebody must speak to Mrs. Shelby, and an old acquaintance could carry off such a mission with better grace."

"Why didn't Graves come on with his wife?" inquired the canon, irrelevantly.

"Don't mention the simpleton! I've no patience with him—or with Ruth for marrying him. We never can see the reason for other people's marriages, but that one above all others was incomprehensible. If ever a woman needed to marry a dynamo to bring out her best it was Ruth Temple. And she married Bernard Graves—a man who has degenerated into a *poseur* before women's clubs. Marriages made in heaven indeed! Give me Darwin and natural selection."

"You really have something of the kind," laughed North. "She was a free agent, his plumage evidently attracted in the old, old way, and so she made her choice."

"Fiddlesticks! Don't tell me that she made a fool of herself of her own free will. That man isn't capable of stirring the emotions of a poster girl with orange skin and purple hair, let alone a flesh and blood woman. Something outside herself—don't laugh; I'm a woman and I know—somebody, not Graves himself, bred that folly. If she were another sort of nature, I'd say she married for spite; but she—"

"For respite, perhaps—respite from herself. I've known cases. But we're far afield from the Shelbys. Shall I approach the governor?"

"No," said Mrs. Van Dam, with decision. "The wife is the one to see, if I know anything of women, and this is a woman's task; I, clearly, am the instrument, and shall not shirk."

"You would have made an eminent surgeon," remarked North, with his slow smile.

The unflinching Good Samaritan selected an hour two days later when the governor's wife was likely to be alone, and sent up her card. Not a few women had sighed for a sight of Mrs. Teunis Van Dam's calling card, and sighed in vain; but Cora Shelby, who had heard of these yearnings, thanked her God that she was not as other women are, and glanced at the pasteboard with indifference.

"Yes; I suppose I'm at home," she said languidly, posturing for the maid, and for a full half-hour left the august visitor waiting below stairs while she turned the pages of a novel.

The influence of Mrs. Tommy Kidder had determined this petty course. This sprightly young person, being herself a real social force, shared little of the awe in which Mrs. Teunis Van Dam was held by most of her townsfolk and by all newcomers, and Cora, with her own ideas of the part which she, as the governor's wife, should play, had taken Mrs. Tommy's frothy nonsense at rather more than its surface value. She was more than ever alive to Mrs. Van Dam's importance—her grandson, the military secretary, was an ever present reminder; but she cherished a quickened sense of her own importance, too, and was vigilantly alert to withstand any sign or symptom of what Mrs. Tommy called "Knickerbocker domination."

Her first shaft, however, fell wide of the mark. Mrs. Van Dam serenely assumed that her tardy hostess meant to pay her the compliment of a more elaborate toilet, and employed the interval in an interested survey of the changes wrought in the reception room's arrangement by its new mistress. So absorbing did she find this occupation, that she utterly missed the glacial temperature of Cora's greeting.

"I must congratulate you on resurrecting that bit of mahogany," declared the old lady, indicating a table. "I've missed that piece for three administrations. Wherever did you find it?"

"Really, I can't remember," fibbed Cora, resolving straight-way to banish it.

The military secretary had suggested its restoration, and she jumped to the conclusion that he had been inspired by his grandmother.

"It's a real link with the past," added Mrs. Van Dam, with a far-away look in her eyes. "I can recall it as long ago as Governor Tilden's time."

The great Mrs. Van Dam's cordiality thawed Cora in spite of herself, and she was well in the way of unconditional surrender to her charm when the caller cut straight into the pith of her errand.

"Without beating about the bush, my dear," she began, "I'm here on a meddlesome business which you mustn't take amiss. As an old woman who has seen something of the world in general, and much of this queer little Albany corner of it in particular, you must permit me to tell you that you have been too generously lenient with a person who has forfeited the right to darken decent people's doors. I mean ex-Senator Ludlow; and I presume I needn't specify his misdeeds."

"No. You need not," rejoined Cora, stiffening. "I'm not interested in scandal."

Mrs. Teunis Van Dam straightened rigidly in her chair.

"I fear that, after all, I must particularize," she replied. "Obviously you can't know the truth of things."

"I know that his wife divorced him, and I have heard a

dozen or more malicious tales about his present life. I doubt if you can add to the collection."

"You put me in a false position."

"And you reflect on mine in assuming to dictate whom I shall receive. This house belongs to the state. Every citizen is welcome."

Mrs. Van Dam had gathered her furs and risen, but at this she paused.

"There," she exclaimed, with a little laugh, "what women we are! I've been talking of one thing, you of another. You have the right view of your official obligations precisely. Of course the man is free to come to your public receptions. The state can't establish a moral quarantine, more's the pity."

"Ex-Senator Ludlow is free to come to my house at all times," cut in Cora, with a brilliant crimson dot in either cheek. "I do not sit in pharisaical judgment on the unfortunate. I've had his story as well as that of you who are against him. I believe him a misjudged man who deserves a courageous friend."

"Oh, if it is a question of friendship—" and Mrs. Van Dam terminated sentence and interview with a shrug.

Yet Cora had not seen the last of her visitor's stately back before she repented her open championship of Handsome Ludlow. Knickerbocker domination, not conviction, had forced her hand. Since she had hung her banner on the walls, however, she resolved to stand fast, and the following Sunday morning issued an unmistakable declaration of war. On her way to service she saw Ludlow crossing the park before the capitol, and stopped her carriage.

"'Nymph, in thy orisons be all my sins remember'd,'" quoted the man, his handsome, impudent eyes on hers.

"I propose that you'll do that for yourself," Cora retorted archly. "Get in."

She had intended going to the cathedral, but withal sudden resolve she ordered the carriage driven to an older church just at hand, which time out of mind had made special provision for the head of the state, down whose central aisle she marshalled Ludlow, and installed him in the governor's pew.

CHAPTER III

Had the protest against Knickerbocker arrogance languished at this pass, history would be the poorer, but Cora Shelby found it impossible to stop with this show of independence. Her ambition was whetted for an exercise of actual power, and the outcome was the famous battle of Beverwyck, whose story still lacks its balladist.

Early in her survey of Albany society, Cora had met with the Beverwyck Club.

"It is the local academy of immortals," instructed the military secretary. "Its judgments may not be infallible, but they're beyond appeal. It is the pink of exclusiveness; it worships etiquette above all other gods; and its receptions to incoming governors demand the reddest lettering in the calendar."

When Shelby's turn for this signal honor drew near, and the military secretary, to whom Fortune, not content with sending him into the world a grandson of Mrs. Teunis Van Dam, had added membership in the Beverwyck Club, approached him to discuss preliminaries, the governor cheerfully referred him to his wife in whose social knowingness he placed an abounding trust. Of Albany other than as a legislative workshop he knew next to nothing. His social progress in the salad days of his first term in the Assembly had begun in a saloon behind the capitol much frequented by departmental clerks, whence through hotel corridor intercourse he evolved by his second session to a grillroom, patronized by public servants of higher cast who gave stag dinners and occasional theatre parties, which called for evening dress. Up to this period Shelby had never found evening clothes essential to his happiness. His little sectarian college had rather frowned on such garments, and he, too, for a time had vaguely considered them un-American. Yet, taught by the grillroom, he assumed this livery, wore off its shyness, and grew to like it for the best it signified. Here evolution paused. Mrs. Teunis Van Dam, Canon North, and the Beverwyck Club, so far as they stood for anything, peopled a frigid zone of inconsequence which he had no wish to penetrate. Washington, influence in his party, and intimacy with its leaders sophisticated him before his return; behind every mask he now discerned a human being; and no social ordeal terrified. Nevertheless, something of his old-time diffidence toward the unknown country beyond the grillroom lingered, and it made for peace that his wife seemed so competent to guide.

On the score of her competency, Cora entertained no misgivings, and the day following Handsome Ludlow's public elevation to sanctity she met the club's representatives, the military secretary, and an august judge of the Court of Appeals, with a self-possession she felt would grace the daughter of a belted earl. The judge, after some ponderous compliments, told her that the committee in charge, having assured itself through the secretary that the governor and herself had no conflicting engagement, had agreed upon a near date for the reception, which he named. Cora promptly decided that in not consulting her the military secretary had been wanting in respect, and to punish him invented a previous engagement out of hand. Withered by his senior's Jove-like frown, the young man apologized in hot-skinned contrition for his ignorance of the unknowable.

"It's barely possible I didn't mention it," dropped Cora, scrupulously fair.

This gracious intercession for the culprit had no weight with the judge, who continued to regard the secretary with severity, and left him wholly out of the discussion of a date which should meet her wishes. This matter settled without further affront to her dignity, the judge expanded under her flattering attention, and gossiped of the reception itself.

"Between ourselves," he confessed, "the invitation list is bothering us unconscionably. You see, it has expanded beyond our space. At the last governor's reception the club-house was invaded by a mob—a mob, madame,—there is no other expression,—which I need not add is out of keeping with our traditions. But how draw the line without offence?"

With the dregs of her wrath against Mrs. Van Dam stirred afresh by the disciplining of the grandson, Cora perceived and seized the opportunity for a swingeing blow.

"There's an absurdly simple remedy," she returned thoughtfully; "but of course it would hardly become me to offer suggestions."

"My dear madame," the judge protested, "it would be an act of charity."

After a politic interval of coaxing, Cora explained:—

"The reception is meant to be official in spirit, isn't it? Then why not make it so in fact? Limit your invitations to the official circle. If all the townspeople unconnected with the government are excluded, no one need take offence."

A few days afterward the invitations went forth, restricted according to Cora's plan, and the heart-burnings which were kindled scorched the club's self-esteem like nothing in its staid career. But while others merely bewailed the amazing fact of their exclusion, Mrs. Teunis Van Dam, with characteristic energy, determined to probe the indignity to its author, and summoned her grandson to an absorbing interview.

"Schuyler Livingston Smith," she inquired, "what is Mrs. Tommy Kidder's relation to public affairs that she should receive an invitation to the Beverwyck Club?"

The secretary named an insignificant board of which Mr. Kidder was a member. His grandmother rapidly instanced a dozen other names, and repeated her question. In most cases the young man had to confess his ignorance of their claims.

"So," she commented in the end; "so. And I, whose people have helped govern this community since there was a colony to govern, am beyond the pale! But who was Peter Stuyvesant beside Mrs. Tommy Kidder's husband? Nobody. Who was Abraham de Peyster? who was Gerardus Beekman? who was Rip Van Dam? And the Schuylers, Livingstons, and Van Rensselaers? All nobodies. My dear child, what lunatic in the Beverwyck Club suggested this official classification, which even the Archangel Michael could not carry out?"

Her grandson, with no friendly recollections, named the judge.

"The silly old man!" exclaimed Mrs. Van Dam. "And who inspired him?"

He cheerfully told her, with the added detail that Mrs. Shelby and the judge had subsequently gone over the invitation list together. She was silent for a time, and then dismissed him. Alone with her thoughts, she elaborated a countermine, whose energy was specially directed against the Beverwyck Club, though she had no objection to hoisting the governor's wife in the explosion, albeit she refused to consider her the real antagonist. The true offender was the exclusive organization which had prostituted itself to such ignoble influence.

Within an hour of her grandson's departure Mrs. Teunis Van Dam despatched an invitation of her own. The Beverwyck Club reception was scheduled to run its formal course from nine to eleven o'clock; Mrs. Van Dam asked the governor and his lady to dine with her on the same evening at the hour of eight.

All hinged now on the personal equation of Cora Shelby, whose vagaries the old lady owned herself quite unable to forecast. Nor in this respect was Cora herself a much wiser prophet. Her first instinct, mixed with wonder, was to decline, and she held to this opinion the better part of an hour. Yet before the impulse could stiffen into resolution, it met the neutralizing influence of the old town, which, partly through the military secretary, partly through the scoffing Ludlow, she had unwittingly assimilated. By these teachings she had learned the flattering, almost royal, significance of Mrs. Teunis Van Dam's dinner invitations. She was seized afresh by a curiosity to observe how they did things in Quality Row, and became of two minds forthwith. Appointed for the same evening as the club reception, the dinner had, moreover, the look of a peace overture, a concession to her power, even an admission of defeat, which was soothing. She could hardly present the matter to Shelby in this light, as she had withheld all mention of the Ludlow business from his ear; but with a generosity which astonished herself, she dwelt on Mrs. Teunis Van Dam's undoubted prestige, and ended by advising acceptance.

Shelby, preoccupied with an appeal for the pardon of a consumptive forger, mechanically agreed.

"Sooner or later we'd have had to endure both functions," he said. "It is time saved to pack them into one evening."

Cora bridled. It was a prodigious affair for her that he took so indifferently.

"Time, time," she reprimanded; "the state doesn't expect its governor to grub like a clerk."

Shelby promised to mend his ways; but the dinner and reception occupied his thoughts so little that he worked beyond his usual hour at the capitol on the afternoon of the appointed day, and, coming tardy home, was late in dressing and late in setting forth. Cora was indignant to the boiling-point. She meant to be behind-hand at the reception, as a display of what she deemed good form; but a dinner was a dinner, as her husband, in the privacy of the carriage, was taught past all forgetting. Yet his fault lost its gravity before Mrs. Van Dam's welcome.

"If you're really late, I'm delighted," she returned to Cora's embarrassed excuses; "for you see, I've just found that I must apologize for a delay myself. What a boon servants run by clockwork would be! But it won't be very long."

It was long, though neither of the guests suspected it. Shelby was diverted by Mrs. Van Dam's unimagined vivacity; while his wife had no immediate room for any impression save satisfaction that this autocrat, who held that punctuality should be the politeness of democracy no less than princes, had been caught napping. It was clear that she meant to bury the hatchet, and Cora, with her own point carried, saw no reason why she should not add a shovelful of symbolic earth herself. Thus, beginning with a trickle, the flow of her good humor presently broadened to the width of the sluice-gate, as she entered upon an absorbing scrutiny of the quaint old house which by tradition had served one of the earlier governors. It was a rambling structure of unexpected turns and endless alcoves stored with curios, art treasures, and trophies of travel.

Perceiving their interest in their surroundings, Mrs. Van Dam gladly played the cicerone.

"That chair and desk came from the Senate Chamber of the old State House," she said, following Shelby's eyes. "They were used by my grandfather, and I luckily got them at the demolition. His wooden inkstand and pounce-box are there too. That Stuart over the mantelpiece is his portrait."

"I've heard of him," answered Shelby, warmly. "He upheld De Witt Clinton's hands in the fight for the canal."

She left him momentarily to give Cora the history of a faded Flemish tapestry that lay in a cabinet, and then included them both in the romantic tale of a Murillo, unearthed in a Mexican pawnshop, which she assumed would interest so steadfast a champion of art as the governor had shown himself in his congressional career. Cora basked in the exquisite flattery of being treated as a person of greater cultivation than she was, and strained on tiptoe to merit her reputation. Had her mind been free to register its ordinary impressions, two things might have struck her as singular; the absence of other guests, and, stranger still, in a temple of punctuality, the lack of clocks.

The same happy atmosphere enveloped the dinner itself, whose perfection of service and cookery betrayed no hint of delay. Mrs. Shelby found her views of life and the sphere of woman sought for and appreciated, and the governor was enticed into political by-paths illustrated by Tuscarora stories told in his happiest vein. He was frankly charmed. Many women had attracted him in many ways, ranging from the earthy fascination of the sometime Mrs. Hilliard to that commingling of girlish impulse, mature good sense, and an indefinite something else in Ruth which swayed him still; but none of them had met him on quite the serene plane of this delightful old woman of the world. By her birthright she seemed to bridge the present and the past, and under her spell the quaint-gabled Albany of another century rose again. Once more Arcadian youth picnicked in the "bush" and coasted down Pinkster Hill past the squat Dutch church; the Tontine Coffee House sprang from dust, and through its doors walked Hamilton and Burr, Jerome Bonaparte, and a comic-pathetic *emigre* marquis, who in poverty awaited the greater Bonaparte's downfall, cherishing his order of Saint Louis and powdering his poll with Indian meal; the Livingstons and Clintons divided the land between them; Van Buren and the Regency came to power.

There was more of this when the dinner had ended, and they lingered in the library over their coffee and Mrs. Van Dam's priceless collection of relics of the time of the royal province and the yet earlier New Netherland.

"A plague on the reception!" exclaimed the governor in the carriage, when the good nights had finally been said. "I could have talked with her till morning."

There was a lively stir and bustle about the entrance of the Beverwyck Club as they approached, which Cora took to be that of late-comers like themselves. She would have preferred that she be conspicuously the last,—the climax. Seen nearer, the flurry was peculiar. If the idea were not preposterous, she could believe that people were actually leaving the club—leaving before they met the governor in whose honor they assembled—leaving before *she* came!

"Your watch, Ross, your watch," she exclaimed suddenly.

"I did not wear it."

She bethought her of a recently acquired carriage clock whose face the lights of a passing trolley made plain. She looked, gasped, and looked again in horrid fascination. The punctilious Beverwyck Club had decreed that its reception should end at eleven, and the decrees of the Beverwyck Club were rigidly enforced. The carriage clock pointed its inexorable hands to a quarter past.

CHAPTER IV

Thenceforth Cora Shelby's respect for the fearless strategist in Quality Row verged upon awe. If Mrs. Teunis Van Dam now deigned to assist at one of the weekly house-openings, the occasion savored of an aroma which the united patronage of Mrs. Tommy Kidder and the ladies of the lieutenant-governor, the secretary of state, the controller, the treasurer, and the entire bench of the Court of Appeals could not exhale. Cora made sure of her good offices for the legislative reception weeks in advance, and in all matters, save only Handsome Ludlow, deferred anxiously to the great exemplar's code.

No one who thought twice about Mrs. Van Dam escaped the reflection that she was a descendant, and Cora with her mind running continually on this shoot of a peculiarly sightly family tree, was as fired by this truism of natural law as if it had lain all the centuries awaiting her discovery. Those delightful magicians of figures, who as easy as asking prove William the Conqueror the mathematical begetter of us all, had hitherto contented her; but such sweets cloyed before Mrs. Van Dam's august line of Dutch and English forebears, who had considerately made history and bequeathed portraits and plate. But the path of Japhet in search of a father was primrose beside the American's in search of an ancestor, and Cora's researches were long barren of result. The labyrinth of Brown, her maiden name, she speedily forsook, though at the outset it seemed to run promisingly to knighthood, literature, and art; Huggins, her mother's name, was impossible, and Hilliard, more sounding, clearly out of the question; while the Shelbys, to whom she turned in last resort, seemed hopelessly commonplace. Ross's father, to her own knowledge, had done little but drink; and the grandfather, though of sterner stuff, as became a pioneer, was handicapped by his unlucky distillery. The governor's own notions about his family were the vaguest. Like many Americans, he had the impression that its beginnings traced to two brothers who immigrated to this country prior to the Revolution in which they served.

"The Revolution seems to be the Norman Conquest of American genealogy," he remarked in the course of his wife's cross-examination.

"But don't you know their names, or what they did in the war?" she queried anxiously.

Shelby shook his head.

"Perhaps they were teamsters," he laughed.

Cora was too pained to jest. Mrs. Van Dam was a "daughter" of this and that society by virtue of descent from generals.

For a time the chase now circled teasingly round a southern branch whose achievements were notable, but the unconcern of the distiller with regard to vital statistics balked a happy union of North and South, and goaded Cora to that last desperate ditch of the ancestor-hunter—a blind leap over seas. In the fortunate isles where choice forefathers flourish thick as buttercups, Cora made her foray with hunger's lawless haste, enlisted the aid of an indigent person skilled in blazonry, and in good season brought her spoils to the governor.

"I've had bother enough getting this," she said, exhibiting a coat of arms; "but I must say it's far prettier than the one we saw in Mrs. Van Dam's library."

"Runs mainly to red, doesn't it?" Shelby ventured, gravely considering the work.

"That's gules," explained Cora, learnedly; "the color of the field. Books of heraldry describe the arms as: 'Gules, two boars' heads displayed in chief and a mullet in base, sable; crest, a dexter arm, embowed, grasping a cimeter—'"

"I took that for a crumb-scraper," put in the governor, jocularly.

"The motto," went on Cora, soberly, "is, 'I achieve.' I think the purple of the mantling highly effective—purpure, that's called—which, taken with the red and black, would give a most romantic light to our hall in New Babylon if we put a window at the turn of the stair. Tomorrow morning I shall order a die made for my stationery."

"So this is ours," said Shelby. "Did the original owner acquire it in the Holy Wars, or was he a rich brewer who endowed a hospital?"

Cora reddened.

"He was Owen Shelby, a Welsh soldier of the Commonwealth."

"A near relation of mine?"

"You are undoubtedly his descendant. Of course I can't supply every trifling link—your people were so careless of their records; but there is no question in my mind that you are entitled to his arms, and you ought to be grateful to me for my pains."

"I am, I am," protested Shelby, with a chuckle. "But before the engraver begins work on the crumb-scraper and the prize pigs let me suggest that you add a detail which has been overlooked. I mean a bar sinister."

"Ross!"

He slipped his arm round her waist with a laugh.

"One of the state library people said that you were trailing the foreign Shelbys, and I glanced at your references. The fact I remember best is that Owen Shelby, late of Cromwell's Ironsides, died a bachelor."

She flung from him in stormy anger.

"I've twice been fool enough," she flashed, "to marry a man unable to appreciate me."

He winced. The reproach, more wanton than any she had ever framed, lashed him on the raw. The manner of his succession to Joe Hilliard's shoes had fostered an almost morbid solicitude for her well being which had not seldom over-topped his better judgment. If he had failed of his duty, it was not for lack of striving.

"I've tried, Cora," he answered bitterly.

Neither broached a formal reconciliation—such crude devices fell into disuse early in their marriage; but the man gave her social hours he could ill afford in the press of the closing session, and presently a tremendous event from the outside patched, if it could not heal, the breach. This was nothing less than the launching of Shelby's presidential boom.

Three factors contributed to this movement: the return of prosperity, the governor's personality, and the Boss. Shelby won his election in a midnight of universal hard times; his inauguration saw the dawn; the legislative session closed amidst a sunrise of splendid promise. By the deathless fallacy which credits or blames the ruling powers for everything, natural or supernatural, Shelby's party reaped abundantly where it had sown with niggard hand. The governor's personal deserts were more solid, the public recognizing his retarding ratchet as the cause of the machine's continence and the lowered tax-rate. Apparently the Legislature bore him no ill will for his curbing hand. A quiet word had issued from the Boss that the governor's vetoes must stand, and Shelby's one pet measure, the appointment of a commission to deal with the improvement of the canals, had passed both Houses by a vote which was almost non-partisan. A spontaneous demand seemed to well from the people that this faithful steward be sent higher.

But Shelby knew something of the rearing of that tenderest of plants in the political garden—the spontaneous demand. In the voice of the people he had so often read the will of the Boss. The inspired laudations of country editors, the resulting echoes in the city press, the interviews with the knowing ones who withheld their names, the genuine momentum lent by the easily impressed—all the covert workings of spontaneity were known to him from the days of apprenticeship at the Boss's feet. The method was transparent, the motive only was hazy; yet he divined the motive itself with sufficient accuracy. The Boss thought he knew too much. It is well to make your own governor, but to make him too well is ill. It was this one's drawback that he had passed the No Admittance sign of the workshop and got the trade secrets of the boss business at his finger ends.

The pupil smiled sometimes when he recalled the first great rencounter with the master. The birch and frown no longer terrified. Evidently the Boss knew this, and failing the birch, dangled a prize.

What Shelby did not divine was the incentive force of pique. While the leader gave his smiling interviews to the reporters on the subject of the governor's vetoes, he had too often had to dissemble that his earliest information came from them. He did not resent the vetoes, if they made party capital; nor did he resent Shelby's popularity, for he liked him. The bitterness of the cup was that the ingrate took no pains to inquire whether he cared or not. It is true that in large questions Shelby had uniformly sought his counsel, and the session had been fairly prolific in legislation redounding to the party credit; but the governor's independence in the lesser matters attainted his loyalty. What the one man considered upholding the dignity of his office, the other interpreted as leze-majesty.

Shelby's attitude toward the presidential chit-chat was frankly human. Too modest to measure himself beside the greater successors of Washington, he yet knew himself to be as well equipped as many who had held the office; and, without troubling his sleep, determined that should the boss-made boom attain genuine popularity, it might drift where it would without hindrance from him. Precisely this occurred. The governor's practicality smoothed the way to his indorsement by men whose foremost interest was business rather than politics, and a banquet given him late in April by a great commercial organization of New York, which approved his policy of letting the city mind its own affairs, set him definitely in the race.

Throned in a gallery above the diners; courted by heroines of by-gone horse shows, the hem of whose garments she had never dreamed to touch; with the White House looming mistily through the sheen of silver and crystal and napery under tinted lights, Cora viewed the taking spectacle as a personal apotheosis. A silly periodical for "ladies" had recently printed an article about her which ascribed Shelby's making to herself, and she, in this rosy hour believing, looked upon her handiwork, and saw that it was tolerably good. Statesmen, diplomats, captains of industry, the smiling Boss—a very parliament of brains—did the governor honor, and the most famous after-dinner speaker in the land proclaimed him New York's favorite son.

To most of his listeners Shelby's reply seemed admirable. A morning paper called it "a little classic of straight-forwardness"; but his king-maker aloft thought his bearing too simple by far. If he listened to her, he would tip his presidential lightning-rod more showily.

CHAPTER V

Summer leaped a hotbed growth from spring, and Cora Shelby, tiring of golf, the country club, and Albany's now mild pastimes, took herself off for a round of fashionable resorts with Mrs. Tommy Kidder. The governor had other occupations. So far as a man could do such a thing, he put his presidential chances out of mind and bent his energies upon a study of the canal problem, whose solving he was ambitious to make the monument of his administration. As a legislator he had been recognized as an authority upon this his hobby; but the knowledge of the assemblyman was shallow beside that of the governor, who asked no fairer laurel than to link his name with the regenerated Erie Canal as the second Clinton had associated his name with its beginnings.

Throughout the languid heated term whose official calm only the occasional request of a fellow governor for requisition papers disturbed, Shelby plodded over the bewildered mass of estimates, maps, and mazy statistics which his special committee was accumulating. A more brilliant man doubtless would have left much of this arid drudgery to subordinates, contenting himself with the sum of things, without a close scrutiny of detail; but this was never Shelby's way. When he mastered a subject it was his blood and bones, and his passion for the Ditch transmuted its story, howsoever told, into stuff that splendid dreams are made on

Mark Lee Luther

and modern empires built.

Those arduous months were the happiest he had known. He toiled mightily, but he wrought at a labor of love, while his leisure hours fostered friendships as novel as they were attractive. Cora Shelby's campaign of the watering-places had not embraced Milicent, and the girl returned from school in June to find her mother already gone. She dutifully made known her arrival in Albany, and in time deciphered from a patchouli-scented scrawl postmarked "Bar Harbor" that Albany was an excellent spot for her to remain.

"She says that summer hotels are no places for young girls," Milicent told her stepfather. "Why then does mamma care about them?"

The governor was nonplussed: but he quietly set himself to make Albany tolerable for this astonishing young person, yet scant of seventeen, who had suddenly flowered into the outward semblance of a woman. He devised excursions on the river and pilgrimages to historic spots about the city and the countryside, acquiring strange antiquarian lore of the Schuyler house, the Van Rensselaer mansion, and the Vanderheyden Palace, and, more curious still, a perception of his deep capacity for affection. This child of the Hilliards' better selves, with her father's frankness, her mother's earlier beauty, and with a winsomeness all her own, awoke his slumbering instinct of fatherhood.

The wholesome new relation quickened his insight amazingly. He divined that however much the girl might care for these wayside rambles with him, her youth must still crave youth, and in this strait he turned to Mrs. Van Dam, who forthwith became Milicent's captive, too, and a fairy godmother into the bargain. So Shelby came much to frequent a vine-screened upper veranda off Mrs. Van Dam's library, where she was fond of serving coffee after dinner, and one could dip down over the red roofs and tree-tops to the stripling Hudson changing its coat of many colors in the sunset. As this corner was a haunt of Canon North's, also, it fell out that a friendship sprang up between the men which strengthened into intimacy. Shelby had never dreamed of making friends with a clergyman. The sectarian college had put him out of joint with priestery. But North was in a class by himself. He had no sacerdotal air or jargon—that negative virtue was his earliest passport; and he was from crown to sole a robust manly man. The governor took to dropping into the canon's book-lined study near the cathedral after office hours, and North would come to the executive mansion and smoke half the night away; for the canon was a judge of tobacco no less than men. Not once in their intercourse did he mention church-going or creeds; he did not "talk religion." Yet, whatever the canon's religion was, Shelby was aware that he lived it. The air was full of little stories of his helpfulness of the sort people told of a man North once alluded to as "Saint" Phillips Brooks.

Milicent went to the Catskills late in August as the guest of a school friend, and after a day or two of novel loneliness, the governor decided to carry out a recently formed plan for supplementing the work of his committee with a personal inspection of a part of the canal system. As it seemed to him that he could get at the best results by quiet means, his journey was presented to the press in the light of a business trip to his old home. For forty-eight hours his leisurely progress with his private secretary escaped remark. Then the newspapers upset his apple-cart. Shelby had become too interesting a figure for the role of Haroun-al-Raschid, and the paragraphers rang astonishing changes on his adventures at the few points where he had succeeded in making observations unrecognized. What he saw thereafter was accompanied by the click of cameras and the fatuity of local bigwigs brimming with eagerness to tie their fortunes to the car of the coming man.

At New Babylon, where he became the guest of the Hon. Seneca Bowers, the minute espionage upon his doings ceased, and Shelby felt less a personage than at any time since his inauguration. The town was proud of him, but too faithful to its ancestral reserve to tell him so. People who had called him "Ross" all his days addressed him in this fashion still; and the Widow Weatherwax calmly imposed an audience in the matter of her last will and testament, which the new-fledged lawyer, William Irons, had bungled, and spiced the renewal of their relations with her old-time candor and a full chronicle of the past, present, and probable scandal of the county. In little ways, however, the governor perceived what close-mouthed Tuscarora really felt. They had hung a crayon portrait of him in the court-house, and the Pioneer Association, which was about to hold its annual picnic beside Ontario, asked him to deliver the address.

Shelby accepted the invitation, and, saturated as he was with the homespun history of his county, excelled himself. But he did something more than retell a familiar tale. A product of this life, he nevertheless saw it from the outside and in its wide relations, and the canal-begotten civilization, which was his immediate theme, led irresistibly to the vast economic problem that lay near his heart, and to a suddenly formulated plan for its solution. By one of those inspirations of the moment which public speakers know, yet dare not count upon, the vexing details of his summer's drudgery shifted and rearranged themselves into a coherent pattern and policy whose fulfilment should place the historic waterway, not merely abreast of the age, but bulwarked for the future. It was a significant utterance which carried far. Shelby could give no copies of his speech to the press, since the speech had largely shaped itself in the making; but the correspondents who covered what had promised to be a purely bucolic assignment, were not slow in seeing their error and retrieving it. What the Tuscarora pioneers and their descendants heard, the whole state read; and the discerning perceived that, wherever the party, the party machine, or the party boss might stand, the governor had scaled the high plateau of statesmanship, where public opinion is less catered to than led.

Late in the afternoon Shelby shook the last brown hand in the serpentine line of country people which coiled in and out the stuffy parlor of the Lakeview Inn, and cutting loose from the reception committee under cover of a headache, slipped away into the trees. The fringe of the wood was defaced with the litter of picnickers, and smelt of lunch; the din of the agents for new-fangled reapers and ploughs, whose gaudy paint was doubly garish against the sober background, had routed the squirrels and birds; but the remoter paths held only silent lovers, and the camp-ground, where the Widow Weatherwax had mouthed and played the prophet, stripped of its tents, its zealots, its wavering torchlights, was full of wholesome sunlight and forest peace.

The spot stirred ghosts, and the governor turned to the murmuring shore with its gentle mimicry of ocean. Half sheltered by a clump of sumach sat a woman upon a bit of driftwood and flung pebbles in the lake. He stared, and then went slowly down to her.

"Ruth," he said, "you here!"

"Your Excellency startled me."

Her banter puzzled him, but the handclasp was warm.

"Forget my office," he petitioned.

"After your tremendous speech to-day? You were his

Excellency the governor of New York with that, and I was properly impressed. It struck me that you would make a benevolent czar."

"Are you mocking me?"

"God forbid, your Excellency!"

"I'd rather be plain Shelby," he said, studying her profile. "I'm glad you heard me—glad that you liked it. It was sincere, and you value sincerity. But I had no notion that you were listening. I supposed you somewhere with the fashionables."

"I reached home yesterday, and came at once to my lake cottage. I heard that you were to speak, and braved the picnic to hear you. I trust you appreciate the sacrifice."

"And—your husband? Is he here too?"

Ruth flung a pebble.

"I believe he's addressing a woman suffrage convention in Chicago to-day." She gave him a lazy glance. "And Mrs. Shelby—is she here?"

"She's in Saratoga, I believe."

"Belief again? We really ought to read the papers."

He tried to search her face, but the pebble-throwing prevented. The Widow Weatherwax had expatiated on the topic of Mrs. Bernard Graves's unhappiness, with tedious variations on the saw about marrying in haste to repent at leisure. He wondered—he scarce knew what. She drew him with all the old attraction, but an elusive something had vanished. He guessed that it was the essence of youth, though the form lingered.

"Are you happy, Ruth?" he asked abruptly.

She looked him in the eyes, and laughed.

"That reminds me of your unofficial self," she said. "You never could invent small talk for the feminine mind."

"You were never the kind of woman who wanted it."

"I better appreciate its uses nowadays. It conceals either the absence or presence of thought. Bless me! there's an epigram. But I'm afraid it's merely an echo of Voltaire."

He was not listening. A midsummer madness rioted in his brain.

"But are you happy?"

"Small talk, small talk," she insisted. "See how that yacht's sails take the sun. Isn't the water a splendid sapphire? Do you like to fish? Do you prefer Tennyson or Browning? Meredith or Hardy? Isn't it warm? Isn't it cool?"

"But are you?"

She rose and faced him with strange eyes.

"What do you want?"

"Want," he repeated mechanically, rising too.

"Why have you come here in your pomp of governorship and promise of greater things to harass me?"

"Harass you, Ruth! If you knew—"

"Know? I know too much. I'm unlearning things now. That's the key to happiness—forgetting. And here come you, as you used to come, an untamed, masterful force— that's what you are, a force!—and instead of forgetting you ask me to remember. What is it you're really seeking in this probing of my happiness? What must you be told?"

"Nothing." With the revelation of the flaw in her armor he conquered self. "I know—God help me!—I know."

CHAPTER VI

The Boss questioned the wisdom of the Tuscarora speech, and the fall widened the unacknowledged breach between him and the governor. The September primaries had assured the leader a firmer control of the state convention than he had ever exercised, and it was well understood to be his, and his alone, made to his order, and the docile register of his will. That this victory clinched his ownership of the delegation to the national convention of next year was self-evident; and that a presidential candidate with New York's backing would attract allies from several eastern and at least two southern boss-ruled states, was well warranted by the tale of the great politician's excursions into national affairs in the recent past. By implication of the April banquet the leader's personal choice, Shelby, had therefore no trivial chance of capturing the nomination; and in the Boss's opinion the favored pawn owed a decent deference to the master chess-player. So Shelby thought, too; but they split over definition of terms in the same old way.

"You juggled millions like a Napoleon of Finance," complained the Boss at a breakfast for two shortly after the state convention. "Is that the kind of talk for people just recovering from hard times?"

His tone chafed the governor.

Mark Lee Luther

"It's the kind of talk for a proper handling of the canal problem," he retorted crisply. "The canal has been the prey of peanut politics too long."

"The speech was ill-advised—ill-advised," persisted the Boss, irritably. "You should have consulted somebody."

Shelby provoked him with a smile.

"That was my idea, precisely," he returned. "I thought I'd consult the people."

A difference springing from the November elections strained their relations farther, and goaded Shelby's patience to its utmost reach. Although they favored the organization as a whole, the elections wrought certain damaging changes in detail, one of which involved the fortunes of Handsome Ludlow. Early in his term the governor had appointed the man to a temporary commission, at the urgent plea of the Boss, who painted the ex-senator in the light of a faithful soldier haply fallen outside the breastworks by reason of the ingratitude of a fickle city constituency. Ludlow had regularly drawn a salary, which his subordinates earned, and divided his abundant leisure between the diversions peculiar to Mrs. Tommy Kidder's coterie and schemes for the recovery of his senatorial seat. In the latter business he met with a defeat more telling than he had yet experienced. But Ludlow was an office-seeker of resource. Through a channel which he did not disclose, he got wind of a judgeship whose forthcoming vacancy was known to the governor and those in his confidence, and promptly undertook a still-hunt for the place. Presently his name came to Shelby with the strong recommendation of the Boss.

The governor was angry to the core. As a lawyer alone he recoiled from raising even temporarily to the bench a man whose activities had been notoriously political, and his law practice innocent of a single case in a court of record; as a husband whose ears tingled with gossip of this same Ludlow's summer attentions to his wife, which the Boss, whom nothing escaped, must have heard too, his hurt was shrewder. His refusal was curt.

The Boss met the governor's move with silence, but under his own roof Shelby had crossed a politician less self-contained. Ludlow owed his fore-knowledge of the judicial vacancy to Cora, who flew in high dudgeon to her husband to demand why he had refused this favor to her valued friend.

Shelby was dumfounded.

"These affairs don't concern you," he said, after a moment's incredulous scrutiny of her face.

"Why did you refuse to make him a judge?" she repeated hotly.

"Ludlow is a discredited political hack. I had no alternative."

"It's jealousy."

Shelby whitened.

"If you mean to press the thing into that region," he answered sternly, "I'll own that there is an element of jealousy. I've had to open my eyes lately to many things which concern you and Ludlow. Bar Harbor stories, Saratoga stories, Albany stories, too, of things you've kept from me—God knows what hasn't filtered my way. I am jealous—jealous for your good name, and mine, and Milicent's."

She wept at that, saying that he misconstrued her warm sympathy with the unfortunate; and he, proof against anything but the feminine tear-gland, as she knew, protested his faith. It was near his lips at this moment to beg her to treat Ludlow henceforth with mere civility, but he refrained. When he broached it afterward her pliant mood had vanished.

"You would have Albany saying that you believe its tittle-tattle," she argued; and he deferred for the hundredth time to her superior perception of the mental processes of the social world.

Till the Legislature met in January, the governor was absorbed in the writing of his annual message, whose recommendations he proposed to devote almost exclusively to the canals. His committee had completed its work, and his great plan was muscular and vertebrate in all its structure, for he contemplated a far-reaching system of legislation rather than a simple makeshift appropriation of the out-worn type; and the ultimate goal of it all was to lift the politics-ridden waterway out of politics altogether. Before he gave his final revision to the printers, he submitted a proof to the Boss, who returned it with the comment that his intellect was of an order quite too everyday to criticise a project obviously framed for the millennium. From the man reputed to own the Legislature, whose committees, certainly, were cut and dried in his office weeks before it met, this sarcasm was gloomily prophetic; but since his Tuscarora speech, Shelby had personally sounded many senators, assemblymen, and representatives of the several canal interests, and he was not dismayed.

The reception given by the newspapers to what they styled "The Governor's Splendid Dream" heartened Shelby, though he deprecated its form. He insisted that the scheme was no more his than the committee's, whose elaborate report he submitted with his message, and that it was no dream at all, but the businesslike remedy for an admitted ill. As in De Witt Clinton's case, however, the public brushed aside the idle question of genesis, and honored the untiring advocate.

There were plenty who agreed with the governor. Famous economic experts and civil service reformers wrote their approval, great financiers wired congratulations, and the public hearings on the bills embodying his ideas, which friendly legislators shortly introduced, were attended by representatives from the exchanges, boards of trade, merchants' associations, and chambers of commerce of every city directly concerned.

A reporter remarked upon this striking showing to the Boss.

"Yes," said the great man, "the governor seems to have the unanimous support of the college professors and the New Yorkers who claim residence in Newport, Rhode Island; but I wonder what the taxpayer thinks."

This figurative taxpayer personified for him the rural vote whose strength was his strength, and whose thought he made his own. He was hearkening to the murmur of the counties which the canal did not touch, but whose memory of its flagrant abuses was long, and the conclusion that he reached the country newspapers of his system began speedily to express. One editor bewailed the "Hundred-Million-Dollar-Millstone" which the governor proposed to hang about the people's neck; another attacked the consistency of the man who would to-day scatter like a prodigal what he had scrimped yesterday to save; while a third pertinently inquired whether such a spendthrift were fit timber to put in Washington as a check upon the waxing extravagance of Congress? By dint of repetition these things attained wide currency.

Shelby was untroubled.

"Millions, to be sure," he replied to a query of his wife's. "The commercial supremacy of a state is perforce a question of millions."

"But they're saying you risk your presidential chances," she lamented. "Do take every care to strengthen yourself. It's the fondest dream of my life to see you President. You must let nothing stand between you and the nomination."

"Thank heaven I'm not stung that badly!" the governor ejaculated.

"But for my sake! If I should ask you—beg you on my knees?"

"I'd say you should be in better business."

He answered her lightly, and playfully pinched her ear, but she saw that no word of hers could sway his purpose, and hated him. For the hour, however, even this teasing vision of herself as first lady of the land paled before the very present topic of Milicent's debut. Despite Shelby's advice and her own pleadings, the girl had not been allowed to return to her school in the autumn; for when they met at the summer's end, the revelation of her daughter's good looks and unconscious girlish charm, by her mother called manner, revived a shadowy project of Cora's for an elaborate coming-out ball which had enticed her in the early days of life in Albany. Neither Milicent's reluctance nor her stepfather's protest against the launching of so young a girl availed.

"Only last week I saw her playing with a doll," said Shelby, routed at every turn.

"What an argument! I played with dolls after I was married to Joe. If you postponed a woman's debut till she tired of dolls, you would conflict with her funeral."

This sally displayed such unexpected humor that Shelby laughed, and his wife seized the favoring moment to end discussion.

"It's my duty to my child," she declared; "and of that, a mother is the best judge."

Although the event was to be deferred till late February, as the crowning glory of the season which Lent would close, Cora's plans were on foot by Thanksgiving Day. Among her earliest preliminaries was the enlisting of Mrs. Van Dam, whose friendship for Milicent she had determined to exploit as soon as she learned of its existence. This was not difficult. Of the wisdom of the thing Mrs. Van Dam said nothing,— she had had her fill of advising Mrs. Shelby,—but her sympathy for Milicent was keen, and it drew her into a rather distasteful share in Cora's programme, in the hope of lessening the girl's ordeal. Where Mrs. Teunis Van Dam led, Albany naturally followed; and with Albany subdued, Cora directed her conquering march toward other worlds. In the year of her publicity she had, through Mrs. Tommy Kidder and other agencies, brushed here and there at the rim of the magic inner circle of metropolitan society, for every inch of which she now encroached an ell. Shelby gained his first knowledge of the astonishing extent of his wife's acquaintance when he scanned the invitation list of a thousand names, and was told by the military secretary that New York's quota was coming by special train.

About five o'clock on the evening of the ball, the governor came home fagged and depressed. Aside from canal reform, still drifting through seas of talk, the legislative session presented several insistent public questions which seemed to have imposed their cumulative worry on his morning hours; later had come an acrimonious hearing over the removal of an incompetent district attorney; then a quarter-hour's fencing with the press correspondents, who wanted to know things which it was inexpedient to tell; and, finally, a rasping conference with the Boss, who, using the ball as a cover for one of his rare pilgrimages to Albany, had, throughout the day, held levee in his hotel parlors with such vogue that at moments both Senate and Assembly all but lacked a quorum.

Mrs. Tommy Kidder's brougham blocked the porte-cochère as Shelby mounted the steps of the executive mansion, and at the door he met the volatile lady herself.

"I've been watching the workmen give the finishing touch, governor," she gushed. "You are about to set foot in fairyland."

Shelby put her in her carriage, and entered the house. It did not seem fairylike. Only a dim light shone here and there through the dusk, and the floors were not yet clear of the rubbish of the decorators. From one of the smaller rooms came the sound of Handsome Ludlow's voice. He too, apparently, had been watching the finishing touch. The governor passed on to his own apartments in quest of peace. It was a vain search. His quarters had been invaded and curtailed for the event, and the corner left him was confused and forlorn. He lit a cigar, smoked a brief moment, heard a feminine cough on the farther side of a door leading to one of the rooms from which some guest had dispossessed him, and desisted.

He went downstairs presently, and left the house for the conservatory, a favorite haunt of his, usually troubled by no one else save Milicent. He scarcely knew one flower from another, but he delighted to potter about, smelling here and there, and the Scotch gardener idolized him as heartily as he detested the wife, who cared nothing for these treasures in themselves, and openly avowed that she preferred the odor of patchouli.

The greenhouses proved rather forlorn too, denuded as they were of so many potted things for the glory of the mansion; but their quiet obscurity ministered to Shelby's jaded mood. Then he perceived that he was not alone. Low voices drifted from another aisle—Ludlow's and Cora's—doubtless still absorbed in the finishing touch. After an instant's hesitation the governor moved toward them, till a vivid little picture framed by the fronds of a drooping fern brought him to a standstill. He beheld a deliberate kiss.

Mark Lee Luther

CHAPTER VII

The scene so nearly paralleled that crucial moment in his own life, under Joe Hilliard's roof, that the quarry owner seemed fairly to twitch his sleeve. Then, as the dead man had done before him, Shelby stayed his hand. Hilliard had respected his hearthstone because it held the ashes of a burned-out love; the governor respected his office. Unseen by the rapt pair, he left the conservatory, and regained his disordered room.

How should he act? There was scant opportunity for reflection. The dinner hour was presently upon him, with a chattering tableful of Cora's friends who were staying in the house. Shelby seldom shone in these mixed companies, and to-night he seemed to himself to stand off in wondering detachment, while somebody clothed in his likeness said and did many things. He made clear a bit of political slang for the woman in yellow on his right; he smiled appreciation of the quip of a young thing in pink three places distant down the left; he explained to a foreign gentleman, whose English was irreparably broken, that Albany was not the capital of the United States; and all this time he watched his vivacious wife at the table's end, and marvelled at her hypocrisy. So Joe Hilliard had probably wondered. Hilliard was very real to him. He seemed to have incased himself in Hilliard's personality. A little later, when Milicent, all exhilaration now that the bursting of the cocoon was instant, came in her bravery for his approval, he kissed her like one who knows no care, and extravagantly admired the roses he forgot that he had sent. The same mechanical self stood beside his wife and stepdaughter at the coming of the guests, spoke its automatic greetings, and extended its automatic hand.

For one brief instant the opiate lifted. The endless smirking procession had cast Ludlow to the front. The man was lingering with easy assurance between mother and daughter.

"Which is the debutante?" he asked.

Shelby could have felled him for taking the girl's hand—Cora's mattered nothing. But what of his own hand? Milicent's fan suddenly escaped its fastening, and as suddenly he caught at the pretext for which he groped. Again in his place, Ludlow had drifted by with no word spoken between them. He sighed with relief, and in the same breath cursed himself and the conventions which compelled such cunning. In a rational world he could have knocked him down.

Once again that evening they came face to face. It was late—past one o'clock—and the governor issuing from the smoking-room met Ludlow at the threshold. No one was within earshot; fate itself seemed to have ordered the meeting, and till that moment Shelby had desired to confront Ludlow with a fierce desire. Yet they passed with a nod. Long uncertain before many offering courses, Shelby on the instant made his choice.

The orchestra hushed, the last good night spoken, Milicent gone to her dreams, the house half in darkness, he intercepted Cora in the corridor leading to her apartments.

"Ten minutes of your time," he requested.

She stared, yawned, and stared again.

"At this hour?"

"Now."

She led the way into her dressing-room and sent away her maid. Shelby waited silently by the open grate till they should be alone.

"You're rather pale," observed his wife, languidly, in passing to a chair; and with finger tip lightly brushed his cheek.

He shrank involuntarily.

"Pale and nervous," she added, "and a fit subject for bed. Was Old Silky disagreeable to-day? I thought him as sweet as peaches tonight. Did you notice Mrs. Van Dam's famous diamonds? It's not often she wears them all. Milicent got her to do it."

"I was in the greenhouse before dinner, Cora," said Shelby, speaking with slow emphasis. "I saw you and Ludlow."

"Oh, yes," returned the woman, glibly, "we were wondering whether the large drawing-room needed a few more palms."

"I saw you and Ludlow in one another's arms," pursued her husband in the same hard staccato. "I saw him kiss you."

She half rose, eying him fearfully; then, reassured by what she saw, sank back in her seat, fingering the long glove she had partly drawn from one white arm. As on that other night, her faultless shoulders rose from a black setting of laces and shining jet, and, manlike, Shelby took the garment for the same which had helped to warp the fabric of his life from its design. The remembrance maddened him.

"Speak, you devil," he charged.

"I love him," she returned defiantly. "I love him."

"And my wife!"

"I was Joe's wife—before."

"You've the right to say it," he owned.

"Well, then, meet me halfway. Since you know the truth, what do you advise me to do?"

"Advise you?" he echoed.

"Precisely. Put yourself in my place. Suppose that you were in love with somebody."

He started.

"I—"

"So hard, is it? Suppose it, anyhow. Suppose yourself a human being instead of—well, say a personified canal; a human being married to another human being—the wrong one—with your love for the right one growing stronger every day. What would you do?"

"Master my passion. Preserve my self-respect."

She laughed at the trumpet note of his answer.

"You've the cocksure remedy of one who has never tried."

He strangled a retort.

"Try to comprehend my feelings," she pursued. "If you were

in love with me, I shouldn't ask it. But you're not in love with me. Frankly now, are you?"

"I am your husband."

"And I'm your wife. Does that prove a love affair? No, no. The naked fact is that neither cares, and because of that I ask you plainly how we can best arrange the matter."

"This is nonsense."

"It isn't. It's common sense. A New York woman I know—I met her at Narragansett—was in the same position. Her husband was broad-minded, and they settled everything without an unkind word. She lived somewhere in the Dakotas for a few months, married again as soon as the judge signed the decree, and made a roundabout journey home her wedding trip."

"And you would imitate this programme?"

"In some respects—yes. I've not thought it out in detail. Your practical mind ought to shed abundant light. If you weren't my husband, I'd retain you as my lawyer."

"By Heaven, I've stood enough of this!" flashed Shelby. "Are you destitute of even the moral rags and tatters a Hottentot may boast? You ask my advice. Have it you shall, and follow it you must. I have forfeited the right to reproach you as man to wife—granted that I never had it; as a man I waive my personal affront. But as the governor of this state to the mistress of this, the state's house, I warn you that this brazen mockery of decency must end. When I am governor no longer you may go your way in such fashion as you will. Till then you must take no step which shall discredit my office or the position to which my office raises you. You will tell Ludlow this, and when you have told him, you will hold no private speech with him until my successor takes his oath. Promise."

His volcanic outburst cowed her flippancy.

"I promise," she said.

Before the week elapsed the newspapers announced that Ludlow had decided to resume the practice of law in New York. Cora made no comment; but Shelby read into the retreat her purpose to keep their sorry truce inviolate, and strove to shut his mind to every thought alien to his work.

The public business was absorbing enough in truth. His great canal project, which during a month of hearings, conferences, committee enmeshments, and the like, had hung in jeopardy, was wrecked beyond repair. Nor was this the worst. The governor's forcing of the issue had convinced the Boss that a popular demand for canal legislation of some sort really existed, and he prepared to respond with a measure after his own heart. A vicious substitute, which it was given out that the organization fully indorsed, glided facilely to its final reading after the manner of bills bearing the mystic sign manual of the Boss. Foreseeing disaster, Shelby sought at least to rescue the wise provision of his plan which looked to the administration of the canals along business lines, and to this end used his personal influence with various members of the Legislature. Achieving little here, he even appealed to the leader himself.

The Boss wrote him in his ironic mood.

"Naturally I cannot forecast the action of the Legislature," he said, following his modest custom of disclaiming foreknowledge of the events he shaped; "but in my opinion any measure which ignores the legitimate expectation of patronage on the part of the party in power is too idyllic for this workday world."

Shelby was at no loss to give this dictum its true inter-
pretation. His own scheme had secured the party's
legitimate rights sufficiently—he was too clear-sighted to
overlook that. It was the party's illicit greed for spoils which
he had failed to satisfy—the greed which the Boss had
framed his makeshift to meet. The opportunity for jobbery
was left as wide as before, perhaps wider; for while under
color of economy the appropriation cut the reasonable sum
Shelby had suggested as a beginning, it was a vast amount
still. So conceived, and at the eleventh hour saddled with an
amendment directing the building of a costly feeder which
the engineers had declared needless, the travesty of all the
governor's good intentions passed both Houses by a narrow
vote, and reached Shelby himself.

Jacob Krantz, whose interest in this particular bit of
legislation was keen, in his own vernacular hit off the
situation.

"It's time for a show-down," said this observer of things as
they are. "The Boss has put it up to the Champion of
Canals to make good his bluff."

Shelby realized this truth clearly enough in the ten days
given him by the constitution for his decision; but he took
no one into his confidence, and fought his dreary battle
alone. It was a hard choice that destiny had offered him in
the end—total shipwreck of his brave dreamings, or a
salvage of what perhaps might better sink. Had his duty by
the people been absolutely plain, he would have acted
instantly, for he had striven to be the people's governor; but
in the ten days of his ordeal the people seemed to speak with
a hundred differing tongues, whose single coherent message
proclaimed what he already knew—that for him there could
be no middle way. The bill was in the form of a concurrent

resolution to submit the appropriation to popular vote; but Shelby had no mind to dodge his responsibility. With his record, with his conception of his trust, he must confront the issue squarely—sign or reject.

One of the most clamorous of the newspapers favoring the bill phrased his choice yet more narrowly, quoting copiously from his speeches and bidding him "sign or stultify." But appeals to his consistency found him deaf. The man who never changed his mind and the man who never changed his coat were to him equally ridiculous; time had its sport with each of them. Another attack, made when he had held the bill for upward of a week and a rumor of a veto was rife, drew blood. Volney Sprague's *Whig* which, without ever thinking good of Shelby, had long since returned to the party fold, embraced the occasion to revive the old scandals linking Shelby's name to unsavory canal contracts, with the insinuation that the governor's real quarrel with the bill which had passed lay in the fact that it exposed too few millions to thievery. The erratic editor's virtual allegiance to the Boss whom he once had flayed, might have caused Shelby a smile, had he not been saddened by the thought that any human being could misunderstand him so completely. To him it was a transparent truth that because he had known the canal's abuses as a politician, so surely must he wish to end them as governor of the state.

The veto rumor, which Shelby neither fathered nor encouraged, precipitated two things: the Boss sent word through his nephew, a not infrequent messenger, that the party's interests plainly required that the party's governor waive his personal disappointment and sign the bill at once; while Cora, for some days past of a repentent mind, requested the same small favor as a reward of virtue.

"Show in this way that you forgive my folly," she cajoled.

"You'll never be President without the Boss's aid—everybody says so. Do as he wishes and as I wish too."

"And give you a chance to intrigue with the Handsome Ludlows of Washington?"

By and by, as he sat writing in his study, he would have unsaid the taunt, and resolved that he would talk rationally with her of his dilemma and of the course he was prepared to take; but no opportunity befell that evening, and on the morrow, the last day left him but one, he breakfasted alone. Partly with the intention of speaking to her, partly for freedom from the button-holing of the grillroom where he usually lunched, he left the executive chamber shortly before one o'clock and set out on foot for his home.

As he turned from the capitol park into his own street, Mrs. Van Dam's carriage halted abruptly at the curb, and the old lady beckoned him.

"I'll not ask you to get in," she said, "for I'm sure you need the walk, but I've news to tell you of a friend of ours. Ruth Graves's husband died in Los Angeles yesterday after an operation for appendicitis."

Time had softened the rougher memories of his brief rivalry with the dead man, and the circumstance that each had in some degree given distinction to their common birthplace threw Bernard Graves into a light which made his early taking off mildly pathetic, but in this moment Shelby's mind could compass only the one great fact—Ruth was free!

Canal, governorship, presidency forgotten, he stared into the muddy street as the carriage whipped away, till a knot of school children gathered at his heels with round eyes centred on the cobbles which apparently engrossed him. Shelby recalled himself, and hurried on to his own door.

"I shall lunch at home to-day," he said to a servant in the hall. "Please tell my wife."

The man handed him a sealed note explaining:—

"Mrs. Shelby went out about an hour ago. She asked me to give you this."

Shelby carried the note to his room before he opened it.

"I can't keep my promise," it ran. "I saw him to-day. He wants me. Good-by."

CHAPTER VIII

He, no less than Ruth, was free! There was no dissociating the two facts. They shouted their message together. He was rid of his incubus—why mince the word now!—rid of her gadfly vulgarity, her shallow emotions, her pinch-beck ideals, her hideous selfishness. By her own rash act she had freed him to marry the woman he loved with all his rugged strength—the woman who that memorable September day had proved loved him. What was the transient chatter of the world beside this verity! What might he not achieve in the new life! What station could he not now find confidence to fill!

A knock distracted, without wholly rousing him. Milicent entered.

"I hear you're to lunch at home, father," she said. "The gong has sounded twice."

He stared vacantly into her young eyes; her very existence had been blotted from his recollection.

"Aren't you well?" She came to him. "I shall be glad when the Legislature stops worrying you and goes home."

He crushed his wife's note into a pocket.

"Yes; I'm well," he answered slowly. "Just worried—as you say. That's all. I thought an hour at home would help— home quiet, you know—home—"

There was a frightened widening of her gray eyes, and Shelby pulled himself together.

"But I can't lunch with you after all, little girl," he told her hurriedly. "I find I must go back. It seems your mother is— is out. Perhaps you know—"

He stopped. What did she know?

"I'm just in from a turn about Washington Park," explained the girl. "The maple buds are all bursting. And you should see the crocuses."

"Your mother has been called out of town. She will be gone all night, probably—perhaps longer. You had best ask some friends in to stay with you. It will cheer us up. Now go down to your luncheon. You mustn't let me spoil it for you."

"But you're *not* well," she insisted.

"I am—I am indeed." Out of a window he caught sight of his wife's coupe. "I'll take that down town," he said.

They descended together. In the hall he warned again, "Don't let your luncheon spoil."

His foot on the carriage step, he questioned the coachman:—

"Did Mrs. Shelby catch her train?"

"Yes, sir," the man replied cheerfully. "I saw to that. A close shave, though. I heard it pull out as we drove away."

"That was at what time?"

"One twenty-five, sir."

"No baggage?"

"Just hand satchels," put in the footman. "Mrs. Shelby said her trunks weren't ready."

"Drive to Canon North's," directed the governor, jumping in. "He's near the cathedral, you know."

The carriage jolted from cobbles to asphalt, rounded the looming capitol with its chateau-like red roofs cut sharply against the pure spring sky, grated the stones again, and halted at the canon's door. The governor had the carriage door open before the footman could leap down, and told the man that he would make his own inquiries.

The maid said that he had missed the clergyman by five minutes. Possibly he could be found at the cathedral; perhaps at the Beverwyck Club.

Shelby bade the coupe follow, and hurried on foot to the church, which lifted its temporary wooden roof above the clustering episcopal buildings near at hand. Two or three cabs waited at the curb, from one of which fluttered a facetious knot of white ribbon tied to an axletree. A smell of stale incense pervaded the vestibule. The murmured words of a liturgy drifted down the long nave as he passed within. North was reading the marriage service. Shelby bided restively in the shadow of a column till the ceremony should end.

It was a small wedding party, merely a handful of onlookers, chiefly teary women, grouped around the courageous pair, whose stanch "I will" woke derisive echoes aloft.

"For better for worse, for richer for poorer, in sickness and in health . . . till death do us part."

The youngsters pattered the awful words so glibly! Then North's prayer went forth over their kneeling figures, they rose, took his hand an instant, and turned to face an applauding world. The watcher pitied them with a great pity.

Shelby followed North from chancel to vestry. The priest had laid aside stole and surplice, and stood meditatively in his cassock as the caller entered. Some men the cassock effeminates; not so North, whose virile shape it emphasized, modelling his muscles like an antique drapery. He seemed to radiate strength.

The canon remarked his friend's strained face, greeted him as if governors made a practice of popping into his vestry unannounced, and bade a negro, who was folding vestments, to finish his task later.

"What has happened to you?" he asked, directly they were alone.

"My wife has eloped."

North started at the bald announcement, but asked quietly:—

"Did she leave by the one twenty-five train?"

"You saw her?"

"I saw him." Ludlow needed no naming. "I came in from

the west at that time for this wedding."

Shelby jerked out his watch.

"That train is an accommodation, making nearly all stops. They were probably too excited to consider the fact, or care. Any one taking the Southwestern Limited twenty minutes from now would make New York half an hour before them—provided they're bound for New York. Of course, there's the chance that they will change at some point to the express, which left a quarter of an hour ago. Somebody must intercept them."

"And it's your present misfortune to be governor of New York," added the canon, ripping at the buttons of his cassock. "Permit me to fill your place."

"It's a hateful thing to ask of you. I could ask it of no other man."

North nodded, and caught up his hat and coat.

"You did right to come to me, my friend."

"Say to her"—they passed again into the silent nave on the way to the carriage—"say that one of the best little girls who ever lived is waiting for her mother to return from—from shopping, what you please. Say that I—" He broke off, and fronted North in the stillness. "By God! no," he burst out suddenly. "No message from me yet. I can't do it yet—"

The governor went back to the executive chamber, and heard, one by one, the stories of the callers who had massed the antechamber during his prolonged absence. From all sections, of all degrees, of all political types, their importunities were variants of a single theme—the thing he could give. Him they gave nothing, not even encouragement. Five o'clock came at last, and he left the plain little work-cell behind the sumptuous panelling of the executive chamber for a ten-minute bout with the press correspondents. Was it true that he had decided to sign the canal bill? Was a veto imminent? Did he propose to let it become a law without his signature? Had he and the great leader severed their relations? Was a breach in the party machine a possibility? What was his position with regard to the presidential nomination? Did he approve of an out-and-out indorsement of the gold standard?

He was through with them finally, and the office-seeking, news-hungry world, supposing him gone to his home, left him alone in his cell to complete his interrupted work. Half-past five o'clock! His thoughts strayed to follow the course of two trains. By now the fugitives were below the Highlands; North must already be entering the city. Fort George and the bridges of the Harlem were above his head, the long, straight streets reeled away like the spokes of a giant wheel. Presently he would pace the platform at Forty-second Street. In an hour they would meet.

Shelby forced his mind back to his desk. The closely written sheets of manuscript which had filled his evening yesterday lay before him. He called his private secretary from the adjoining room.

"Have the stenographers all gone?"

"All but one, governor," said the secretary. "He is working past hours on a personal matter for me."

"Let me borrow him."

For an hour the governor slowly dictated from his sheets.

"You will miss your regular dinner over this," he said to the man, at the end, and pressed a bank-note upon him. "We'll need several copies, of course."

The stenographer went to his typewriter, and Shelby walked out to his secretary's desk.

"He's working on this," he explained, showing him a page of the manuscript. "I suppose he doesn't leak news?"

The secretary flushed a little over the hasty reading.

"He is wholly trustworthy," he replied.

"There is nothing of the Star Chamber order about the matter, but I always prefer to be the source of information. I should have put this through to-day if a personal affair hadn't prevented. Have the formalities in readiness for the morning. Good night."

He again consulted his watch. They had met! Without seeing him he walked past an orderly with a telegram. The man overtook him at the elevator.

"So soon?" said the governor, absently.

The orderly exchanged glances with the elevator boy.

Shelby tore open North's message. It said "Come," and named a Forty-second Street hotel. One of the fastest trains in the world was due in less than a half-hour. In fifteen minutes he gained the station. With the time which remained he wired North of his coming, and telephoned Milicent a cheery message that he should not return till late. She told him that she had her friends with her, and he even caught a gay little echo of their chatter.

It occurred to him that he had eaten nothing since morning,

and as the train cleared the river and raced southward on its long flight, he ordered food. But he scarcely tasted it. No food could appease the hunger of his mind, the starvation of a lifetime, which the canon's message prefigured. His ugly thoughts kept pace with the roaring monster which bore him; but, unlike the monster, he made no real progress; spun vainly, rather, like a top. After all, what was he, what was human striving everywhere, but a vainly spinning top. He dozed over his drear philosophy, and from dozing slept.

He woke as the train swung at Spuyten Duyvil from the valley of the Hudson to the valley of the Harlem, freshened his face with cold water, and stepped from the car at his journey's end clear-eyed and alert. Beyond the iron barrier of the train shed stood North.

Shelby caught his hand.

"Well?"

"It is well."

"Where is she?"

"Waiting at the hotel—waiting for the word you could not send."

They made an intensely quiet islet amidst the buffeting human tide. The governor's face was drawn, and in the electric glare looked pasty white.

"That is why you sent for me?" he asked.

"That is why. Believe me, it was necessary."

"I believe you," Shelby answered slowly. "Tell me what you have done."

"It's a short story. About five o'clock I passed them. Their train was at a standstill, mine was running slowly because of a washout. I saw your wife at a window. Then we made an unexpected stop near a station, and I left my train for theirs."

"Then?"

"That's all. I think neither was sorry to see me. I came at the reaction—the psychological moment."

Shelby thought North wished to spare him the recital, which was true in a measure. Yet the canon's reticence had its taproot in the natural man who perforce did his strong deeds simply.

"Good night," he added cheerily, putting out his hand. "I find that I can get a train back soon."

CHAPTER IX

A few minutes before eleven o'clock Shelby and his wife got out of a carriage at a west-side ferry. With North's assurance that her husband was surely coming, Cora's thoughts turned to the conventions which in the morning she had blithely whistled down the wind. It happened that a friend in the Jersey suburbs had within the week suggested that they visit Lakewood together, and the invitation no sooner recurred to her than she sent a message saying that she had found it possible immediately to join her at her home. Shelby had assented to this plan, and directly set about escorting her to her destination. No dread of Ludlow prompted this vigilance. He discerned that that glamour had forever waned. The woman's jerking nerves made him fear a collapse. Stripped of shams for once, she had his pity.

As he paid the cabman at the ferry-house entrance an incoming boat discharged its passengers, who from habit scurried forth as if it were morning, and the day's work lay all before. Two men issued with the foremost, one of whom spied Shelby as he followed his wife through the dingy swinging doors.

"Great guns!" he said; "the governor!"

The Boss wheeled.

"What's that, Krantz?" he demanded sharply.

Without replying Jacob Krantz darted into the ferry-house, slipped into the waiting line before the ticket-office, and watched Shelby make his purchase. The governor left the window without noticing him, and joining his wife at the wicket passed on to the boat.

Krantz shot out of doors with his heavy lids propped wide.

"He bought tickets for Orange, and there's no return train before daylight—I heard him inquire. Do you see what he has done for us? He's out of the state—*out of the state*! See? The lieutenant-governor can sign the bill!"

The Boss drew him quietly aside.

"No, no," he returned. "This is New York—not Montana."

Staring out at the clamoring cabbies, the leader reflected. If this secretive governor intended either to veto or to sign the canal bill, he would scarcely leave Albany the evening before the last day given him to act. Did his absence not argue that he meant to let the measure become a law without his signature? Despite his representations to Shelby, this was the course the Boss actually expected the governor to take. It was the course which he, given the man's difficulties, would himself follow were he in Shelby's place. But he had found it unsafe to forecast this man's actions by his own, and by temperament he counted nothing certain till he knew it as a fact accomplished. The governor would undoubtedly return to Albany sometime to-morrow; it therefore behooved him to delay that return until the time for hostile action should expire. Searching out a telegraph office, he ascertained the point at which a message would intercept the train, and wired Shelby a peremptory request for a meeting in New York on the morrow at ten o'clock.

"I'm making a morning appointment with the governor," he told Krantz.

The satellite slanted his head knowingly. Past midnight the answer reached the club where the Boss made his bachelor home. If Shelby was amazed at Old Silky's intimate knowledge of his movements, his message did not betray it. Nor did the Boss betray his own amazement at his too apt pupil's prompt evasion of a snare. What he read was this:—

"The governor's office hours are nine to five."

Krantz in his eagerness would have laid profane hands on the missive, but the Boss permitted him neither to touch nor see.

"It seems that he intends returning to Albany to-night," he said calmly. "It occurs to me, after all, that he can reach New York by trolley. Probably he'll take the paper train which leaves about three. Energetic man—very."

"Then you'll see him to-night?"

"No; not to-night," rejoined the Boss, dryly. "I'm going to bed."

Krantz watched the reverend figure out of the smoking-room with his narrow eyes, and for a time sat as motionless as a dozing crocodile. Finally he roused and lounged toward the door, where he received a revelation. Bag in hand, the Boss, whom he imaged above stairs between sheets, was unostentatiously letting himself out into the night.

Shelby went directly to his berth on reaching the station, and while the car remained in the train shed, slept. The departure wakened him, and after useless striving he resigned himself to his insomnia, raised his window curtain, and lay watching the staid procession of Dutch-named towns picketting the river banks. A mimic tempest fretted the Tappan Sea, whose bravado dwindled to mere guerilla marauding in the Highlands, and vanished altogether where the Storm King held the pass and heralded the dawn. Presently the purple Catskills marched and countermarched into line with cloud banners streaming rose-red in the sunrise. Yesterday was blotted in to-day. The watcher also put yesterday away, dressed, and left his train all in a tranquillity which even the knowledge that a stateroom door neighboring his berth had just emitted the Boss could not have ruffled.

At his accustomed hour the governor entered the executive chamber. Like the steaming earth and the park elms without in their tender green, this stately room seemed swept by the breath of spring. The warm tones of the hangings, the Spanish leather, the lavish mahogany, glowed responsive to the fingering sunlight, and the painted simulacra of his predecessors looked down almost benignantly from their gilded frames. The little cell behind the wainscoting, into which the increasing complexity of affairs had forced the recent executives, claimed him during most of his working hours; but it was as rightful tenant of this vast chamber that he felt most the governor of New York. It epitomized for him not merely the commonwealth of the present, huge as it was, but the whole historic past since the September day when Hendrik Hudson's *Half Moon* dropped anchor down yonder in the stream. He felt himself no more the successor of these frock-coated moderns whose oil presentments covered panelling and frieze than of the periwigs who ruled before them. He was the heir of Stuyvesant, Dongan, and Lord Lovelace no less than of Cleveland, Van Buren, and John Jay. There had been sturdy souls among that company; men who had hoped mightily, striven mightily, sometimes achieved mightily. Some few had attained the presidency of the United States; some barely missed the prize; some pursued it to their bitter graves. Where would he rank? According to a newspaper he carried in his hand, it lay with him this day to determine. Yet for one so omniscient, the editor was chary of counsel.

Shelby went on to his little inner room and took up the day's routine with his secretary, who casually dropped the news that the Boss had that morning arrived in Albany and begun to receive the faithful at an early hour. Whether owing to this cause or not, Shelby's own quota of legislative callers was small. At ten o'clock he met briefly the delegates of a labor organization, who in an embarrassed fashion had much to say of plutocrats and trusts; and with their departure came a fluttering invasion from a young ladies' boarding-school, headed by a chaperone laboriously intent on improving the girlish mind. All requested autographs, which were readily supplied from the stock in hand, and a round half-dozen asked the private secretary in strictest confidence if the governor were a married man.

He had but just returned to his desk when an orderly handed him the card of the Boss.

"You'll see him here?" asked the man.

"No. In the executive chamber," answered Shelby.

The Boss stood beside the massive fireplace, gazing pensively up at a portrait of Washington.

"Ah, good morning, governor," he called, turning slowly. "I trust I'm well within the official hours."

"Quite."

"Mahomet is somewhat stricken in years, and night travel impairs his digestion, but if need be, he can come to the mountain still."

"It was the governor of the state your message offended," said Shelby, quietly. "Personally I'm not thin-skinned, as you know."

"Yet, in my poor way—" the Boss included the chamber in a comprehensive gesture.

"Yes; in last analysis you put me here. I don't forget that."

The leader shrugged.

"You were always so devilishly direct, Ross," he let fall good-humoredly. "It's your besetting sin, and spoiled the making of a clever politician. You lack the diplomatic instinct."

Shelby proved him in the right immediately.

"You've come about the canal bill," he said. "Sit down."

"Yes; the canal bill—and other matters."

He laid his hat and stick upon a desk, and drawing a chair beside Shelby's near a window embrasure, leaned to him, chin in hand, as in the days of their hand-in-glove intimacy. "Between us two plain speech after all is best," he went on. "You've no mistaken notions about me. You recognize the newspaper bogy which goes by my name as a caricature. You know that I am as proud of this state in my way as you are in your way. You know also the manner and method of my ascendency in state affairs, and by the same insight you know its scope."

"Yes. I know its scope."

"So far as knowledge of method goes, you are as capable of

party leadership as I. Indeed, if that were all, you might set up a rival shop, as some of the editors kindly suggest, and attempt to put me out of business. Naturally you don't share that delusion."

"No."

"No; you're too sane. My tenure doesn't rest on mere control of the purse-strings. My great asset is forty years' dealing with all sorts and conditions of men. Nobody else has quite my equipment."

"Why tell me what I know? All talk of my setting up a machine of my own is idle. I am aware of the extent of your influence. You have tacitly offered me the state delegation to the national convention in June, and it is within your power to deliver it—probably to name the candidate. Have you come to withdraw the offer?"

The Boss straightened.

"I have come in a spirit of compromise," he returned. "We've differed widely on this question of a greater canal. You have evolved a plan best suited to Utopia; my own is aimed to meet the human nature I know best—the human nature De Witt Clinton, in whose steps you evidently aspire to tread, comprehended and took into the reckoning. Be practical as he was practical—as you were in the early days of our acquaintance. I no longer ask you to sign the bill; I respect your punctilio. I only beg that you will permit this measure which your party has espoused to become a law without your signature. Everybody will understand your position. You will occupy an honorable middle ground."

"For me there is no honorable middle ground. It lies with me to approve or reject."

The Boss got upon his feet.

"I dislike coercion," he said.

The governor rose.

"You need use none. No amount of it could hypnotize me into seeing a bad bill as a good bill."

"Do you count the presidency so lightly?"

"No American can count it lightly."

"You face political suicide. Do you fancy your renomination for this office possible?"

"No. I have weighed that, too."

"And your virtue is unshaken?"

The governor smiled at the sneer.

"Oh, I'm past all that," he said. "I took the precaution to veto the bill before you came to tempt."

With uncertain step the old leader turned and made his way to the door, where he paused to vent his bewildered, yet sincere judgment.

"I've never met anybody quite like you in politics, Shelby," he owned, almost kindly. "You are a paradox—a sort of admirable fool."

Choose from Thousands of 1stWorldLibrary Classics By

A. M. Barnard
Ada Leverson
Adolphus William Ward
Aesop
Agatha Christie
Alexander Aaronsohn
Alexander Kielland
Alexandre Dumas
Alfred Gatty
Alfred Ollivant
Alice Duer Miller
Alice Turner Curtis
Alice Dunbar
Allen Chapman
Alleyne Ireland
Ambrose Bierce
Amelia E. Barr
Amory H. Bradford
Andrew Lang
Andrew McFarland Davis
Andy Adams
Angela Brazil
Anna Alice Chapin
Anna Sewell
Annie Besant
Annie Hamilton Donnell
Annie Payson Call
Annie Roe Carr
Annonaymous
Anton Chekhov
Archibald Lee Fletcher
Arnold Bennett
Arthur C. Benson
Arthur Conan Doyle
Arthur M. Winfield
Arthur Ransome
Arthur Schnitzler
Arthur Train
Atticus
B.H. Baden-Powell
B. M. Bower
B. C. Chatterjee
Baroness Emmuska Orczy
Baroness Orczy
Basil King
Bayard Taylor
Ben Macomber
Bertha Muzzy Bower
Bjornstjerne Bjornson

Booth Tarkington
Boyd Cable
Bram Stoker
C. Collodi
C. E. Orr
C. M. Ingleby
Carolyn Wells
Catherine Parr Traill
Charles A. Eastman
Charles Amory Beach
Charles Dickens
Charles Dudley Warner
Charles Farrar Browne
Charles Ives
Charles Kingsley
Charles Klein
Charles Hanson Towne
Charles Lathrop Pack
Charles Romyn Dake
Charles Whibley
Charles Willing Beale
Charlotte M. Braeme
Charlotte M. Yonge
Charlotte Perkins Stetson
Clair W. Hayes
Clarence Day Jr.
Clarence E. Mulford
Clemence Housman
Confucius
Coningsby Dawson
Cornelis DeWitt Wilcox
Cyril Burleigh
D. H. Lawrence
Daniel Defoe
David Garnett
Dinah Craik
Don Carlos Janes
Donald Keyhoe
Dorothy Kilner
Dougan Clark
Douglas Fairbanks
E. Nesbit
E. P. Roe
E. Phillips Oppenheim
E. S. Brooks
Earl Barnes
Edgar Rice Burroughs
Edith Van Dyne
Edith Wharton

Edward Everett Hale
Edward J. O'Biren
Edward S. Ellis
Edwin L. Arnold
Eleanor Atkins
Eleanor Hallowell Abbott
Eliot Gregory
Elizabeth Gaskell
Elizabeth McCracken
Elizabeth Von Arnim
Ellem Key
Emerson Hough
Emilie F. Carlen
Emily Bronte
Emily Dickinson
Enid Bagnold
Enilor Macartney Lane
Erasmus W. Jones
Ernie Howard Pie
Ethel May Dell
Ethel Turner
Ethel Watts Mumford
Eugene Sue
Eugenie Foa
Eugene Wood
Eustace Hale Ball
Evelyn Everett-green
Everard Cotes
F. H. Cheley
F. J. Cross
F. Marion Crawford
Fannie E. Newberry
Federick Austin Ogg
Ferdinand Ossendowski
Fergus Hume
Florence A. Kilpatrick
Fremont B. Deering
Francis Bacon
Francis Darwin
Frances Hodgson Burnett
Frances Parkinson Keyes
Frank Gee Patchin
Frank Harris
Frank Jewett Mather
Frank L. Packard
Frank V. Webster
Frederic Stewart Isham
Frederick Trevor Hill
Frederick Winslow Taylor

Friedrich Kerst
Friedrich Nietzsche
Fyodor Dostoyevsky
G.A. Henty
G.K. Chesterton
Gabrielle E. Jackson
Garrett P. Serviss
Gaston Leroux
George A. Warren
George Ade
Geroge Bernard Shaw
George Cary Eggleston
George Durston
George Ebers
George Eliot
George Gissing
George MacDonald
George Meredith
George Orwell
George Sylvester Viereck
George Tucker
George W. Cable
George Wharton James
Gertrude Atherton
Gordon Casserly
Grace E. King
Grace Gallatin
Grace Greenwood
Grant Allen
Guillermo A. Sherwell
Gulielma Zollinger
Gustav Flaubert
H. A. Cody
H. B. Irving
H.C. Bailey
H. G. Wells
H. H. Munro
H. Irving Hancock
H. R. Naylor
H. Rider Haggard
H. W. C. Davis
Haldeman Julius
Hall Caine
Hamilton Wright Mabie
Hans Christian Andersen
Harold Avery
Harold McGrath
Harriet Beecher Stowe
Harry Castlemon
Harry Coghill
Harry Houidini

Hayden Carruth
Helent Hunt Jackson
Helen Nicolay
Hendrik Conscience
Hendy David Thoreau
Henri Barbusse
Henrik Ibsen
Henry Adams
Henry Ford
Henry Frost
Henry James
Henry Jones Ford
Henry Seton Merriman
Henry W Longfellow
Herbert A. Giles
Herbert Carter
Herbert N. Casson
Herman Hesse
Hildegard G. Frey
Homer
Honore De Balzac
Horace B. Day
Horace Walpole
Horatio Alger Jr.
Howard Pyle
Howard R. Garis
Hugh Lofting
Hugh Walpole
Humphry Ward
Ian Maclaren
Inez Haynes Gillmore
Irving Bacheller
Isabel Cecilia Williams
Isabel Hornibrook
Israel Abrahams
Ivan Turgenev
J.G.Austin
J. Henri Fabre
J. M. Barrie
J. M. Walsh
J. Macdonald Oxley
J. R. Miller
J. S. Fletcher
J. S. Knowles
J. Storer Clouston
J. W. Duffield
Jack London
Jacob Abbott
James Allen
James Andrews
James Baldwin

James Branch Cabell
James DeMille
James Joyce
James Lane Allen
James Lane Allen
James Oliver Curwood
James Oppenheim
James Otis
James R. Driscoll
Jane Abbott
Jane Austen
Jane L. Stewart
Janet Aldridge
Jens Peter Jacobsen
Jerome K. Jerome
Jessie Graham Flower
John Buchan
John Burroughs
John Cournos
John F. Kennedy
John Gay
John Glasworthy
John Habberton
John Joy Bell
John Kendrick Bangs
John Milton
John Philip Sousa
John Taintor Foote
Jonas Lauritz Idemil Lie
Jonathan Swift
Joseph A. Altsheler
Joseph Carey
Joseph Conrad
Joseph E. Badger Jr
Joseph Hergesheimer
Joseph Jacobs
Jules Vernes
Julian Hawthrone
Julie A Lippmann
Justin Huntly McCarthy
Kakuzo Okakura
Karle Wilson Baker
Kate Chopin
Kenneth Grahame
Kenneth McGaffey
Kate Langley Bosher
Kate Langley Bosher
Katherine Cecil Thurston
Katherine Stokes
L. A. Abbot
L. T. Meade

L. Frank Baum
Latta Griswold
Laura Dent Crane
Laura Lee Hope
Laurence Housman
Lawrence Beasley
Leo Tolstoy
Leonid Andreyev
Lewis Carroll
Lewis Sperry Chafer
Lilian Bell
Lloyd Osbourne
Louis Hughes
Louis Joseph Vance
Louis Tracy
Louisa May Alcott
Lucy Fitch Perkins
Lucy Maud Montgomery
Luther Benson
Lydia Miller Middleton
Lyndon Orr
M. Corvus
M. H. Adams
Margaret E. Sangster
Margret Howth
Margaret Vandercook
Margaret W. Hungerford
Margret Penrose
Maria Edgeworth
Maria Thompson Daviess
Mariano Azuela
Marion Polk Angellotti
Mark Overton
Mark Twain
Mary Austin
Mary Catherine Crowley
Mary Cole
Mary Hastings Bradley
Mary Roberts Rinehart
Mary Rowlandson
M. Wollstonecraft Shelley
Maud Lindsay
Max Beerbohm
Myra Kelly
Nathaniel Hawthrone
Nicolo Machiavelli
O. F. Walton
Oscar Wilde

Owen Johnson
P.G. Wodehouse
Paul and Mabel Thorne
Paul G. Tomlinson
Paul Severing
Percy Brebner
Percy Keese Fitzhugh
Peter B. Kyne
Plato
Quincy Allen
R. Derby Holmes
R. L. Stevenson
R. S. Ball
Rabindranath Tagore
Rahul Alvares
Ralph Bonehill
Ralph Henry Barbour
Ralph Victor
Ralph Waldo Emmerson
Rene Descartes
Ray Cummings
Rex Beach
Rex E. Beach
Richard Harding Davis
Richard Jefferies
Richard Le Gallienne
Robert Barr
Robert Frost
Robert Gordon Anderson
Robert L. Drake
Robert Lansing
Robert Lynd
Robert Michael Ballantyne
Robert W. Chambers
Rosa Nouchette Carey
Rudyard Kipling
Saint Augustine
Samuel B. Allison
Samuel Hopkins Adams
Sarah Bernhardt
Sarah C. Hallowell
Selma Lagerlof
Sherwood Anderson
Sigmund Freud
Standish O'Grady
Stanley Weyman
Stella Benson
Stella M. Francis

Stephen Crane
Stewart Edward White
Stijn Streuvels
Swami Abhedananda
Swami Parmananda
T. S. Ackland
T. S. Arthur
The Princess Der Ling
Thomas A. Janvier
Thomas A Kempis
Thomas Anderton
Thomas Bailey Aldrich
Thomas Bulfinch
Thomas De Quincey
Thomas Dixon
Thomas H. Huxley
Thomas Hardy
Thomas More
Thornton W. Burgess
U. S. Grant
Upton Sinclair
Valentine Williams
Various Authors
Vaughan Kester
Victor Appleton
Victor G. Durham
Victoria Cross
Virginia Woolf
Wadsworth Camp
Walter Camp
Walter Scott
Washington Irving
Wilbur Lawton
Wilkie Collins
Willa Cather
Willard F. Baker
William Dean Howells
William le Queux
W. Makepeace Thackeray
William W. Walter
William Shakespeare
Winston Churchill
Yei Theodora Ozaki
Yogi Ramacharaka
Young E. Allison
Zane Grey